CHASING SHADOWS

HARVEST OF THE UNBORN

C.C. SULLIVAN

Copyright ©2025 Harvest of the Unborn - Book One - Chasing Shadows

FIRST EDITION: 2025

978-0-6458432-5-5 (pbk)
978-0-6458432-6-2 (ebk)

First published by Hot Doggy Press, 2025

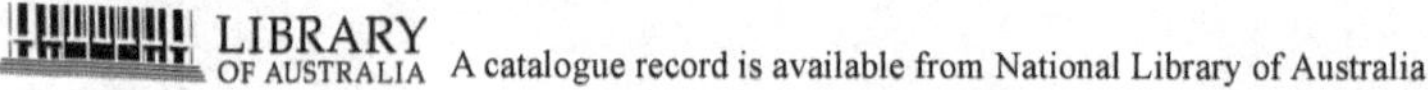

LIBRARY OF AUSTRALIA A catalogue record is available from National Library of Australia

Cover Illustration by Eileen Rigby - Rigmarole Studios
Interior and Cover layout by Christine Titheradge - Radgelan P/L

Harvest of the Unborn

Book One: Chasing Shadows

Book Two: Beyond the Tunnels

Book Three: Redemption Path

REWIEW

"Review for Chasing Shadows"

Chasing Shadows by Cheryl Sullivan is a thrilling page-turner set in the heart of Sydney, blending mystery, suspense, and heart-pounding drama. The story follows a strong and empowered female novice investigative journalist, whose determination and resourcefulness make her both relatable and inspiring. Cheryl Sullivan does a fantastic job of creating likeable, well-rounded characters, drawing readers into their lives and keeping us invested in their journey from start to finish.

The Sydney setting after WW2 adds a rich, atmospheric backdrop that feels authentic and vivid, making the city almost a character in its own right. The twists and turns of the plot are perfectly paced, keeping you guessing until the very end. The story tackles thought-provoking themes without losing its edge as a gripping mystery.

If you're looking for a book with a strong lead, a cast of likeable characters, and a story that will keep you hooked, Harvest of the Unborn is a must-read. Cheryl Sullivan has delivered a memorable and empowering novel that will leave you eagerly awaiting her next work.

Highly recommended!" - Juliet Potter - Journalist

Acknowledgements

The highlight of my writing journey, was when this story was twice shortlisted to the Queensland Writers Centre's, Adaptable *Turning the Page to Screen program* in 2019 and 2021.

There are not enough descriptions to cover the support I received from my three adult children, their partners and children, my sisters and their families. Also, my parents, in particular my mother who in her last hours told me to keep writing.

The following people are not in any order but because of their support and contribution I extend sincere thanks to Lori-Jay Ellis, CEO of Queensland Writers Centre, whose support is unsurpassable, and Sandra Makaresz who edited my drafts - I followed her advice without exception. To the past staff of Queensland Writers Centre including Meg Vann, Aimée Lindorff, and Katie Woods, who encouraged me to write this story. Special thanks to my friends and my writing buddies.

Special thanks to Christine Titheradge whose expertise re-published this book on my behalf with the help of Charmaine Clancy and Hot Doggy Press.

Thanks to Peter Yard, whom I met at the Qld State Library where the idea originated, and Lee Finn who welcomed me to join the Brisbane Writers Group where I practised the craft and later became one of the coordinators when she retired. To the SLQers (slackers) who helped outline the sequel. To my partner, special thanks for providing a quiet place in his home to allow me the space to write.

Thanks also to Anna Campbell, a prolific author of romance novels, whose writer's surgery advice suggested included re-writing the first few scenes. And Louise Cusack, whose manuscript assessment gave me the confidence to continue the story.

Extra special thanks to Eileen Rigby, at Rigmarole Studio in Samford Valley, who created a piece of art depicting my vision of the cover.

Without the assistance and encouragement from all of the above, and possibly some I've forgotten (my apologies), Chasing Shadows, the first book of the Harvest of the Unborn Series, may still be a seed in the making.

Chapter One

Shadows crisscrossed the two-storey sandstone brick boarding house where Lailah O'Brien had rented a room before her disappearance. Charlotte Tyrell rubbed her eyes with her gloved fingers. A sudden drop in the early afternoon temperature sent a chill through her bones, or was it the premonitions of the future flashing inside her head? Dark clouds broiled overhead in readiness to unleash a burden of electrical energy upon the unsuspecting. An icy wind brushed past her. She buttoned her overcoat. Winter had arrived in Sydney in June 1946.

The rhythmic *ta donk* of the train rolling along the tracks during the night failed to lull her to sleep. Unrelenting chatter and laughter between men and women returning from war in economy class had kept her awake all night. The journey left her fatigued in every part of her body. She stared up at the awnings over the verandah casting shade across the boards in front of closed French doors, and shuddered. Too late in the day to change her mind after accepting the position of crime reporter. She opened the iron gate to face whatever imagined dread awaited.

A wayward branch snagged her glove, and to her annoyance, a thorn pulled a thread. Once free of the sharp stalk, she swung the gate hard. In defiance of her anger, the bottom bars snagged a rose bush on the opposite side, stopping the gate halfway between the fence posts. She shuffled sideways through the opening. Charlotte hurried along the path between frostbitten rose canes. Within reach of the doorbell, she paused. Images of dark Gothic lead-light panels decorating either side of the wide entry prickled her spinal nerves. Both panels, which seemed out of place on the house, depicted ugly scenes of devilish creatures holding odd looking weapons. Ruby coloured eyes glared even undercover. She chose to ignore the ugliness depicted in the panels without understanding why they bothered her senses. Charlotte shrugged off the eerie sensation to prepare herself to meet the landlady.

Before she composed her thoughts, the front door burst open. She jerked with fright. A youngish woman rushed past and over the few steps. A black headpiece, held in place by a beaded hat pin, barely contained the woman's flame-coloured curls bouncing over her shoulders. Charlotte's charcoal trouser suit was in sharp contrast to the bright green wool dress whizzing past. Unstable on her back foot, she grabbed the nearest post and rail to avoid the impending collision. A melodious voice sang an apology. "Ooh! Sorry!" The woman rushed by with a wave. "Bye, Mrs Park, got to go."

A response came from within the dim entrance. "Bye, Love, remember, dinner is at seven tonight and don't go anywhere on your own. You've heard the news!"

Taps of heels on floorboards grew louder behind Charlotte. As she turned about, a woman appeared in the door frame scrutinizing her with menacing eyes, which opposed her cheerful greeting.

"And you must be Charlotte. My apologies for being informal. I like to make my girls feel at home." Charlotte nodded and half-smiled. With the door held ajar against the wind, the woman ushered her in. "Come in, come in love. You'll meet Magda later. She's not always in a rush."

"Thank you," Charlotte answered as she stepped inside, eager to see her room. She surveyed the foyer, absorbing every detail. An undersized chandelier offered a soft glow. The dark colours in the panels did little to lift the gloom. The fringed edge of the threadbare carpet runner stopped short of an ornate hall stand opposite the stairwell. An assortment of overcoats, scarves and hats hung above a receptacle for umbrellas. Charlotte added her overcoat to the rack next to a small mottled mirror with its fractured light from the chandelier's dust-covered crystals.

Beneath the elegant staircase, a cabinet with a keyed lock displayed an odd array of ornaments and an uncut opal. Charlotte recognised the gemstone and thought it out of place among the finely sculptured bric-à-brac and bent to inspect. "You can look but not touch, dear; these are my personal trinkets."

Charlotte noted the change in the landlady's voice. Not wanting to earn any mistrust before she moved in, "I understand,

Mrs Park," she replied between yawns, "cherished pieces, I am sure."

Mrs Park invited her new boarder into the parlour on the left of the hallway. "This is the common area for my boarders." She removed a used cup and saucer from the table with a 'tut tut' and placed them on a tray. Charlotte understood by the landlady's tone she expected her tenants to keep the room tidy. An elegant fireplace adorned the chimney breast. Hand-cut logs and pine cones aflame in the hearth lifted her spirit. Two young women engrossed in whispered conversation occupied chairs in the corner. They leaned so close their foreheads touched. Neither changed positions until Mrs Park introduced her daughters Lily and Violet. The whispering ceased as they eyeballed the newcomer.

Mrs Park continued when she had their attention. "Lily is the youngest by two years. Violet celebrated her coming of age party last year." She pivoted back before the sisters asked questions, "Charlotte will move into the empty room opposite Magda, so please make her welcome." Neither girl responded in any manner of acknowledgement. Their style of clothing was of simple cut dresses, and Charlotte wondered if their behaviour equalled their appearance.

The sisters appeared as twins clothed in similar styles of blue and grey. High collars covered any sense of exposed flesh. Buttoned to the waist, bodices and straight skirts fitted snug around their small frames. "Mummy, when's dinner? We plan to see a film today." They both stood to leave the room.

"7.00pm sharp," a curt reply exhibited the woman's mood.

Lily snubbed her mother and took Violet by the hand, showing unity. "C'mon, Violet, there's plenty of time if we go now."

"Never mind them, love," said Mrs Park in response to their outburst, "good manners are not one of their qualities. Magda is a vibrant young lady, and I'm sure you two will be friends."

Charlotte brushed off that remark. Perturbed by the girl's reactions, she wondered what else they lacked. Like a belligerent child, Charlotte followed Mrs Park throughout the house in a sluggish fashion. Not a word penetrated Charlotte's dull, weary senses. Oblivious to her new tenant's need for rest Urtha Park led her boarder through the halls.

"The kitchen is behind the dining room. Everyone is welcome to make supper after hours. My quarters are beside the kitchen, and I'll show you the washroom tomorrow. Come, I'll take you upstairs to your bedroom."

Sleep on the train trip had eluded Charlotte. To save money, she travelled in the seating carriage where her mind filled with excitement and trepidation about the move to Sydney. The rumble of wheels over tracks, the rattle of windows and shutters, and the chatter of other passengers kept her awake until near dawn. Her waking hours extended into the afternoon.

Charlotte's mood revitalized with the promise of sleep, but her legs grew leaden as Mrs Park urged her to follow up the stairs. Each knee bend brought hope as she drew closer.

The landlady retrieved a set of keys from her apron pocket to open the first door on the left. The woman entered first to show her boarder the room. "Small, but serviceable," she said, handing the keys to Charlotte.

The word 'twee' jumped into her head as she entered her room and spotted the kidney-shaped dressing table. Lace curtains tied back at the window formed a heart at the centre. A chest of drawers and a mismatched wardrobe big enough to hold her meagre belongings completed the room. Not her ideal decor, but suffice for a cheap rental. Charlotte plonked her suitcase on the floor with a thud, eager to test the mattress.

She agreed to read the list of house rules before the evening meal and acknowledged rent was due each Friday at supper. Disappointment turned to frustration when told that the 'charming' daughters shared her bathroom. Dinner was served on Saturday nights around 5.00pm to allow time for social engagements. "Tired after your journey?" Mrs Parks asked, her hand on the doorknob.

"I am," replied Charlotte, grateful the landlady was leaving the room. She continued, "The train was filled with servicemen returning home. A cheerful few displayed their happiness; others wore masks of unforgiving sadness. Most were too young to fight a war."

Mrs Park dismissed any further conversation by opening the door. "I'll be downstairs if you need anything." She left Charlotte on her own.

Charlotte discarded the outer layers of her outfit. She hung her cardigan over the bedhead and her trousers and blouse over the chair by the window.

The editor of City News expected her in his office Monday morning, giving her a couple of days to settle after the long trip. She slid beneath the sheets, closed her eyes and yawned.

Her thoughts drifted to the reasons for moving interstate. She left nothing behind except an ex-boyfriend and shattered dreams. The four-year relationship soured when she discovered he was unfaithful with her best friend.

Free to make a new start, she accepted a position in Sydney as a crime reporter. A career she worked hard at and put her own life in jeopardy more than once. This new editor had checked her credentials and was not concerned about her gender or her age. At twenty-two, she had mastered the skills for investigative reporting. Her placement in this boarding house was not by coincidence. The editor believed the disappearance of a boarder was somehow connected to this house. Charlotte's telephone conversation with her new boss prior to her relocation to the city highlighted the failure of the police to establish the missing girl's activities after her supposed departure. Charlotte's youth and experience would enable her to pursue her editor's suspicions.

Anything for a great story. Sleep before dinner brought images of a dance with menacing creatures whose red glazed eyes invaded her dream. A cry for help pierced her heart as death knolls clamoured through her dream state.

She sat bolt upright. Sweat on her brow. Her breathing was shallow; her mouth dry; she inhaled deeply and exhaled to slow the pounding in her chest. Her vision adjusted in the fading light. Charlotte squinted her eyes. Had she imagined the door handle twist? No. The dinner gong echoed through the house as she jumped off the bed, interrupting whoever tried to access her room. Initial instincts to yank the door wide open were pushed aside. Voices from other boarders mingled in the hallway. Too late to identify whoever might be close by. This little incident would not be forgotten.

8

CHAPTER TWO

With no trust in premonitions, the effects of her dream did not linger. Floorboards creaked beneath the weight of footsteps throughout the house, adding a disturbing reminder of her dream. A floorboard near her door groaned as if pained beneath the weight of someone paused on the other side. Could she have imagined that someone had tried to enter her room earlier? Her wits returned, she cried out, "Is anyone there?" No answer. But the shadow beneath her door faded away.

She rose from the bed to open the window and poked her head through the opening to inhale the fresh air, but her lungs expanded with a rush of cold air. She gasped and spluttered, trying to catch her breath. The wind whipped at her hair; her skin prickled with goosebumps. She shivered as she closed the window. Wintry weather had turned the evening sky into a whirling mass of dark clouds.

The temperature had dropped while she slept. The room was cold compared to the warmth of the bed. A quick rub over her shoes removed the surface dust. She whispered to her shoes as if they were animate things. A good spit and polish for you both before I turn up for work on Monday. Well placed bobby pins secured her mid-length bob along both sides over her ears. Her trousers were clean, though crushed from the overnight travel. Hard as she tried to pat them down, the creases showed where her cardigan hemline finished.

She locked her bedroom door and placed the key in her cardigan pocket. She paused a moment to once more rub her hands down her thighs before heading downstairs.

"Ah! Here she is. How are you, dearie? Did you get your things unpacked?" Mrs Park stood in the hall holding a tray laden with a platter of various slices of cakes and a jug of what looked like milk. The government had eased on supply of ration cards. Jelly, tin cream and condensed milk made delicious slices. Charlotte, herself, baked with the same ingredients back home.

"Not yet, Mrs Park," replied Charlotte.

Mrs Park nodded her head toward the parlour. "You go in first, love. Don't want to lose a grip on this tray." Charlotte stepped into the parlour. The chairs by the fire were empty and inviting. She sat and held out her palms to catch the warmth. Fresh pine cones crackled on the fire.

Charlotte watched Mrs Park set the tray on the centre table and proceed to pour tea. A petite girl helped herself to a slice of jelly cake. She stood in front of Charlotte. "Hello! I'm Sophie. My room is in the attic above you. I hope I won't disturb you."

"I'm sure you won't, Sophie." Charlotte smiled back and admired Sophie's simple hand-knitted pullover. The lemon colour suited the girl's complexion. Sophie's skirt of navy coloured wool added contrast to the paleness of her skin. She wore house slippers of black satin with ruby-red flowers stitched across the front. "You look warm," complimented Charlotte.

"Oh! Don't mind the slippers. My feet get colder than a frog on a rainy day." They chuckled at the thought.

"How do you like your tea, love?" Mrs Park asked Charlotte.

"Black, please, no sugar, thanks. But I can get it." Charlotte made to stand, but the landlady handed her the cup and saucer before she had a chance.

"Thank you, Mrs Park. No need to wait on me."

Mrs Park ignored the remark, her head turned toward the entry hall as the front door opened. Dried winter leaves swirled past the parlour's doorway to settle in a whimsical pattern on the worn rug. A red-haired beauty burst into the room with flair. Charlotte recognised the young woman who almost tripped her earlier in the afternoon.

Magda's entrance was loud and grand. Her voice a cheery tone, "Hello! I'm home! What a day." She plopped on the nearest chair and kicked aside her shoes.

Sophie responded first. "Tough day at the office, dear?"

"No, the sailors escorted a few of us from work over to Luna Park. What a place. I might lose my voice from screaming on the roller coaster."

Lily and Violet entered the room, and obvious to Charlotte, not in the mood for frivolity.

Magda winked at Charlotte, who responded with a meaningful smile. Mischief was afoot. "Of course, the Tunnel of Love was a must."

"Spare us the details of your escapades with the opposite sex." Violet shook her head in disgust.

Magda poured a cup of tea for herself and added a splash of milk-like substance plus a tiny sprinkle of sugar, part of her tea-making ritual. The drought in the west caused havoc in the dairy industry. With the scarcity of milk, powdered milk became a common substitute. She stirred the sugar minus the tinkle of silver spoon against china. Within moments, she lifted the cup to her lips; pointed her 'pinkie' outward before sipping without smudging her painted lips. Between sips, Magda acknowledged Charlotte.

"Hello, you must be our newcomer. I'm Magda."

"Yes, I know. You almost knocked me down the stairs this afternoon. I'm Charlotte." She couldn't stop herself from smiling at the contrast of quiet tea-sipping and rushing out of the door.

"Yes, sorry about that." Magda placed her cup and saucer on the table nearest her to clutch her hands to her heart. "A date with the most handsome American sailor I've ever met."

Mrs Park interjected, "Be wary of those sailor boys, love. They promise the world to a girl in every port." They laughed together at the thought. Charlotte listened to the banter between the two women.

"It's all right, Mrs Park. Yes, he will sail off into the sunset. Anyway, I have no desire to go to America."

"I've heard that before. Our neighbour's daughter said the same thing. Now she's living over there in some bible belt with one child and another on the way."

"Don't worry so, Mrs Park, I'm having a little fun now that the war is over." To change the subject, she asked Charlotte, "What are you doing here in Sydney?"

"I start my new job at the City News."

"Are you a journalist?"

"Yes, but I won't be doing anything important for a while, except mail and filing." Her reply was light-hearted, but she noticed Lily and Violet's scowled faces. *Why would this upset them?* Charlotte continued to smile while she studied the sisters across the room. For now, her previous work with the police forces back home remained secret.

Magda's cheery voice brought her attention back to her surroundings. "Hey, Charlotte, come to the dance Saturday night at the Town Hall?"

"Sounds great, Magda, love to." They sat in the parlour, getting to know each other's backgrounds and ambitions. By the end of the evening, a friendship sprouted.

Chapter Three

Joseph Moody shuffled toward St James Rail Station. At twenty-five years, he looked like an old man dressed in well-worn army gear. He was cold and miserable. Late afternoon shadows darkened the pathways through Hyde Park, where homeless remnants of society commenced their evening rituals wherever they sheltered for the night. Stooped beneath the weight of his khaki overcoat and woollen army blanket on his shoulders, another storm broiled overhead bringing icy southerlies to assault the city and all those who traversed its streets.

He wrapped his hand around the rum bottle inside his coat's left pocket fighting the temptation to indulge in a swig. His other pocket bulged with cigarette packets, courtesy of his friends. An open packet and box of matches filled his inside breast pocket. Nervous tension welled from within. He needed shelter for the night, a place from the outside world, but he knew his nightmares would impinge on his sleep.

He ignored the grunts of recognition from the regulars. Newcomers, with their meagre belongings searching for spaces to rest, wove through the mass of bodies bobbing up and down. A sea of shadows from blankets and canvas sheets flicked up and down, wavered across the floor and ceiling. The movements reminded Joe of a convoy of ships laden with troops coursing paths beneath a midnight sky. He shuffled on past the society of hopelessness.

The grumbles and moans as each person spread out on the floor irritated Joe. A dormitory of misfits. A woman's hushed voice soothed the cries of her infant. He turned to watch the baby suckle on its mother's breast and wished he had known a mother's love. Fate wove a different thread to lead him in directions opposing his life choices.

By the time he reached his particular spot, his legs faltered. Tired and unfit, he begrudged the distance to his own space, where he sought solitude deeper in the tunnel. Joe was not in the mood for a cold bath in the water hole left by early engineers. He retrieved his few belongings from the recess close to where he slept. Preparation of his makeshift bed consisted of initial layers of canvas scraps to ward off the chill of cold concrete, followed by layers of wooden pieces from fruit crates and, finally, his army overcoat. The grey blanket he wrapped tightly around his body. A knitted balaclava kept his head, ears, face and neck warm. Before he sat, he pulled his wallet out to examine the contents. The battered leather folds held a crumpled letter, a photo and a small amount of cash, thanks to his friends Michael and Nora.

He unfolded the last letter his fiancée Madelaine had sent before she disappeared. He knew it off by heart, but he imagined her seated at her writing desk and penning the words I love you. He touched his fingers to his lips then pressed them close to Madelaine's photo. *I should've been there Maddy. I should've been there.*

He slumped atop his bed, leaned against the cold wall tiles, and tucked his wallet and its memories inside his coat pocket. Joe set up his most prized possession. A kerosene lamp gifted by Michael with a note that read - 'Something to put a little light back in your life.' With unsteady hands, he managed to strike a match in one swipe to light the kerosene-soaked wick. He preferred the mesmerising dance of a naked flame to a battery-operated rail guardsman's torch, which he kept on hand for backup. If he could find solace in the silence triggered by alcoholic stupor, this was his space for sleep. The abandoned rail tunnels at St James offered isolation. His transition to fit back into society was more difficult than he imagined.

Unspeakable haunting memories of a Godforsaken time plagued Joe at night. He fought against the well of voices from dead comrades. His first gulp of rum released a melee of painful screams from dying men. Worst times invoked the silence before a battle. He could taste the fear inside the landing craft. He could no longer pray to a God who had forsaken him and his fellow soldiers. He sought refuge in rum. The effects of alcohol quietened his inner turmoil and stifled his nightmarish demons without comfort.

Joe settled into his space with no expectation of a good night's sleep. He remained seated against the solid wall. To save his supply of matches, Joe lit a cigarette from the flame of the kerosene lamp. The first drag was long and slow to allow the buzz of nicotine to work its magic. He tried to blow a smoke ring, then gave up. The rum bottle stood between his bent knees. The flickering light projected hideous shapes onto the opposing wall. His own dark shadows splayed like ghouls across the subway tiles with each movement of his arms.

He took a last puff of the cigarette then stubbed it out on the floor. He grasped the bottle tight around the neck. The bittersweet flavour of the amber liquid passed his lips. Vapours of rum mingled with the fumes of the burning kerosene. The first swallow teased his taste buds before slipping over his tongue. "Thank you, my friend," he said as he raised the bottle in salute to his shadows.

Each swallow soothed his senses until silence filled his brain. Rum extinguished the tormenting nightmares of desert and jungle battlefields. Numbness seeped through his nervous system by the time he drained the last drop. Resting on his makeshift bed, sleep devoured him until a sudden whirring noise jolted him back to consciousness. Vibrations pulsed beneath him and around him. Light flashes pierced his closed eyelids. He stirred, stretched, and rolled over to face the wall. Each nerve cell responded with muscle spasms. Unable to control the sensations in this position, he rolled back. An ache inside his head thumped to the rhythmic beat. He blinked before he opened bloodshot eyes behind the balaclava openings. *Christ!* The back wall glowed with hues of blues streaming in circles. He checked his lamp, but the flame had long died.

His senses shifted - he could taste the sound and hear the colours. His heartbeats increased. Sweat oozed from every pore. He wanted to tear at his clothing but could not move. The bizarre kaleidoscope of colours filled him with a mixture of fear and awe. He was scared, as scared as when he warded off the enemy outside the sand bagged trenches in the desert. He wrapped himself tight into a cocoon, hoping he would be invisible in the shadows. Cowardice did not fit well in

Joe's nature, but nervous tension racked his body. Was he back on the battlefield where the Angels of Death took away the dying and dead? He willed his blurry eyes to close. They refused to obey.

Undefined forms began to evolve from deep inside the haze. Eerie patterns stretched from floor to ceiling the length of the tunnel. Colours of blue, aqua and purples weaved into a blur, obliterating the tiled walls. Wide-eyed and trembling, Joe shrank deeper under the blanket. What new nightmare invaded his soul?

Three distinctive shapes emerged, faceless men wearing Trilbies tipped low over their brows. Tall men in dark trench coats who looked nothing like his battlefield angels of death strode past. Bewildered by the scene unfolding, he wondered if the image was real. Who were they? Is it possible he was crazy? Fear held him rigid, his muscles taut. He dared not move. Darkness seeped into the tunnel within minutes. He grabbed his torch from his coat pocket. Silence embraced Joe as he fumbled for his cigarette packet to extract one. In his haste, the rest spilled out. He mentally cursed, afraid his voice might echo.

Before despair set in, he roughly scooped up the cigarettes then tossed them aside in a heap. He steadied his hands enough to relight the kerosene lamp. He trembled like a schoolgirl on her first date. His mind, beneath the spell of alcohol, filled with dread. A new nightmare invaded his already tortured soul.

Chapter Four

Saturday afternoon was alive with preparations for the dance. The girls hustled for a position close by the fire to dry shampooed hair. Charlotte wrapped strands of her hair around hot curling tongs to enhance her bob style cut. Satisfied with her efforts, she left the fire to Magda, whose thick hair needed more time. "I'll be upstairs if you need me, Magda."

"Won't be long myself."

Inside her room, Charlotte stood in front of her open wardrobe and frowned. Four trouser suits for work, one day dress, and another frock for after five wear filled the small hanging space. She removed the garment from its confines and draped it over the bed. Seated in front of the mirror of her dressing table, she prepared to apply face powder and a soft pink lip colour. A knock on her door interrupted the routine. Poised between adding a second puff full of powder, she answered with a yes and heard Magda's voice.

"I need help."

Charlotte eased off the chair and moved to open the door. She came face to face with Magda leaning against the door frame with her head hard against the timber. A collection of dresses hung precariously over her shoulder, threatening to tumble to the floor. Magda looked forlorn and in need of a friend.

"Whatever is the matter?" asked Charlotte.

"I don't know which frock to choose for tonight. Can you come and help?"

"Sure, why not."

"Great."

Charlotte felt the tug on her arm as her friend dragged her across the hall. Inside her friend's bedroom, Charlotte sat on the bed after negotiating a path between dresses and shoes strewn across the floor. Floral and striped styles burst with colours to complement her pale skin and red hair. "I see your problem."

"You do?"

"If we collect all the garments and hang them around the room, we might have a good chance to select one for tonight."

Together they collected the stray garments. After deliberating on the choices, Magda chose the blue floral, a reminder of springtime. "Good, you're done; now I have to finish getting ready." Back in her room, Charlotte stretched her arms over her head to pull on the prettier of the two dresses she owned. *Time to release my feminine side, and with no full-length mirror, how can I well.* She scolded herself, remembering the words of the nuns at high school. 'Vanity is a sin'. She smiled.

She wanted to give herself the once over before venturing out. The dress did look damn good in the store. She spun about on the spot. The skirt fell soft about her body, then widened at the knees to curl about her mid-calf. The off the rack style suited her shape. A soft curvature of a seam gathered under the bust line enhanced her female attributes. The finishing touch was her mother's pink pearl brooch pinned beneath the lace collar and pearl earrings attached to her lobes. Happy with her outfit, Charlotte crossed the hall and knocked on Magda's door. "Are you ready?"

"Yes. Come in." Magda was turning this way and that, watching the movement of the upper skirt expose the pale blue tulle petticoat. She stopped to study her new friend before uttering a compliment, "That suits you; you look lovely."

Charlotte's pastel hue contrasted with Magda's vibrant floral of blues. The bodice plunged low enough to hint at cleavage, and the wide collar emphasised the size of her bosom. Shiny clips set with bright blue stones held rolls of her hair firmly in place.

"Are they real diamonds around your neck?" Charlotte asked.

"Don't be silly; they're paste stones. Not the real things." Her fingers slid over the stones, "They do catch the light on the dance floor, though." She winked at Charlotte. Both laughed at the innuendo.

After an early supper, Magda and Charlotte, dressed in overcoats against the cold, stepped out for a night of dancing in the Town Hall ballroom. The sun set behind a build-up of dark clouds, which indicated more heavy rain in the city. On their way to the bus stop, Charlotte turned up her collar and knotted her neck scarf tighter to block the rush of cold air coursing along the avenue.

"Can't wait to tread the boards to warm up," Magda said as she snuggled close to Charlotte.

"It's been a while since I went to a dance, Magda, and I'm sure I have two left feet."

"You'll be fine, Charlie. With your looks, you won't be short of a dance partner. Here's our stop."

"I'm glad you know where you are going."

"Not hard when you travel to work every day."

Before Charlotte knew it, Magda hooked her arm with Charlotte's. Together they climbed the stairs to the main street. People chatted about the new dance routines as they jostled along the footpath toward the building. Excitement spread through groups rushing beneath the portico. Music bellowed through the huge open doors. Bodies huddled on the outskirt of the dance floor where men twirled their partners in step to the music.

After they checked their coats at the cloakroom, a tall American sailor grabbed Magda. He twirled her about and the flash of her legs and tulle petticoat raised a few wolf whistles. "Hi, babe, been waiting for you." He leaned in for a kiss.

She turned her head for a peck on the cheek. "Not now. Stop. Please." she giggled. "Let me introduce you to my new friend, Charlotte from Queensland, and fresh to the city life," before she could say anymore.

"I'll get a buddy of mine to look after her tonight."

"No need, mate. This one's taken." Charlotte turned her head. The local accent belonged to a tall, handsome man with onyx-coloured eyes and his hair cut short back and sides with a single curl over his forehead. He held out a bent arm to escort Charlotte to the dance floor. Butterflies filled her stomach, her knees wobbled, her heart pounded when he asked her to dance. Stripped of control of her emotions in the presence of this man, she fumbled her words, "I'm afraid I'm a bit rusty on the dance floor."

He looked down at her. "Me too. Name's Michael, by the way."

"I'm Charlie." Her stomach flipped, and her hands shook at his touch on the small of her back. Her usual bravado disappeared. This new feeling was disconcerting. She trembled as he took her close in his arms for a slow dance. For the first time in her life, tremors streamed through her body. This man affected her in ways she had never encountered. She willed her body to relax before he noticed. Beneath his charm, she relaxed enough for his expert guidance through the dance steps without mishap. Their bodies aligned with the rhythm of the music. Dancers cleared the floor when the set finished.

They both attempted small talk at the same time. Charlotte conceded to Michael's wishes to speak first, and she shared why she moved to Sydney to work with the City News. She noticed he raised an eyebrow in query about her chosen career, but an American interrupted and asked her for a spin on the dance floor. Charlotte was none the wiser about Michael's career.

Charlotte caught up with Magda and her sailor friend, whose buddies were polite but loud. She had a couple of dances with one or two of them. Aware of Michael's frequent gazes in her direction, she noted he danced with no one else but a young and pretty woman with blonde hair. Not the type of female to interfere in relationships, Charlotte wondered if the besotted woman was his girlfriend.

The MC announced the last dance. Another sailor whisked her onto the floor before Charlotte had a chance to look for Michael. After a few steps into a waltz, Michael cut in, "Sorry mate, the lady saved this one for me. If you don't mind." The American released Charlotte with all the chivalry of an English knight.

Charlotte smiled at Michael, then laughed when he said, "You couldn't have the last dance with a foreigner on your first night." The gap between them widened as the last bars of the waltz floated across the room. The lights on full signalled the end of the evening. "Thank you, Charlotte; perhaps we'll meet again."

"That would be nice, Michael, and thank you for helping me find my way around the dance floor." Charlotte looked about for Magda, but Michael spotted her.

"There she is, with your coats. She seems in a hurry. I'll walk you over."

Surprised, she asked, "Do you know Magda?"

"Yes, I do." His response lit her inquisitive mind. Magda acknowledged Michael between short bursts of goodbyes with the Americans. He helped both girls into their coats.

Aware of Michael's gentleness and nearness, Charlotte asked, "What's the rush, Magda?" The dance was over, but she was disappointed the evening had come to a close. Small talk between each dance had been one-sided. She was positive he held secrets. A glimmer of light manifested in the dark onyx pools beneath his brow when he smiled. She wanted to know him.

"We've got to catch the last bus; it's a long walk home." Magda grabbed Charlotte's hand and led her away. "I've no wish to disappear like those two girls in the news, thank you."

"Of course not, but there are two of us." Charlotte kept her business to herself. Too early to reveal the truth about her residence in the boarding house. Reality reared with the shift into reporter mode but not before she said goodbye to Michael. Neither noticed the frown form on Michael's face. Magda dragged her down the steps into the cold air. "Slow down, Magda. What happened back there?" She wished she had more time to say goodnight to Michael. Perhaps another time.

"Oh, nothing I couldn't handle. I didn't want to get bogged down with those sailors. I don't trust them. Their ship sails on Wednesday. Thank goodness." She giggled. When they're gone, maybe I'll have a chance to find an Aussie guy just like Michael."

Confused and embarrassed by her remark, she said, "It was only a dance, Magda, and besides, you already know him."

"Only a dance. You say that so casually. I'd a like a dance like that, and I certainly don't know him the way you are suggesting."

Home before curfew, they drank a cup of hot cocoa before going upstairs to bed. Charlotte asked how Magda knew Michael.

"He comes into the mayor's office now and then, and if you think I am interested in your handsome dance partner, he's not my type. You can dream all you like about Michael Devlin."

"I'm sorry, Magda. It's all new to me."

"What is?"

"Oh, you know, the move to the big smoke; the emotions run wild at times."

"You're okay, Charlie. Hang in there. It won't be long before you get settled and able to handle everything that comes your way."

"I'm not so sure, Magda."

"Go to bed, silly."

"You go up while I wash up these cups. Won't be long." Charlotte checked the kitchen before she flicked the light switch. The entry hall chandelier with its faint glow camouflaged the worn carpet and dull painted walls. The street lamp radiating through the glass panels summoned the glass-eyed ghouls' shadows to dance.

The familiar scent of Divine7 lingered about the stairwell. To her, it smelled of death surrounding her grandfather's body laid out in a room on a summer's day. She would never get used to the scent of that cologne.

Caught between the entrance and her room, she dashed up the stairs two at a time.

CHAPTER FIVE

An evening shift proffered a chance for Michael to meet with Joe in Hyde Park. His satchel held cold chicken, fresh damper, and two containers. The flasks contained hot tea for himself and rum for Joe. The bag weighed heavy over his shoulder. "G'day, mate."

"What do you want, Mick?"

Joe's gruff voice did not deter his friend. Michael ignored the tone. "Just a friendly hello." The satchel landed softly on the bench seat beside Joe. "Here, I brought you some tucker. Not much of a meal. Thought we might share." He spread the food out on a tea towel he placed between them before picking up a piece of chicken and a slice of damper. "Don't know about you, Joe, but I hate to eat alone."

Joe's saliva glands worked overtime. The smell of fresh damper made his empty stomach growl. He had no immediate recollection of when he last ate. A staple diet of soup, sardines or anything in a tin washed down with water was wearing a little thin. "I could think of better company, but you'll do." He reached out for the chicken.

"Tuck in then," Michael suggested.

"Did you cook this?" Joe asked as he chomped into the flesh.

"Sure did! I have your aunt to thank for the Sunday lessons."

Joe nodded in agreement. He remembered the lazy days at the Devlin house, especially Sundays. Joe's aunt worked as a cook and housekeeper for the Devlin family. The money she earned provided everyday comforts for them both and Joe's education. Though she loved him like her own, she had little free time to spend with him. Fortunately, Michael's family welcomed him anytime. His home was with his aunt, but Joe's childhood revolved around his friends, Michael and his sister, Madelaine, and her friend, Nora. The four children spent as much free time together as possible until the war.

Michael dabbed a clean handkerchief across his mouth. He flinched when Joe used the back of his coat sleeve. "Forgotten your manners, I see."

"Let's not get into that, please, not tonight. I'm exhausted."

"Are you sick?"

"Nuh."

"Why are you so tired? Not like you. Are you getting enough food?" He filled a mug with hot tea for himself.

"Yeah. The soup kitchen's Italian Chef offers a-la-carte menus. For afters, the ladies hand out sweet French pastries topped by with Belgian chocolate syrup."

"Very funny. I'm serious." Before Michael sipped on his tea, he handed a small flask of rum to Joe.

"Since when did you ever get serious, mate?"

Aware of the tension rousing inside Joe, Michael replied, "I care, mate, I care."

"Well, if you cared so much, how come you didn't find Maddy?"

"C'mon, Joe, rehashing the past isn't going to solve anything. Maddy's gone; accept it. You think I don't miss her? God, she was my sister. I was happy when she accepted your proposal. No better brother-in-law than my best friend."

"Leave it, Mick, not another word. I need to get into the tunnel to sleep. That blue light woke me twice last night."

"Blue light? What blue light?"

"The one in my dreams."

"That reminds me, Joe. I met a wonderful girl at the dance last night who has the voice of an angel. My dream girl, I want to spend the rest of my life with this one."

"Did you manage to get her name, or just your hands all over her?" Joe looked sideways at his friend.

The comment prickled Michael's temperament. "You've been living it rough too long, Joe. This one is special and new in town. She's agreed to meet up soon."

"Good for you, Mick! Maybe it will give you some time to yourself instead of looking after me."

"Ah! Joe, things will get better for you in time. Let go of the past and face life head-on. It isn't easy, I know. Something will happen to burst these bubbles you've put around yourself."

Michael refilled his mug. "I've known you since childhood, and there is a good man inside that frame somewhere. I would give anything to bring you safely home."

Joe fidgeted when Michael wiped moisture from his eyes. "Bloody hell! Mick! What am I supposed to say now? Time's not right for me, not until I can look at myself in the mirror and see a friend instead of blood on my hands."

"It was a war our country fought, Joe. Not a backstreet gang fistfight." Michael pulled the bottle of rum from his satchel. "Here, this might help. Against my better judgement, though, I'm sure you'll make short of it."

Joe snatched the bottle. "I'm not sure if that means you care or not, but thanks anyway." He rose from the bench seat and headed for the tunnels.

As Joe walked away, Michael shouted. "Remember our signal. I'm here if you need me."

"Yeah! Yeah! See you! And thanks for the rum." Joe raised his arm in a wave without turning.

Rum helped Joe forget about his war experiences and the loss of Madelaine. Not knowing was the worst of all. Joe couldn't handle life back home and chose to live on the streets and in the tunnels at night. His excuse was his search for Madelaine in the abandoned spaces. He wasn't about to give up except when the angels of death called him.

Michael walked away, wondering why Joe made past events personal. Others suffered or just got on with their lives. He missed his sister too. Husbands, sons, wives, and daughters died on battlefields or in planes falling from the skies or trapped inside bomb ravaged ships. War affected families from all walks of life. He turned around to watch Joe weave through the traffic and disappear into the shadows. Joe is a mate, albeit a drifter at the moment. Michael picked up his pace to start his night shift on the crime-infested streets of Sydney.

Joe hesitated inside the tunnel where nightmares plagued his subconscious. He questioned why the blue lights disturbed him more than battle scars. His hand clasped the bottle of amber liquid, his travel companion into the depths of despair.

34

Chapter Six

"Read all about it!" The paperboy bellowed out the headlines from the curb. "Young woman missing for two days. Read all about it!" Mindless, Joe pushed through the queue and past the grubby little fellow standing beside his rack of newspapers. The lad waved the headlines in every direction to gain a sale.

"Yesterday's news," Joe shouted. *The police have no idea, according to Michael. The bastard thinks it's me. Mates. Who needs them?*

Joe spun about when a shadow fell beside his own. His fists raised in defence. "What the fuck do you want now? I answered all your questions. Leave me be."

"That's not true, Joe. You misunderstood. I want to know what you actually saw on Saturday night."

Michael tucked his hands inside his trouser pockets to hold his suit jacket back behind his elbows. His stance portrayed a formidable investigator dealing with a suspect. Without consideration of Joe's reactions, he questioned his friend. "Where were you on Saturday night?"

On the defensive, Joe replied. "You think I had something to do with that girl?" He glared at his friend, then hunched his shoulders in shame. "Jesus Christ, Mick, I wish I had been anywhere but in those fucking tunnels that night." He sat on the bench with his head skyward. Michael was beginning to get on his nerves. "Yeah, how do you like that. The tunnels are usually my sanctuary away from the crowds."

"Yeah, drunk and in such a state that you wouldn't remember anything." The jaded look on Joe's face sought an apology. "Sorry, mate. I'm bewildered by this case; it reminds me so much of when Maddy disappeared. I couldn't find Maddy, and now…" he shrugged and sat beside Joe. "I have to find this one. It's my duty." Michael pulled a bottle of rum from his satchel. Joe snatched the bottle away before his mate changed his mind.

"Don't talk to me about duty. I've had my fill of obeying orders and hasty decisions which caused unnecessary deaths." He tucked the bottle into his coat pocket and continued. "Besides, my nightmares are more real than ever."

Michael shifted in the seat to look sideways at Joe. "Whatever are you talking about, Joe?"

"The angels of death in the tunnels at night." Joe tensed.

Michael withheld a laugh. "No such thing, Joe? Probably some kids playing a trick."

"Yeah, sure. I've seen two of them carry what looked like bodies over their shoulders. I watched them disappear into a shimmering mass of blue lights at the end of the tunnel. If I remember to look in the morning, there's nothing but a blank wall." Joe shuffled his feet to stop the nervous twitch in his leg.

Eager to elicit more information from his friend, Michael asked, "When did this happen, Joe?"

"Must have been a couple of nights ago, I suppose." His vague recollection did not help as he had been out of sorts. "I drank too much over the past couple of days, but they fuckin' scared the hell out of me."

Michael sighed. "And because you don't wear a watch, you don't know what time, do you?"

"Christ, Michael, you know how I hate to know the time. Besides, I wouldn't be able to focus on its hands in my condition. Have enough trouble focusing on my own."

Michael berated himself. If he had clues or witnesses, his job would be easier. In this case, Joe's constant state of inebriation made him an unreliable witness. Like his sister Madelaine, Dorothea Langdon disappeared without a trace and was last seen waiting for a bus at Hyde Park.

His men searched the area and lost valuable time interviewing the homeless in the area. *Nothing! Nil! Zilch!*

Chapter Seven

Down near the Sydney dockyards, Charlotte stood on the opposite side of the street to the City News building. She ascertained her career as a crime reporter would flourish inside those walls. After all, the editor placed her in a boarding house to investigate the disappearance of Lailah O'Brien from the premises. The landlady had given Charlotte the missing girl's room. Lailah's disappearance was exactly why she moved to Sydney.

The dark side of human nature fascinated her even at times when fear sometimes held her back. This was not on her agenda today. She straightened her stance and squared her shoulders. She took a deep breath. With a brashness that frequently irritated members of the opposite sex she strode across the road.

The lift to the Editor's office was an old, unstable iron cage that moved sluggishly past the stairwell. Nobody took any notice of her. On level one, a teenage girl carrying a bundle of files in her arms stepped inside the cage. Charlotte stifled a smile as the bundle of files deftly moved to the crook of one arm to rest against the youngster's hips. With one hand free of the paperwork, the girl raised a side frame of her glasses, as her narrow red lips stretched open, "Hello, are you a visitor here?"

"No, I'm new staff." A bell tingled. The level four indicator light flickered as the lift shuddered to a stop. "My floor; see you around." Charlotte stepped out of the cage and watched it ascend to the upper levels before she turned around to observe the layout of the room ahead. Inside the expanse, desks aligned in groups of four covered the wooden floors. Smudge covered windows prevented natural light from streaming into the space. Telephones rang at intermittent times. Men with loosened ties and long shirt sleeves rolled back, manned the desks. Most held telephone handsets close to their ears while the pen in their free hands scratched notes on paper pads. Three rooms on the back wall separated the chief of staff, editor and assistant editor from the reporters and typists. In bold print on the door of the middle room, she read the words Editor and the name of Rory Calhoun.

Before she announced her presence, she heard a man's voice, "For God's sake Rory, she's a woman. What would she know?"

"Ease up, Brian, she has the skills to shape this newspaper into the future, and I am giving her a damn good chance."

"She's a rookie, Chief! Why do I get stuck with her?"

Without a second thought, Charlotte moved close to the door to eavesdrop. Something she often did in her career. Charlotte heard the strike of a match. The rich odour of burning pipe tobacco, which seeped through the decorative panel above the door, caused her nose to twitch. She sneezed, a dead giveaway of her presence. Telephones began relentless ringing from all areas in the open section. A man stood at his desk and shouted, "There's another disappearance!"

The door behind her swung open. She boldly stated, "Looks like I got here in time!"

A man of medium height and dressed in a shabby grey suit and neat striped tie stepped aside. His green eyes sank beneath bushy eyebrows scrunched together in a permanent frown.

He refused her extended hand to shake in greeting. "Women reporters, what next? Soon they'll be flying planes and commanding ships!"

Charlotte had heard this remark before, but her rebuttal was sharp, "We already do, mate!"

The editor guffawed. "I think you two will get along just fine." Rory leaned back in his chair to placate an imagined itch in his curly hair. He scratched at his crown while he puffed on his pipe. "Now then, Miss Tyrell, it is good to have you on our team."

"Thank you, Mr Calhoun, I look forward to working here, and you can call me Charlie."

"This is Brian Winslow; he will work with you on the disappearance of local girls. Colin, the photographer, is on call for when you might need him. Before you arrived, Detective Michael Devlin notified the press about a news conference."

The revelation that her dance partner was in the police force unsettled her. *He's a detective; why didn't Magda tell me? Surely she knew. Will he be a hindrance or an ally?* She assured herself it was a minor detail, and she would manage any situation that might bring them together.

The editor looked at his gold watch. "You got half an hour. I expect you two to be there and have a report on my desk before day's end." As the two reporters turned to leave, Rory added, "And be nice to one another! Take Colin with you!" He followed them to the coat rack. Colin heard the shout and raced to the lift.

Eager to build a working relationship with her colleague Charlotte asked the obvious question. "Where was the last place this girl was seen?"

Brian replied, "At the Hyde Park bus stop late Saturday night after the dance in the Town Hall."

"I was there on Saturday night and was unaware of any disturbance. Everyone seemed to be in good spirits. A few stragglers wandered off down the street toward St James station. Nothing to worry about; it was just a little noisy."

"What did I tell you, Brian? You two get your heads together, and, after the press meeting, talk with the investigators."

They both donned their overcoats and walked toward the entrance. "Do you know your way around town yet, Charlie?" Brian asked.

"No, I haven't had the time to explore." She was a little miffed with his familiarity with her nickname but let the moment slide as she needed to work with this reporter.

"Well, let's go. The walk will do us good." He lengthened his stride. Charlotte kept up with her colleague's pace.

Morning rush hour fulfilled her expectations of a city street chock-a-block with pedestrians and cars and buses edging beside trams. The cacophony of motors and horns saturated the air like an orchestra trying hard to find a note and failing. Reporters crowded outside the police station blocking the footpath. Several policemen guarded the entrance.

"Don't look so worried, Missy. We have to wait until Mr Devlin appears." Brian nudged Charlotte with his elbow.

"It's a press conference. Why should I be worried?" She batted her eyelids at him.

The huge cedar doors opened, and a buzz of whispers echoed around them. Detective Michael Devlin and his Senior Officer stepped up to a microphone. The crowd hushed but not the traffic. Before the officer's address began, Brian spoke to one of the guards and requested a private session with Detective Devlin. Colin busied himself with his camera taking photographs from all angles of the press conference. Brian and Charlie wrote notes for tomorrow's issue. The crowd dispersed before the two reporters entered the reception to wait for a private interview.

A few local citizens waited on bench seats. One young man collected his personal belongings after spending a night in the lock-up. She heard the duty sergeant tell the young man he was lucky no one wanted to press charges. Charlie wondered if anyone in the room saw or heard anything about the disappearances. Most of them looked street savvy by their furtive glances and attire. Before she could speak to anyone, a man appeared in the doorway of the station's inner sanctum.

A soft hue of pink covered both her cheeks as soon as Michael entered the room and gestured for them to approach him. If only she had asked Magda more about this man, perhaps she would have been prepared. Somehow, he had avoided conversation about his career while they spun around the dance floor.

Brian spoke first, "G'day Mick, what's been happening? Anything we can print today about the young woman?"

Michael looked past him to smile at Charlotte. "Hello, we meet again."

Her blush deepened. *Oh, God, why now?* "Have you got enough heat in this room?" Her remark was a feeble attempt at distraction from the flush on her cheeks.

Brian interjected before Michael had a chance to respond. "You two know each other?"

Without shifting her gaze away from Michael, she answered, "We met at the dance on Saturday night. That's all. We had a couple of turns on the floor, nothing more. Close your gaping mouth and keep things professional."

Her tone unsettled Brian, who rocked back on his heels. "Okay, Missy, I got the message. Professional it is."

To dismiss the temptation to laugh, Michael turned to Brian and invited them into the inner sanctum of the police station. Charlotte followed the men into a room with Michael's name in gold print on the door. Manners in the male domain fell by the wayside. In a polite social event, she would have waited to be invited to sit, but as the men showed no inclination to do so, she plonked herself in the chair nearest to the desk. After the two men made themselves comfortable, she decided to get on with the meeting. "Detective Devlin" She paused and looked at the ceiling then set her eyes on the detective. "Please, no questions until after you hear the story."

Both reporters nodded in agreement, although Charlotte had a list prepared.

"All I can tell you at the moment is that we know her name is Dorothea Langdon. Both her brothers died in the war, so she remained at the family's Paddington home with her parents who encouraged their daughter to go out Saturday night. They felt the time for grieving was long overdue. They suggested she reunite with friends. She met them at the Town Hall dance and, according to witnesses, was there for the last dance and left with the group of six friends for the bus stop." He paused to look at the mound of files on his desk.

"The last time anyone saw her was at 12.30am. Her bus was the last one scheduled to stop at Hyde Park. After boarding their bus, which was on time with ten minutes spare for the last one, Miss Langdon's companions realised their friend would be on her own. She assured them of her safety. Her transport was on time, and, according to the driver, nobody waited at the stop, so he drove on. We are interviewing passengers who might have seen her between arrival and departure." Michael paused and looked at Brian.

"As you would know, Brian, the homeless who usually hang around the area, settle in the tunnels early at night. With no immediate witnesses, our investigation has come to a full stop." Michael had been standing behind his desk with his head bowed, tapping his pen all the time he was speaking.

"Do you think this incident links to your sister's disappearance?" The tapping stopped. The pen was held in mid-air.

Charlotte's jaw dropped. Her journalist instincts ignited like a tuppeny-bunger. Questions she had for Michael streamed through her mind on both personal and professional levels. This was turning out to be some story. *How old was his sister? What's her name? Why was she in Hyde Park? Did he fail as a detective, or is he still looking for his sister?*

Could her disappearance be connected to the current two? She hushed her thoughts to listen to Michael.

Michael shook his head as he answered. "Can't honestly say, but there may be. It's been over six months, and like the recent ones, disappeared without a trace from the same spot. We did everything we could to locate her, but the search was called off." Michael tapped his pen against his desk. He explained about his dismissal from the case and how the investigating officers determined she had left of her own accord when they found personal items such as her purse, hat and gloves in a rubbish bin. Michael added, "Their reports stated she had found another boyfriend and didn't want to be around when her fiancé returned."

Charlotte and Brian could only nod their heads as if agreeing with the detective. Michael rested on the corner of his desk in front of the reporters. "You understand that I tried everything to convince them otherwise. I put patrols in place to protect women in the park area. Still, my senior officers declared them a waste of valuable manpower and time. Hyde Park was of interest to the investigation. After several debates, a few men were spared to patrol at intervals. I maintain my sister was abducted, but at the moment, my job is to focus on the disappearance of Dorothea Langdon and Lailah O'Brien and not my sister Madelaine. If there is a connection linking all three, perhaps the boys may stumble onto some lost clues." His eyes diverted to Charlotte. "Do you have any questions?"

Charlotte answered, "Lots, Michael, but I need to write this up for tomorrow's paper first. Can we make another time for questions?"

"Contact me through the station, please." Michael, with his right arm pointing at the door, stepped away from his desk to escort them from his office.

Not exactly the answer she expected, but she understood the professional attitude behind his statement. Brian and Charlotte rose from their seats and shook hands with Michael in a gesture of goodwill. Michael moved to open the door of his office, but Brian reached the handle first and released his grip to shake hands with the detective. "Bye, Mick. Hope you find the girls in one piece."

Michael's telephone rang. Before he accepted the call, he closed his office door behind the two journalists with the hope of solving the abductions uppermost in his mind.

Chapter Eight

After a week of investigations, Dorothea Langdon's file lay flat, thin and unopened on his desk. Saturday's morning fog brought nothing but misery to Detective Michael Devlin. Snippets of garnered evidence led nowhere towards a resolution of the girl's disappearance. Constant telephone rings and chatter between colleagues within the main office invaded his own space. To distract himself from the perplexing case, the detective decided to catch up with his friend Joe.

Dampness clung to Sydney without a sign of a shift from the murkiness shrouding the city and Michael's mood. Raindrops beat on his hat brim, similar to the sound of fingers tapping on a child's drum. He settled into a rhythmic walk from police headquarters to St James Rail Station. He straddled the puddles on the pavement; leftover rain from the previous night. Awareness of the plight of the homeless struck hard as he neared Hyde Park. He thought Joe was somewhere nearby.

He believed Joe needed guidance more than anyone he knew. Would he have been able to take the same path as Joe and ignore civilized living and undertake self-destruction? Michael was stronger than those ideas. But he couldn't ignore his childhood friend, a nerve-damaged veteran - anxiety neurosis the doctors diagnosed - and a drunkard. From boyhood to adulthood, their friendship surpassed guilt when he supplied rum more frequently than necessary. He knew Joe drank himself into oblivion. *How could anyone believe anything he said? Blue lights in the tunnel; angels of death, Bah!* Michael brushed these thoughts aside.

A blanket of fog clung to trees in Hyde Park. Wet and slippery thoroughfares impeded unwary pedestrians. Every few steps, a homeless person walked past. Stale body odour mixed with unwashed clothes. His stomach recoiled. Breakfast of a quick gulp of black tea proved insufficient. He dry retched. A nearby water fountain offered cold water to splash his face and the opportunity to rinse out his mouth. He cupped his hand beneath the flow to dampen the sweat building on his forehead. Green lawns in summer would have been the ideal spot to spread his body out, but the fog dampened everything. Instead, he wiped across the moist surface of an empty park bench and stretched out his body across the hard surface. Not comfortable to lie on, but it offered respite for a short time until his stomach settled.

If Michael intended to locate his friend, he would need to ask the park regulars if any had seen Joe. When asked, nobody had noticed if Joe surfaced that morning. The many who lived in the park knew Detective Michael Devlin. What did he expect? Open arms and welcome. People of this kind kept to themselves or kindred.

Before making his way into the tunnels, he purchased sandwiches from the station kiosk. Michael found Joe huddled beneath his blanket, still wrapped in his army coat. The temperature in the tunnel was mild, but the stuffy air unsettled him. "Hey, Joe! It's Michael! How are you?"

Joe stirred. He sat up, rubbing the sleep from his eyes. "What the hell! What time is it?"

"You still don't own a watch, do you?" Michael turned his arm about to look at his watch. "10.30am."

"Too early, Mick, go away." Joe lay back on his makeshift bed, pulling his blanket beneath his chin. "I need to sleep after the other night."

Curiosity swelled. "What happened to make you tired?"

"You don't want to know. Anyway, you wouldn't believe me." Joe tilted his head, "Besides, who's going to take the word of a drunk?"

"I will, mate."

"Don't mate me, mate!"

"C'mon, Joe, something's troubled you. I want to help. Here, I got you a sandwich." He waited until Joe sat up to pass the sandwich. Joe put it on his blanket.

"Gotta piss first."

"Okay, I can wait."

Joe came back to see Michael with his back against the tiles and elbows resting on bent knees. "You look comfortable there. Maybe you'd like to move in?"

"Nah, I prefer the creature comforts."

Joe sat away from his friend to avoid confrontation about personal hygiene. "Sandwich is good. Just what I needed. Thanks." Joe lit a cigarette. He blew smoke rings up to the ceiling. "I've plenty of practice on the technique."

Michael rolled his eyes. "Tell me about the other night, Joe, when you couldn't sleep." His request was half-hearted. He would listen to anything to veer away from his thoughts.

"You sure you want to hear about my nightmare?"

"Distract me from the serious investigation I'm involved in." He turned to Joe, "C'mon, spill!"

"The angels of death came through here on Friday night, I think. I lose track of time." He lit another cigarette, dragged and exhaled slow.

"What do you mean? No such things."

"I'm telling you; I saw them. At first, I thought three of them were coming for me. Funny, I know artists paint wings on their angel's backs. These blokes wore coats, not wings." Joe stubbed out his cigarette with detailed care. Twisting the butt about until a black ash mark stained the floor. His breathing slowed, but the clarity in his voice bewildered Michael.

"I've seen them before. First, pulsing lights of blue and aqua fill the tunnel over there." Joe pointed to the end wall, "then the angels stride out of the light as if on a mission. After the colours fade, I wait in the dark for them to take me, but they don't." Joe released an audible sigh. "I'm left alone, and nothing happens. I'm left to a deathly silence." A slight grin smeared his friend's face. "You don't believe me, do you?"

"It's only a dream, Joe, only a dream."

"You think so? I don't. They came back later with a woman slumped over one shoulder. Glad it wasn't me." His jittery fingers flipped out another cigarette from the packet. He dragged until the tip ignited. A quick movement of his hand extinguished the match. His tongue twisted to form smoke rings that floated high, widened and twisted before surrendering to oblivion.

"Did I hear you right? They came back with a woman?" Michael's senses sharpened as he realized the timing was coherent, but not the story. He needed to know more. "I believe you saw something, but in your state of mind, you've created another scene." He shifted his position on the floor closer to Joe.

"I saw one of those angels place an object against a wall tile. A small bubble of light pulsated until blue colours filled the tunnel. They walked into the centre, and then the light disappeared."

"Did they see you?"

"Can't be sure, but for some reason, they didn't want me, else, I wouldn't be chatting with you." Joe took a long draw on his cigarette. "Tell me, are you a little intrigued?"

"I suppose. The time frame is parallel with my investigation, but I believe your nightmares have evolved beyond comprehension. You need help before reality collides with your dream time." He had no time to retract his statement, which was intended to prompt his friend into action and not offer insult to an unstable mind. Silence wove between the two men as each pondered how to resurrect the conversation. Michael could see the hurt bleed across his friend's face. The expression altered with the closing of eyes, downcast head, clenched lips twisted upward to one side, then dropped. A frown between his brows deepened when Joe lifted his head to speak.

"I'll walk you out, Mick. You are my friend, and I am but a blight on your soul." Joe stood and saluted his friend with grace and mockery of a court jester.

To avoid further conflict, Michael ceded to Joe's wishes. Michael allowed Joe to escort him out. This standoff reminded Michael of when they were boys and Joe won at cricket or tennis. *Inside the man, the boy lurks.*

By the time the two men exited the station, bright winter sun dazzled in a cloudless sky. Southerlies, straight from the Antarctic ice caps, dispatched a warning of cool temperatures. Michael hoped the icy weather forecast might entice people to remain in the warmth of their homes, in particular the young women. "Call me if you need me. Joe; I'm still your friend regardless." He said before walking away.

On the footpath opposite St James Rail Station, Michael turned to watch Joe head for the sanctuary of the tunnels. He knew his friend to be a fearless soldier on the battlefield, but the visions Joe described were beyond belief. Michael decided to wait a day or two before another meeting, but this was Saturday. Another dance was scheduled at the Town Hall. He headed to the nearest hotel for a drink - a Sherry - plagued by questions of who the trespassers were and where they came from.

He was still thinking as he gulped the first glass and ordered a second, but the next two questions bothered him the most. *Who was the woman Joe saw taken into the light? Was it our missing woman - Dorothea Langdon?*

Chapter Nine

Rory Calhoun stood in the doorway of his office facing his two crime reporters. His gold watch was visible beneath the rolled cuff of his shirt sleeves. "Well, how did the press meeting go?"

Brian flopped into his desk chair. "As usual, the cops parted with titbits of information and not enough facts. We grabbed a chance for a private meeting with Detective Devlin. Bloody good that did!"

Without her own space, Charlotte stood beside Brian's desk. *Who the hell does this man think he is?* "That's not true, Brian. Michael shared important details."

The Editor queried the details. Neither reporter was forthcoming. Though both Charlotte and Brian were at loggerheads, the conspiratorial looks in their eyes displayed a professional attitude they refused to acknowledge. The Editor raised one eyebrow then looked back at Brian. "A disagreement already. I asked you both to reach common territory and produce note-worthy articles for the front page. Make sure your stories are ready for print ahead of the deadline. If that means working late, so be it." He turned about and closed his office door.

Annoyed by Brian's attitude, she remained motionless until he reacted. "What? Do you want something?"

"A desk would be nice?" There was no time to spare when she first arrived in the office. "Where am I supposed to work?"

"Ah! Red Alert! Damsel in distress. Find one yourself!" He waved his arms in a circle within his small space, "got a deadline to meet."

Charlotte took the lead, found a paper bin, and swept all the paper files off the workstation behind Brian. "Hey! That's my stuff!"

"Keep it off my space then. Now, let's get down to business." Charlotte got his attention. "You and I will find a way to work together, and I need your help."

"My help? Whatever for?"

"Can you get me into a male only area in a seedy pub near Kings Cross?"

"Whatever for?" Brian displayed a disregard for Charlotte's idea.

"What do you think? I want to find these missing girls." Charlotte stood tall with her hands on her hips. Brian's eyes widened then his brow crinkled into a multitude of little frown lines.

"Well? I smell disbelief."

"Why put yourself at risk, Charlie? Not the sort of environment for the likes of you."

Riled by his tone, she clenched her fists. "What do you mean by the likes of me?"

"Jesus, you get riled at the slightest thing. I didn't mean it that way. The Cross is full of men who have no regard for life, plus, a high percentage of 'working ladies' are living in seedy places. Some of those sheilas are willing to sell their children to the devil for any price."

Charlotte altered her demeanour to get on the reporter's good side. "Yeah, I'm sorry for jumping at you, but I'd like us to work together because you know the area. Someone in the neighbourhood knows something about the disappearances and no better place than the heart of the underground." She relaxed her stance to persuade Brian to agree to her request. "Besides, on the positive, we'll have a great story if we manage to solve this before the coppers."

"Yeah, yeah, Charlie, I admire your intentions, but..."

"Honest to God, Brian, you and I both know, only barmaids are allowed in the public bar. It's illegal for women. Besides, I'm new in a town where nobody knows me." Determined to have her way, Charlotte sat beside her colleague and raised her eyebrows. "Well?" she asked.

"All right then! Leave it with me. We get this story out for tonight's print and go for a drink in downtown Kings Cross. Why don't I do a pub crawl around the district and share any information I find?"

"Ha! How long do you figure you would stay sober? No thanks. This is my idea, but I expect you to cover my back." Charlotte's plan scared her. Charged with determination, her fears subsided. Confident that Brian would find a proprietor to permit her into the bar if she wore trousers and little make-up.

"Do you drink beer?" He half-turned in his chair, expecting a negative response.

"Of course I do. But I much prefer rum." She commented as she pulled her chair back to her desk. Charlotte mumbled a thanks beneath the sound of her fingers tapping sharp and fast at the alphabet on her typewriter. A deadline to meet.

CHAPTER TEN

"**M**ummy, the call is for you." In the downstairs hallway of the boarding house, Lily stood with the phone's mouthpiece in her hand, her fingers gripping it tightly.

"Coming." Before she left the kitchen, Urtha Park slung her apron over a hook on the pantry door. She took the mouthpiece from her daughter. "Good evening –"

"– Urtha, you are to come to Zerona at once. Sacrof is waiting." She heard the click before she could answer. *How dare he demand my presence in that God-forsaken place.* Hatred for her brother spewed through her mind, but she feared the consequences of disobedience. Within the hour, Urtha entered the small realm of her people, locked in time and servitude to a tyrant - her brother - Sacrof. Survival at any cost became her mantra.

"Urtha, my dear sister. It pleases me to see you here." The words lacked sincerity. Affection and trust between the siblings disappeared years ago.

Urtha Park grunted a response. "Liar. I am here under your orders." Tired of his murky moods and demands, she antagonized him further, "So, explain why you insisted on my presence when you know I hate this place." In a slight gesture of protest for the inconvenience, Urtha flung her woollen overcoat over the back of the spare chair before lowering her body on another more comfortable seat. Her fingers brushed along her thighs, straightening her dress over her knees. Puffy stockinged flesh bulged over the sides of her chunky shoes. She crossed her ankles out of sight beneath the seat.

When Sacrof spoke, his voice dripped with malice. "It is time, Urtha, to start the program." She was aware what this statement meant. Urtha was quick to impart that she was more than ready. Her small amount of motherly instinct was unashamedly put aside. Urtha regarded her boarders as pawns in Sacrof's scheme to manipulate the genetics of his people. "Our colleagues choose the girl in the attic first, then the red-haired girl followed by the nuisance journalist you know as Charlotte. You will need to be careful. Since humans moved into the tunnels, we changed the routine and took advantage of a couple of young women left alone at a bus stop."

"Why? Did you not consider the consequence of open abductions?"

"Do not question my authority. These random disappearances will remove interest from your boarding house."

Disobedience to Sacrof was useless. As master and executioner, any act of defiance meant death to the offender. Urtha squirmed in her seat, pressed her lips hard and pressed her tongue between clenched teeth in case any reckless words escaped. The taste of blood in her mouth brought her attention back to her brother's speech and her mantra.

"Transportation of sperm cells from our men proved unsuccessful. So, this time, the females in the boarding house will be brought to our side of the tunnel, and, after the procedure, returned to the human world. Doctor Zegrobbe will check on their well-being for approximately three months. After that, we will bring them back to our world until they are no longer needed. It is imperative that our mission remains on schedule. My scientist will explain the details."

The scientist handed the herbs to Urtha with instructions to add the dried blend of tasteless, colourless, and odourless ingredients to their morning meal or tea. A nauseous sensation was expected to overwhelm the recipient within days. One week apart, the girls would fall victim to the concoction to ensure the doctor's diagnosis did not arouse suspicion. Urtha Park was uncertain if the girls might suffer. Aware of the flaws in his idea, she tried to explain the girls would know of their body changes. "But..."

"You will see to it, Urtha!" Sacrof shouted. "Just follow my orders and ask no questions. The doctor has the necessary instructions to follow through with our plans." He held up his hand, palm facing outward. "No further discussion, sister, just obey." He turned abruptly and left the room. The scientist followed suit in case the woman asked more questions.

Several failures occurred before 1946. The old techniques risked the loss of sperm cells or the surrogate, or worse, birth imperfections. Failures threatened his existence. Some imperfects were sent to the outer borders to the lowlifes. Sacrof knew descendants of the exiled resided near the extremities of a world his forebears constructed. These people lived a primitive lifestyle with permission to procreate. The villagers were forgotten until the experiments began. Under the threat of death, the parents of young women escorted their daughters to the Inner Sanctum for experiments.

Subjected to this custom, the villagers began to instil a sense of rebellion among the young men. Thus, a small band of rebels, the Elder, Seth, his two warriors and a few young men and women, formed under the guidance of Harold, who moves between the two worlds.

Chapter Eleven

From across the country, Australian men and boys had answered the government's plea to enlist in the defence forces. A career in with the New South Wales Police Department placed Michael in good stead within the military police. The soldier's life for Joe. The army wanted soldiers. Eighteen-year-old Joe was elated. He passed the fitness test and more so on parade dressed in a private's uniform. The reality was extremely frightening. Rudimentary training found most of his companions with limited military skills. Inexperience showed its ugly face on the battlefields. Heroes died of wounds as fast as anyone else. There was no discrimination under gunfire.

The daring of the young soldiers consisted of childhood games, cops and robbers and cowboys and Indians. Hardly wartime experience. Farmers knew how to use a rifle; a butcher - knives. A baker became an army cook. Joe studied architecture. He loved the old houses, and the convict-built structures appealed to his creative senses. With no formal type of employment, he took his place in the infantry division. He aimed to understand weapons. He rarely missed targets while training.

When Joe returned after the war, he read the report of Madelaine's disappearance via Michael. To learn there were no witnesses stunned him. Those few words implanted themselves in his brain. On the night she disappeared, Madelaine left the hospital after finishing her rostered late shift. She was last seen by other staff heading toward her bus stop at Hyde Park. Madelaine was not at the stop when the next bus arrived, according to the investigators. The report concluded Miss Devlin discarded personal items in a nearby bin and left of her own accord. Nothing such as scuff marks in and outside the bus shelter marked a disturbance of any kind.

Dumb arse dicks were Joe's initial thoughts about the police team. Joe heard Michael's plea to believe he tried to keep the investigation open. For whatever reason, the detective's superiors blocked every move. Joe trusted his friend to remain vigilant. The mission became a constant search for Joe's fiancée at all costs, whatever that brings.

These Trilbies, as he nicknamed the intruders, these Angels of Death may be the same ones who took his love. Joe convinced himself that the wingless creatures in their dark clothes and trilby hats were behind her disappearance. His recent nightmares were not subconscious creations. He needed a drink. *No, at least a bottle or two for tonight, in case.*

Joe's mental state hindered his ability to begin a normal life. He accepted Madelaine's brother, Mick, and their childhood friend, Nora, did their best to help but his need for solitude went far beyond their comprehension. He knew too few men and women who seemed untouched by wartime experiences.

Joe insisted his friends agree to his terms to occasionally meet in the park and not interfere with his choice of lifestyle. He lacked the desire to cope with life. Joe believed a mate is a mate no matter what. Joe ignored Michael's recommendations to seek professional help and live a normal life.

On Sundays after church service, Joe and Nora maintained vigils observing passers-by. When their soirees began, Nora confided losing Madelaine sheared away a part of her own being. He could comfort her but not himself. His relief came from the bottom of a rum bottle.

By 11.30pm, most of the nomads of the park ventured off the streets in the vicinity of Hyde Park. The police presence made them uncomfortable. Extra foot patrols edged in and out of the dark lanes and paths around the park. The vagabonds deemed themselves safe amongst others yet feared the shadows. The street lamps were few and far between. The homeless desired solitude and detachment from the transgressions of society.

The tunnels, one level away from the surface, harboured the many who sought shelter and safety. A place where personal peace was often shattered by the thundering roar of a passing train.

Joe chose his space further inside the tunnel away from the groups who huddled together for safety. Their ever-watchful gazes over garnered belongings created a misplaced sense of security in the dim lights. Sometimes an altercation disturbed the false sense of serenity. Joe preferred to be alone in his area with its limited access to intruders.

He puzzled over how his angels of death moved past the others without disturbance. After a few swigs at the bottle, he decided to take a closer look at the dark recesses along the wall. He was unsteady on his feet after hauling his body upward with his bedraggled coat heavy over his shoulders. He rested a hand on the tiled wall for balance to aid his forward advance. In a drunken fashion, he saluted forgotten men who built the strong arched ceilings and walls and admired the workmanship at each recess.

"Bloody Hell!" He cursed as he stumbled and fell through a gap in the wall. It was wide enough for two, perhaps three, to pass through. He edged into the space of a tunnel he'd not noticed before. No shadows lurked inside the darkness. A whisper of fresh air passed his nostrils.

This unexpected find left him dumbfounded. The alcohol began its foggy twist and tumbled through his system, weakening his muscles. He turned about and tried to count the crevices as he struggled to steady his legs. *1, 2, 3... Oops! Steady!* He toppled over.

He rose from where he fell, dazed, groggy and sore. No blood on his fingers when he touched the bump on his head. In a dream-like state, he managed to get to his hands and knees to crawl back to his makeshift bed. *Look at the damn hole tomorrow.*

The headache in the morning overpowered his senses. The shaving mirror reflected a bruise on his head. He had no recollection of the previous hours. He checked his belongings, all accounted for. The headache strengthened, obliterating all he encountered on his search.

Joe wished he was dead. At least his headache. He reached for the bottle lying on its side. The hair of the dog that bit, as his aunt used to say. He wondered if he inherited alcoholism and decided his problem was self-inflicted. He dragged himself to the lake to wash his face. Body functions called. He would never allow himself to leave the tunnel without combing his hair and washing his hands and face. Each movement took its toll on his body. Bruises formed on his upper arms from when he fell onto the floor. Pain struck the muscles in his back as he reached to do his hair. The comb felt like a brick running over his scalp; his headache increased to an unfamiliar level. The rest of him could wait; nobody would notice him in a crowded street. Each step stretched his muscles to their limit. Time was of little importance, but he needed something to ease the pain. His gut tightened with the strain of walking, but if he stopped, he thought he might never move again. The steps from the underground were the most difficult to manage. Like a frail old man, he dragged himself up toward the outside world one step at a time.

Sydney was alive on the streets above. He surfaced from the tunnel screwing his eyes closed against the glare of the wintry sun. His head thumped. He needed a drink. The Town Hall clock chimed ten bells. "Aagh! Mr Hickory Dickory is awake and making too much noise!" He shouted while he cupped his hands over his ears.

Pedestrians, afraid of his appearance and uncertain of his behaviour, detoured wide around him. On his way to the nearest soup kitchen for a cup of hot tea and a bowl of hot porridge, he muttered to himself. "Never liked the damn stuff, but it fills my stomach for most of the day; beggars can't be choosers." He shuffled onto the street amid the clamour of tooting horns and screeching tyres. He gave the drivers a gentleman's bow followed by a two-finger salute.

He walked on the shady side of the street, beneath the overhang of awnings. Every now and then, he hugged a post for support to regain his breath. He saw Harold, on a seat in the park, talking to a few vagrants. He wondered why they huddled close like a footy scrum. The group parted as he drew near. "Got a *Bex* powder in one of your pockets, mate? My head is breaking in two."

"It won't, you know, but your liver might give up the ghost."

"Ghosts! You see any ghosts? I have. In the tunnels." He poked a finger at Harold's chest, adamant that his visions were real.

Harold asked him to keep his voice low in case the children heard. "What children? I don't see any. Only thieves and beggars live here." Desperate to be rid of the ache in his head, Joe spun a 180-degree turn to collapse on the seat beside Harold and hunched over with his head in his hands.

"See! It's only the demon drink doing this to you. Here's the Bex. Take it over to the water fountain and wash it down slow."

Joe teetered to the water fountain and tipped the powder off the paper onto his tongue. The bitter taste tested his need to swallow or spit and suffer the headache. His height proved awkward with attempts to put his mouth to the spurt of water. After two or three bobs, he managed without falling forward. The powder tingled on his tongue before it dissolved. The headache would take longer to dissipate. He sat beside Harold to breathe in the fresh air and garden fragrances.

A shadow loomed over him. He shivered. *Am I asleep? Where am I?* His heart pounded fast. A hand reached to touch his shoulder. He jumped to his feet, fists high and ready to fight.

Michael moved to the left to avoid a fist to his jaw. "Calm down, Joe!" Michael's voice broke through the tension, "By all the saints! You are jumpy." One glance at the appearance of Joe, Michael apologised. "Sorry, mate, I thought you were asleep; I didn't mean to sneak up on you." Remorseful, Michael added, "C'mon! I'll buy you a decent meal and some tea before anyone else spooks you." A friendly tone penetrated Joe's dulled mind. He liked the suggestion.

Memories muddled in his mind. Images of dark shadows wearing trilbies zigzagged through shimmering hues of blue. He could make no sense of his nightmares as he walked with Michael to the nearest canteen. Aromas of baked cakes and steaming tea teased their taste buds, and Joe's stomach growled, but he hungered not for food but for the truth behind his visions.

Chapter Twelve

The thought of dancing with Michael enhanced her happy mood. "Dinner was divine, Mrs Park." The others nodded in agreement, still devouring mouthfuls of a creamy rice pudding.

"Thank you, Charlotte. I'll tidy up and bring back some hot tea for you all." Mrs Park ran her hands across her apron as she left the room. *Nervous tension or the habit of a cook.* Charlotte clamped her mouth shut to stop the escape of idle words. Lily and Violet followed their mother to the kitchen to start their assigned chores.

Charlotte waited until she and Magda sat alone in the dining room before speaking. "Have you seen Sophie?"

"Yes, I did this morning. Actually, she looked ill."

"What do you mean? Was she sick? She never said anything about feeling ill last night."

"Don't worry so much, Charlie. Mrs Park will look after her and, if needed, will take her to the doctor. C'mon, you have enough to worry about with your work. Let's play some board games."

Charlotte followed Magda's lead and thought a good game of monopoly might be what she needed. Anything to shift the constant parade of scrambled thoughts. She smiled to herself, imagining disjointed strips of string before a knot blocks the thread. She could wait until a connection formed.

Someone had left a game of checkers on the table in the parlour. Not quite the level of difficulty she intended but an easy task to outwit an opponent. Mrs Park returned. The aroma of fresh-brewed tea permeated the room. Charlotte noticed the tray held a pot of tea and five cups and saucers. "There should be six settings, Mrs Park." She saw the woman's face contort in surprise. "A cup for Sophie. Where is Sophie, by the way?"

"Yes, poor Sophie's not feeling well tonight. I'll take some soup up to her room."

"I'd like to take it, please." Charlotte pleaded.

"No! She's not well enough for visitors. And stay away from her door." Shocked by the tone, Charlotte's face reddened.

Magda leaned across to Charlotte and whispered, "Leave it, Charlie. We can sort this out later."

Charlotte's breathing eased to submission. She noticed the wink from Magda and acknowledged she understood. She smiled and changed the subject, "whose turn is it anyway?"

"Yours, of course." The game continued. When the girls decided to pack up and make their way to their rooms, Mrs Park took her leave. Lily and Violet had set off upstairs earlier.

Am I a suspicious busybody? Her gut recoiled as a shiver rippled along her spine. Charlotte resolved to visit Sophie after lights out, no matter what.

Magda and Charlotte turned at the top of the stairs and eyeballed Mrs Park, who stood at the bottom stair, watching their ascent. Charlotte stifled a gasp in the pretence of a yawn. The odorous Divine7 lingered in the upstairs hall. *Why here? It makes me sick. Must find out who wears the repulsive scent.*

Magda embraced Charlotte to say goodnight but whispered, "Twelve o'clock sharp, be ready. Be a good girl and say goodnight to me." Charlotte obeyed and turned toward her door. Neither of them looked back. Magda's words echoed in her ears as she stood by her bed. Should she dress for bed or stay as is? She considered the dilemma for a moment, then decided to change for bed in case they got caught out on their sojourn to visit Sophie.

Moonlight streamed through the windowpane, forming a shadow of a cross on the floor. Mesmerised by the curling and uncurling lace curtains in the draught, she drifted off to sleep.

After lights out, as arranged, a gentle rap on her door indicated Magda was ready. The grandfather clock in the entry chimed midnight. Charlotte and Magda stole upstairs to Sophie's room to confront a locked door. Charlotte tapped on the door, and Magda called her name. No response from behind the door. Magda's voice raised with excitement.

"We'll need to pilfer the master key off the old woman, Charlie." Magda stood back from the door with her hands on her hips.

Charlotte clasped a hand over her companion's mouth, wary in case one of the landlady's daughters lurked in the hall shadows. "Shoosh! Magda. We don't want anyone to hear us." They looked at each other at the sound of an opening door.

"Wonder who that is?" Magda whispered.

Not a light or any further sound indicated anything amiss. They peered through the open balustrade on the top landing to ensure they were alone. The noise played on their jittery nerves; they edged down the stairs back to their rooms. Charlotte screwed her nose to stifle a sneeze. The familiar perfume of Divine7 tickled her nostrils. Magda looked at her, consternation in her eyes. The scent hovered around both of them. Charlotte intensely disliked the aroma and the linked memories.

Charlotte sensed a slight movement behind the linen press door as they crept past the closet. *Strange. One unresolved puzzle. Who creeps about the house in the middle of the night? More questions without explanation.* Safe back in her room, she did not flick the light switch. She snuggled low under the covers. Her cold bed linen raised goosebumps on her skin.

Dark clouds shrouded the sky, hiding the moon. Soft shadows from the lace curtain and the sound of wind whistling through the eaves added to her angst. Her last thought before sleep suggested the wind frightened them outside Sophie's door. *Perhaps not.* She dreamt of tunnels and her body being dragged into a surgical room. Strange hands tugged at her. She woke before her nightmare ended. The wind eased. The slow pitter-patter of raindrops beat a soft rhythm against the windowpane. *Another dismal day to go to work.*

At dinner the next evening, Mrs Park announced Sophie had left the boarding house, and the room was available to rent. Charlotte held her cup of tea mid-air, "When?"

"Yesterday, Charlotte, she said she would write when she could. That's all I can tell you." The landlady turned about-face and left the parlour.

Charlotte looked at Magda for a clue. "Don't look at me. I know as much as you do."

"Hmmm...That explains the lack of noise from her room last night."

Magda nodded in agreement - she slurped her hot tea. "Wonder why she didn't leave a note." Excitement lit her face. "Maybe we should get the room key and check out if she left a message inside."

"Good idea Magda and how do you propose we do that?"

"You're the crime reporter; you figure it out." As an afterthought, she added, "I'll help, though."

"Oh! No, you don't! It's your idea. You do the groundwork. I do the investigation. Remember, I am the investigative reporter."

"Right, Charlie, I'm up for that!"

76

Chapter Thirteen

To Charlotte's surprise, Mrs Park advertised the vacant room within days of Sophie's absence. A tidal wave of suspicion swelled inside Charlotte's head. With two boarders missing from the house, Charlotte indulged in a bubble of speculation until her thoughts settled. Armed with her diary and trusty pen, she wrote the names of the women and the dates of their disappearances, including Madelaine Devlin. She folded a Sydney city map small enough to see the proximity of St James Rail Station, Hyde Park, the Town Hall and St Mary's Cathedral. To her observation, Kings Cross wasn't too far away. How safe were the current boarders within the household? Charlotte decided to investigate deeper into the incidents that occurred within the walls. Puzzled by Sophie's unexpected departure, Charlotte revisited her previous notes. Nothing about Sophie hinted at a falling out with the landlady. Charlotte inserted a piece of ribbon between the pages and closed the book.

Kathleen moved into Sophie's room within the week. In the parlour before dinner, the new girl jumped with fright when a car, further up the street, backfired a couple of times.

Charlotte reacted to the sound as well and jumped out of her seat, thinking she had heard gunshots. "Oh, sorry, I got a fright too." Charlotte dropped back into the chair by the fire. Kathleen apologised with an explanation of how her country upbringing lacked the buzz of a busy city. Charlotte brushed aside her reporter's mind to study the new boarder knowing that Kathleen may be a new friend in the making.

For days Lily and Violet avoided Charlotte, Magda and now Kathleen. Back in the quiet of her room after dinner, Charlotte reopened her notepad to enter her questions about the disappearances. She entered each question as a heading, leaving ample space for future notes. Questions like - How much did the sisters know? Did they know where their mother went, other than shopping? Was Mrs Park behind the disappearances? If so, why?

The grandfather clock chimed eleven bells. A yawn stretched her clenched teeth. After closing the notebook, she remained seated at the dressing table to conjure up sweet dreams. Charlotte sank into bed, where her covers folded around her like swaddling. She felt safe in that moment. The house creaked, trying to release secrets she swore to uncover. She whispered, "not tonight."

Chapter Fourteen

The evening of twirling about a dance floor with strangers gave Charlotte little peace of mind. Her thoughts drifted through a maze of new faces. Sophie's face popped into her mind's eye between sets, unsettling her. She worried she might have missed a clue as to why Sophie left without mentioning her intentions.

Michael arrived later than expected with the blonde he had spent time with last month. When Michael introduced the two women, neither exchanged more than a courteous response. Although Charlotte heard the phrase 'childhood friends', she detected the Nora's peeved look of jealousy, which contributed to her emotional discomfort. Surely Michael noticed the adoration from his companion. Fraught with the possibility she had feelings for Michael, she decided it was best to ignore the temptation and avoid any confrontation with Michael and his companion. Nora accepted an offer to dance with a man she knew, allowing Michael to lead Charlotte onto the dance floor before she had a chance to walk away. Michael remained by her side for the rest the evening as much as possible. As a gentleman, he stepped aside whenever another tapped him on the shoulder during a dance.

An invitation after the last dance shifted Charlotte's emotions to another level. His question about going back to his place threw her off guard. Her body betrayed her mind, which fought the urge to submit to his request. "Not tonight, Michael; I'm with Magda. It wouldn't be proper."

"I'll take that as a maybe, Charlie." Michael withdrew his arms from around her to lead her off the dance floor.

Near the exit, Charlotte found Magda backed against the wall and hemmed in by a semicircle of admirers. Charlotte nudged past the men and grabbed her friend's hand. "Ready for home, Magda?" The question posed a distraction from Charlotte's thoughts. Michael took the hint and walked away to retrieve their coats from the cloakroom. Charlotte dragged her friend away from the group of men. "Time to go, Magda." *Where has this mood come from?*

Magda tugged against Charlotte. "Let me say goodbye to the blokes first."

"No time. Our bus leaves soon."

"Looks like I've got to go. Bye. See you all next week." Magda waved with her free hand before asking Charlotte why she was angry.

"Sorry, Magda. I didn't mean to sound awful. I'm in some sort of mood."

"Have you and Michael had a fight?"

"No, why would you think that?"

"Just a guess. C'mon, there's lover boy with our coats."

Charlotte shrugged her coat over her shoulders and adjusted the collar beneath her hairline while Michael helped Magda into her coat. Charlotte refused to give Michael time to exchange a farewell in case she weakened and agreed to his offer. "We need to hurry, Magda. Please."

"All right. All right. I am going as fast as I can."

Do not look back. Charlotte repeated those words to herself several times until she considered she and Magda were further along the footpath. Regret brought forth a fresh argument against her decision to deny herself the freedom to be alone with Michael. Charlotte remained silent on the way home.

Magda's curiosity about Charlotte's mood change remained unsated. Charlotte refused to discuss her relationship with Michael. Was she ready for another relationship, or should she put her career first? "Drop the subject, Magda. I'm not going to fulfil your need to know everything when I don't have the answers myself."

"Well then, when you are ready to talk, remember, I'm your friend." Magda pulled the cord to remind the bus driver to stop. Neither spoke until they exchanged goodnights to one another in the upstairs hall.

Work activities often brought Charlotte and Michael together. Charlotte managed to keep the meetings on a professional basis. By chance, they happened to be in the licenced café near St James station one evening after their shifts had ended. Caught by surprise, Michael sat next to Charlie. "I feel lost, Charlie. What happened between us. I hope my friendship with Nora hasn't given you the wrong impression." He ordered another round of drinks before Charlotte could react. "I understand how confusing it all seems. Please give Nora a chance; my sister was her best friend. We've supported each other and Joe as well. I keep her informed and take her out when life gets to her. That's all. We are friends and nothing more."

Charlotte reached out to Michael. "I'm sorry, I didn't realize how you two were connected, and I suppose the little green goblin surfaced. My mind was on other things that night, and I wasn't thinking straight."

"Can we start again?" he asked, reaching out for her hand.

Unsure how to respond, she hesitated with, "Let's see how we go."

"I can live with that. We have lots to catch up with."

"Hmm... and where do you propose we start?" she asked with her eyes lowered and one hand touching her hair.

"Let's start from when we first met. Drink?" He asked.

"Last drinks," the barman called.

"Let's go," Michael said. He leaned closer to Charlotte. His lips brushed her ear.

Despite the quiver inside her body, her voice sounded calm. "I mustn't miss curfew else Mrs Park will have my hide."

"Come on." He said, sliding off the barstool. "I've parked behind the pub and can get you home in a flash."

To Charlotte, the drive ended too soon. Her heart wanted more from this man. Could she trust him? She believed they could start over and build the friendship toward the next step, but if that meant not working, could she give up her dream? Confused and uncertain about the direction her life was taking her, Charlotte chose to get to know the man first as a friend. The what ifs could come later. She was unprepared for what came next.

When Michael parked his vehicle, he turned side on to her and indicated the boarding house with a tilt of his head. "Are you aware that your boss Rory Calhoun knew one of the boarders here?"

Her involvement in the case of the missing women was supposed to be kept secret. She would have words with her boss in the morning. At first, she denied any knowledge of his comment. Her sharp instincts powered up. "Who was she?"

"How do you know I referred to a she?"

"Oh, Michael, surely if you checked out the house and residents, you would know that only female boarders are welcome." Used to dealing with facts, Charlotte's feeble attempt at teasing did not get past Michael.

"Come, come, Miss Tyrell. Rory told me everything." He leaned toward her, but she pulled away. "I know why you are here, in this particular house. You're the crime reporter, aren't you? Lailah O'Brien disappeared not long after moving in, and Rory got you here to investigate."

"Now, Michael. I am not at liberty to divulge anything at the moment. Same as you." She smiled at the detective.

"Same here, Charlie, but perhaps we can work together." He turned to get out of the car before either said anything else.

Charlotte opened the passenger door before Michael reached the other side. He offered a hand to help, but she brushed it away. "I can do things myself; you know."

Michael raised both hands above his head. "I surrender, but if you need any help, perhaps we can work together. I hear you were good at undercover work in your hometown." Michael straightened up and added, "we can keep our personal life separate if that makes your life easier."

His driver side door closed before she could respond. *So, you've been doing some homework, Mr Devlin. Maybe, we can work together, but our personal life no doubt might overlap.*

Chapter Fifteen

Sleep eluded Magda long into the night. Silence saturated the boarding house. No longer pressed by winter winds, the external walls ceased creaking. The cold air nipped her ankles each time she exposed a foot to descend the stairs. Magda was not the only person denied sleep.

In the kitchen, Charlotte sat on a chair with her back to the door. Absorbed with her own thoughts and unaware of Magda's approach, she reacted when Magda whispered "Gotcha!" behind her ear.

"Christ, all bloody mighty!" Charlotte jerked with fright dropping her teacup smashing the handle. "Blast you, Magda. Look what you made me do?"

Magda spun from behind and plonked herself on the opposite chair, pleased the cup was empty. She was in no mind to mop up any spillage. Aware she frightened her friend, she expressed remorse. "Sorry, Charlie didn't mean to scare you that much." She blew a kiss to Charlotte.

No longer shaking, Charlotte explained, "I didn't hear you come downstairs. Stealth is not your usual forte."

"Yeah, I know, but I didn't want to wake anyone, and when I saw you here, I couldn't help myself." Magda's face beamed, and she moved to the stove to make more tea. She tilted the kettle and decided it held enough hot water for one more pot of tea. "Another cuppa?" she asked.

"Thanks, Magda," Charlotte said. Her cup was beyond repair. Replace it tomorrow. "What's the time?"

"One o'clock. How long have you been here?"

"Don't know. Restless mind and overtired, I guess. Tossed and turned in my bed, so I wandered down here for some tea. What about you?"

"Oh, kept thinking about Sophie and why she didn't mention her plans to leave."

Magda let the pot stand; rotated it three times clockwise and once in the other direction to allow the tea to brew. The ritual of pouring and leaf straining into the cups proved the old wives' tale held some truth.

"Me too. I'm sure something's happened to Sophie. Anyway, the investigation starts tomorrow. I'll make an appointment with the great Detective Michael Devlin." Soft sipping sounds matched the clink of china cups placed on saucers in the silent house. Silence stretched beyond their space to the street outside. The atmosphere unsettled Charlotte. Too quiet. She nudged her friend. "Thanks for the fresh cuppa but no thanks for the fright."

"What were you thinking about when I came in? You were so still and seemed to be in another world."

"Nothing, nothing at all." Charlotte wrapped her hands around the teacup as if the action might keep her together.

Magda shrugged. "Of course, nothing, Charlie. C'mon share. Loosen up and tell me about what disturbed your beauty sleep."

Charlotte cast her eyes to the locked door in the kitchen. "Do you ever wonder what's beyond that door? I heard scraping and thumping the other night. Noises were generated from here and on the staircase outside my room the night Sophie left. What do you make of that?"

"Of what?" Magda's flushed mood eased with each sip of tea.

"The door over there?" She indicated past Magda, "Beside the pantry." A locked door in the kitchen puzzled Charlotte more than Magda. Instincts rarely abandoned the reporter.

The lodgers often shared a light supper in the kitchen before retreating to their rooms. Charlotte wondered how many hands pulled and pushed the Bentwood chairs in and out of the table over the years. Someone apart from Mrs Park knew what secrets, if any, accumulated in the cellar. The marked floor area closest to the locked door showed recent dents in the oak timber. Her intuition sparked. Her curiosity ignited. "Who's passed over that threshold? More to the point, how many have passed through the doorway?" Charlotte's questions piqued Magda's curiosity in what lay beneath the kitchen floor.

Magda agreed about the fresh scuff marks and indents on the floorboards "Why do you suppose she has it locked at all times?"

"Come on, Magda, time for bed. We need to look behind that door as soon as possible. If you can, try and locate the key."

"Me?" a bewildered Magda replied.

"Yes, you're the opportunist. You'll get the glory."

A few days later, Magda noticed Mrs Park's apron hanging over a hook in the corner of the kitchen. The sagging pocket intrigued Magda enough to warrant a closer inspection while the landlady was out. Magda pulled aside the pocket opening and saw a heavy bundle of keys. She thought if one of the four keys on the ring opened the cellar door, why would these be kept separate from the household keys. The temptation to try one was thwarted when Magda heard the front door open. Moving quickly to the sink to rinse a cup on the sideboard, she grabbed a tea towel and wiped it dry. Mrs Park entered the kitchen none the wiser of Magda's discovery. Magda had agreed with Charlotte's idea to open the cellar and see what secrets, if any, might be unearthed. Mrs Park's evasive answers to questions about the cellar encouraged suspicion.

"We must find out what is going on in this place." Charlotte insisted.

"I agree, Charlie, and I know where to find the keys. We need a plan."

The next evening, Magda watched Mrs Park leave the house and decided to take advantage.

"Charlotte." She whispered huskily at the door.

Half asleep, Charlotte ran her hands through her hair. Her winter pyjamas were still warm, but her feet tingled on the cold bare boards. *Must get a mat off Mrs Park.* She stumbled to unlock her door. "Is there a fire? What's so urgent? What is the time anyway? Why are you whispering?"

Magda raised both eyebrows. "It's midnight, and Mrs Park is out. Now's our chance!" She pulled on Charlotte's arm to drag her from her room.

"Our chance?" A frown appeared across her forehead.

"Shh! Hurry! Time to search the cellar!"

They crept along the hall without disturbing Lily and Violet and avoided the creaking boards on the stairs. Mrs Park's apron, stretched by the weight of a ring of several keys in a pocket hung in its usual place. "Fingers crossed, Charlie. One of these keys must open the padlock."

"I'll keep a lookout, Magda. You try the keys." On the third attempt, the lock turned. It was an odd-looking key and turned counterclockwise. The door creaked open to reveal a solid set of stairs leading down into darkness.

"Wonder if we find any bottles of port or brandy here." Charlotte attempted to make light of their cloak and dagger activity.

"I found the light switch!" Magda said. The cellar unveiled its secrets beneath the naked bulb. Rows of suitcases stacked neatly on racks.

At the top of the stairs, Charlotte asked, "What can you see?"

"Ports! Not the bottled variety either. Several of them - stacked high to the ceiling - boxes too." Magda turned over a label attached to the handle of one suitcase. She gasped. "Lailah O'Brien," she read aloud, "Sophie's belongings are here too."

Magda's discovery intensified Charlotte's suspicions. She entered the cellar. Her friend had opened a suitcase filled with folded old fashion dresses dating pre-war. They looked at each other. Their questions died while their eyes scanned the contents on the shelves.

Charlotte broke the silence. "We've stumbled onto something the police ought to know about. What do you think Magda?" A car door slammed outside. The sound of Mrs Park's footsteps on the porch disrupted their search.

"Quick, Charlie, back to the kitchen before she finds us here."

The front door closed as Magda replaced the keys in the apron pocket. Charlotte heard the glass cabinet open and shut. *The rock is back on the shelf inside the display cabinet. Why does she take the rock off the premises?*

Two empty cups of tea sat on the table as Mrs Park came through the door. The stove fire spat and hissed in a mark of betrayal. To Charlotte, Mrs Park seemed surprised to see them in the kitchen so late. The grandfather clock chimed 2.30am. Charlotte signalled to Magda to remove a visible smudge of dust from her face Mrs Park simply smiled. Charlotte noticed Mrs Park's discomfort. Tension rose between all three. *Do we look guilty?*

Magda's voice soothed the friction rising in the room. "Well, I suppose it is time to go back to bed. What about you, Charlie?"

"Yes, I guess so." Charlotte rubbed her eyes with the back of her hands. "What about yourself, Mrs Park? Most unusual for you to be out so late." Charlotte's question hit the mark.

The landlady nodded in agreement. Her eyes narrowed as she evaded the question. "I'll turn off the lights. Shoo, away with you both."

At the top of the stairs, worried about the items in the cellar, Charlotte shared her concern. "Magda, I'm not sure we closed the suitcase. What if we didn't, and what if she knows?"

"Don't worry so much, Charlotte; your frown lines are deepening. What if? So what! We know the reason behind that locked door." Magda reached for Charlotte's hands. "To see Sophie's stuff stored there shook the living daylights out of me."

Charlotte wanted more information. "Do you realise, Lailah's and Sophie's belongings are here? Did you notice other names on the ID tags? All women. I have lots of questions for Mrs Park." She leaned closer to avoid being overheard. "I know there's enough evidence to connect her to the disappearance of both girls. Something weird happens inside this house."

"Please, Charlie, there has to be a rational answer to the mystery. We'll get to the bottom of things sooner or later. Concentrate on getting some sleep, and don't go near Mrs Park."

"I'm not giving up. I have a meeting with Michael Devlin tomorrow. Goodnight Magda, see you in the morning."

"Night, Charlie."

Apprehension wavered to and fro to the point where sleep became an illusion. *How will Michael react to this information? Will he listen? More importantly, will he pursue the find in the cellar?*

Chapter Sixteen

T he next morning breakfast was behind schedule. Charlotte rose out of bed and dressed earlier than usual. At first glance, she'd noticed dark circle lines in her reflection. Magda appeared none the worse for wear, except for the tell-tale sign of yawns. Lily and Violet looked fresh and, for once, pretty when they entered the room. Her vision through bloodshot eyes distorted their appearances. Charlotte tapped the back of her fingers in punishment for nasty thoughts. *Focus. Focus.*

The investigation of two missing young women had been turned upside down last night. She hoped Michael might unearth proof linking her findings with the others. To avoid any conversations with Magda, she left early for work. Doubts wove between frequent questions bouncing inside her head. *What plausible decision made the landlady store the suitcases? Secrets to expose.*

Commuters from each stop jammed inside the bus. *Suffocation under duress.* What a *headline*. Rivulets of grime riddled condensation trickled down the glass panels as if the bus wept. Passengers coughed and sneezed within her space. Charlotte alighted at the next stop, where freedom from the odours of crushed bodies released her tension. Fog muffled the sound of traffic. Headlights, like outlines of lost souls, penetrated the damp shroud smothering the city. She stepped inside her workplace. Her mood matched her limp felt hat, her damp shoes, and her rain-streaked coat. Her trouser hems stretched by muddy waters dragged along the ground. *Could my day get any worse? Oh, yes.*

Brian noticed her. "You have a bad night?" Sarcasm spat from his mouth.

Charlotte refused to play the game. "Could say that. Let's talk before I meet with Michael Devlin. I have new information to share."

Brian straightened his stance in anticipation of the news. "Do we need the chief?"

"Yes, of course, he needs to know." Charlotte tightened her trouser belt before the hems dragged the waistband to her hips. "Is he in?"

Inside the Editor's office, they sat on chairs opposite the huge cedar desk. Charlotte recounted the discovery in the cellar at the boarding house. Rory Calhoun reached for a cigar. He bit away the tip and spat it into the wastebasket. The shift of his weight on his leather chair was the only sound before the flick of a lighter disturbed the stilled interior. Brian coughed behind his hand. Charlotte sat studying the floor pattern on the carpet.

"The police need to know what you found, Charlie, especially Lailah's suitcase. Job well done." Rory put the cigar between his lips to drag in the aromatic smoke. He exhaled. "Hmm! What do you think, Brian?"

"I agree, but where's the proof?" Brian crossed his arms across his chest. His legs were unable to extend due to the proximity of the chair to the desk. He looked uncomfortable.

"That'll be their job." Rory rested his forearms across the desk. The cigar protruded between his stubby thumb and forefinger as ash from the tip smudged his blotting paper. Deep in thought, he waved away the slowly curling upward smoke.

A memory stirred inside Charlotte. *Dried blood on a victim's bedding.* The recollection of her first crime scene stirred her nerves. A slight tremor shuffled along her spine.

Rory aimed his next statement at Charlotte. "You, Miss Tyrell, could be in danger. If you take this to the police, make certain no one, and I mean no one connects you to that cellar. Is that clear?"

Charlotte nodded at this outburst. Her worry now increased.

"Brian, arrange a meeting with the detective and take Missy here with you." He waved them to leave as his telephone began to ring.

Brian guided Charlotte to his desk and arranged to meet Detective Devlin at 2pm. Brian noted the weariness in his colleague. He wondered if the job might be too much for a young woman but dared not say that aloud. He suggested they have coffee and biscuits in the office lunchroom or by their desks.

Charlotte agreed without complaint. Tired from the previous night's escapades, she was glad she didn't have to walk out into the crowded streets. The shoppers would be in full swing at this time of day, including mothers with prams and screaming toddlers. No, she wanted a familiar space, and the office supplied the right environment for their discussions.

Brian asked if she wanted tea or coffee. He brewed the coffee for himself and a black tea as requested. He then grabbed some cream-filled biscuits and sat opposite Charlotte at the lunch table. "Bloody women sticking their noses in places they're not supposed to." Brian laughed. "What prompted you to look in the cellar?"

"My intuition." She shrugged off his remark about women. "Something beyond a man's belief." She curled her lips in a grin.

"Wish I'd been there. Weren't you scared you might get caught? You said that you and your friend got hold of a key to unlock the cellar door and found suitcases belonging to the two missing boarders?"

"Yes, we did." She perceived Brian's intentions by the brightness in his eyes and the flush of his face. "It's my story, Brian." She said with an emphasis on the 'my'. She leaned toward him to add, "Keep that in mind. Michael Devlin will undoubtedly inundate me with questions from which I may gain a little insight into the police research of the missing girls."

Another staffer entered, interrupting their conversation. Brian nodded his head to the side, indicating the newcomer take his morning tea elsewhere. The young cadet left in a huff closing the door behind him.

"Brian, there's more to tell you," Charlotte said resolutely between bites of a biscuit. "We saw stacks of suitcases, not just the two I mentioned. I wish there had been more time to take notes of all the labels."

She hugged her cup of tea to occupy her hands. Coddled in the warmth of the room, she started yawning. It was all she could do to stop herself from falling asleep. She needed her wits when they met with Michael. "Hey, can we get a drink somewhere nearby? I need something stronger than tea at the moment."

"Sure! There's a bar handy. Women aren't allowed, but we can get around that." Brian confidently agreed. The hotel he chose was nestled between two old buildings opposite the police station. On arrival, she took herself off to the Ladies' Room at the end of the corridor past the Ladies Lounge.

Dismayed by her reflection, she powdered her nose, pinched her cheeks and added a touch of colour to her lips. She ran her fingers through her hair in a ploy to fluff the style out. She was past caring about her shoes and her dirty trousers. Brian waited for her in the hall between the bar and ladies' lounge that separated women from the males only area. A sign over the bar door warned – No females allowed past this point. Brian ignored the sign and guided Charlotte toward a table for four adjacent to an external window. Charlotte hesitated inside the room, expecting to be asked to leave. The barman nodded permission for them to sit inside. No other person acknowledged their presence.

"What's the time, Brian?" Charlotte asked.

"After ten," he replied. "I'll get us a drink." Brian went to the bar and brought back a beer for himself and a rum for Charlotte. "Bottoms Up."

Charlotte thanked Brian for his ability to gain her access into the domain of men. "Time we were on our way."

"Finish your drink first. Let the rum slide across your tongue and down your throat. It's a great drink to calm the nerves."

One gulp and the contents emptied without touching her lips. "Thanks, I feel better already."

Shift changes coincided with Michael leaving the police station for lunch. Amid the hustle and bustle of constables, plainclothes detectives and public members filing in and out of doors, Michael managed to cross the road to the hotel and spotted Charlotte and Brian in the bar area. "Nice to see you, Charlotte. And you, Brian." Michael removed his hat and spun the brim between both sets of fingers. "Mind if I sit down?" he asked, indicating the spare chair between the two reporters.

"Well, this is cosy." He waved to a waiter to place an order for the three of them. "Same all around, I'm guessing." After he placed his order, he asked, "What's important enough to arrange a meeting this afternoon?"

Bugger, he's not in a good mood. Sparks of intuition fired her neurons. "Please listen, Michael. What I have to tell you is important, and this is as good a place as any to fill you in with events of last night."

"I'm all ears. What's this all about, Charlie?"

He listened attentively to Charlotte. Amused at first at the amateurish plan to gain access to the cellar, he chided her for not seeking help. "Stupid woman for going alone. What if you were caught.? Did you not think about that?"

"Stop it, Michael, I'm a crime reporter, and the time was right." Charlotte leaned back in her chair and defiantly crossed her arms.

"He's right, you know." Brian agreed with Michael.

"Oh, don't give me that business about women shouldn't do things without a man's help." Charlotte stood, turned around to look at the others seated in the room. She bowed, then raised her glass and toasted, "To all the independent women in the world."

Patrons at other tables ceased talking and turned to stare at the woman who appeared drunk. Young barmaids giggled while the men sneered at her remark. Michael pulled her back down. "Behave yourself, or I'll arrest you for disturbing the peace."

Brian shook his head from side to side.

Charlotte quietened down immediately. "Sorry, I'm tired. I tossed and turned all night." Her inner strength welled. "To tell you the truth, I was scared. When I saw Sophie's and Lailah's belongings in that cellar along with other labelled suitcases I couldn't think straight." Charlotte shook off the realisation of how close they came to being discovered by the landlady. "Look, late one evening, I couldn't sleep so I went to the kitchen and questioned myself about the disappearances. Magda got all fired up about getting into the cellar after I told her about the noises that I heard downstairs on the night Sophie disappeared." Charlotte held their attention. "And I use the word 'abducted' with confidence."

"What else don't I know?" Michael raised his eyebrows. He had to put a stop to Charlotte's shenanigans and get her to open up more about what went on in that house.

"Well, as far as I can figure out, Sophie was in her room, but neither I nor Magda were allowed to visit. Whoever abducted her took her downstairs late at night." Charlotte twirled her empty glass on the table.

"More drinks?" asked Brian. Michael made a move for his wallet, "It's okay, Mick, my shout."

Michael leaned across the table to clasp Charlotte's hands in his. "Charlie, my love, you took a great risk last night." His fingertips caressed the back of her hands. "But I need you to be more careful."

Charlotte pulled away from his touch. "I've heard all this from Rory, Brian and now you." A tear escaped down her cheek.

Michael dabbed the tiny drop away with his thumb. "It's okay now, but I'm worried as hell that something might happen to you while you are in that house."

"The bastards wouldn't dare."

Brian returned with beers and a rum. "Have I missed anything?" He asked. He noticed the tension between the two at the table. No response from either person. "Good health," Brian said. Charlotte and Michael raised their glass and responded accordingly. "What's next, then?"

Chapter Seventeen

Patrons sat at tables near the windows to the street. Afternoon drizzle descended, highlighting grubby smears on the glass panels blocking any view of the street. The trio sat where several neglected framed photographs and sketches of the city hung crooked on the wall behind them. Charlotte leaned back in her chair and crossed her arms to curb her temper. *What's it going to take to capture this man's interest and follow up on the contents of the cellar?* Attempts aimed at Michael fell short of their mark. Brian relaxed back in his chair and waited for the waitress. Michael fidgeted. He ran his hands through his hair, touched his collar and straightened his tie.

Charlotte clasped her hands on the table then leaned toward Michael with the first words that came to her. "Those missing girls are as unloved as those pictures on the wall for all you care." She demanded answers. "Explain to me why rows of labelled suitcases are in that cellar. Sophie's case was the first, and we saw one labelled Lailah O'Brien. You do remember her, don't you? How much evidence do you need?" She slumped back in her chair, furious that neither man took her accusations seriously. Charlotte's instincts breathed and sighed of their own accord. "Sophie did not leave of her own free will. I know it. I sense it. I believe it."

"You need to stay out of this, Charlie and leave the inquiries to the police." Brian failed to soothe her temper.

"Stay out of it! What the fuck don't either of you understand?" Murmurs from the other end of the room intruded on her outburst. She lowered her voice. "I'm at my wit's end. I write about crime, and I want to find out what happened to Sophie."

"Of course you do, Charlie, but there is no evidence of foul play. You, yourself, heard the excuses. She left at night to avoid teary farewells and a misunderstanding about rent payments." Smooth and mellow as fine sherry, Michael tried to placate her by asking if she needed another drink.

"Don't patronise me." She hissed.

Charlotte looked at Brian for support, but he shrugged his shoulders in defeat. "He's right, you know. Your evidence is circumstantial. Your landlady did say Sophie would collect her things after she found a suitable place to live."

Michael stood up. He gulped the beer down in one go. "It's getting late. I have to go back to work. I'll discuss all this with my superior first. I have a report to file, and I'm sure you two have more to discuss about articles for the newspaper."

"And what about Lailah? Her suitcase is still on the shelf. What are you going to do, Mr Detective?" Flushed with anger, she stood upright. "What if I told you I saw something that might belong to Madelaine. Would that make a difference?" She shouldered her handbag; stormed out without looking back.

On the street outside, her skin prickled. A familiar odour wafted from nearby. The strong scent of Divine 7 cologne smothered her. Someone shoved her from behind. A man grabbed her before she fell. A sneer splashed across his face but disappeared in a blink when Michael relieved him of his grip. "Thanks, mister, I got her. It's okay, Charlie, I'll take you home."

"Brian –" Charlotte struggled to catch her breath.

" – Don't worry. I'll let the chief know."

"I'm fine Michael. Please don't fuss." She tried to stand on her own, but for some reason, her legs were weak.

"What happened?" She asked.

"You tripped, and someone saved you from falling." With one arm around her waist, her elbow cradled in the other, he guided her closer to the building. Away from the gutter edge, he said, "Catch your breath. You've had too much to drink."

"Will you stop fussing?" She brushed him aside.

"Now, listen to me, young lady. I will have you taken downtown for resisting arrest if you don't start behaving. You gave me a fright."

"All right, take me home if you put it that way." Neither spoke during the short drive to the boarding house.

Michael looked across at her. Satisfied she no longer looked angry or otherwise, he touched a fallen lock of hair.

"Don't, I'm still angry at you."

"Charlie, don't be like that. You know how the job goes. I need evidence and strong evidence, but if it makes you feel better, I will visit the landlady tomorrow."

"Thank you."

She got out of the car. Michael leaned across the front car seat to say goodbye, but she had turned her back and walked away as soon as she closed the door. He drove away slowly and watched her in his rear vision mirror for as long as he could without losing control of his vehicle.

Windows wide open on the top floor of the house reminded her of blinkers on a horse. Wisps of smoke from the chimney matched the vapours of the warm breath escaping her lungs. A brisk walk along the path brought her to the front door and those ghoulish panels. If she was a cat, the hairs on her back would be straight up, her claws outstretched, ready to pounce. Her mood remained intact inside the house. Mouthwatering aromas from the kitchen permeated the house. Hunger growled in her stomach, but the temptation of hot food turned sour when Lily and Violet pranced down the stairs. At the sight of Charlotte, the sisters exchanged whispers. Charlotte's appetite dissolved.

"What is it with you two? You pretend I'm a stranger in this house. Well, get this, girls, I intend to uncover the secrets stored within these walls." Charlotte glared at them; her acerbic tongue hit its mark. She brushed past to move upstairs. She never turned back for reactions, but silence followed. She slammed her bedroom door, sat hunched on the floor, and burst into tears.

Frustration zoomed in and held tight. Unstoppable tears sliced her tension and dampened her temper's fiery edges.

A distant sound thrummed in her head - the signal for dinner. She lifted her head off her knees and wiped her face with the back of her sleeves, then rolled to a kneeling position and hauled herself upward. A flushed bulbous face in the bathroom mirror reminded her of a character from a childhood storybook. Cold water soothed her skin and reduced the puffiness of her eyelids. *A bit of lip colour, and I'll look brand new.*

"Ah, there you are, love." Mrs Park greeted Charlotte in the dining room. "I was about to ask someone to check if you were in, but I see all is well. Dinner is ready."

Caught between instincts and curiosity, Charlotte's response lacked emotion. "Thanks." Seated opposite, Magda raised one eyebrow. Charlotte managed to lift one corner of her mouth in acknowledgement. Amused by the interaction between members of the household, Lily and Violet giggled. Kathleen entered the room. "Sorry, I'm late. Hope I haven't missed anything."

"Not at all. You're just in time." Mrs Park said, oblivious of the exchange between the different personalities at her table.

Dinner passed without bother or conversation. Between mouthfuls of roast chicken and vegetables, Charlotte watched the sisters. To distract Charlotte, Magda tapped her foot against Charlotte's shin. The staring game was obvious to all, especially Mrs Park. Lily suggested they have their dessert in the parlour. Mrs Park agreed and sent her boarders ahead while she and her daughters cleared the dining room and prepared trays for tea and dessert.

The atmosphere in the room altered Charlotte's mood, which pleased Magda. Her friend made herself comfortable near the closed French doors. Lily and Violet entered with two trays and served Kathleen first. Violet bumped Charlotte's cup and saucer as she handed the dessert over.

"Oops, sorry, Charlotte."

Charlotte answered without malice in her voice though she seethed inside. "No harm done. You spared my clothes."

Wary of any outbursts between the sisters and her co-conspirator Magda asked Kathleen to join her and Charlotte in a game of cards. Grateful for the distraction from the pending confrontation, she agreed. "If it's poker, I haven't any coins."

"Neither have we," Charlotte said. "Can you play Canasta?"

"Who doesn't?"

Magda fetched the pack from the sideboard while Charlotte tossed the cloth over the table. "You first, Kathleen."

The card game went three rounds before they packed up. Charlotte complimented Kathleen on her skills which her brothers taught her before they enlisted. She added she hadn't played for a while as only one came home.

"How sad for your family, Kathleen. But you're here now and showing us up."

The grandfather clock struck the 10.45pm chime as a reminder of bedtime. Upstairs the girls shared the usual 'good night, sleep tight, don't let the bedbugs bite'. Charlotte was last to enter her room. She waited until she heard Kathleen close her bedroom door.

The next morning, from the warmth of her bed, Charlotte watched the sunlight fracture the condensation on the glass window. Patterns on the rug changed in an instant as trickles of moisture linked and changed direction. She fixated on the performance until shadows inched into her room. *Time to get up.*

Dressed and ready for the day and without her usual enthusiasm, she went to the kitchen for a cup of hot tea and toasted damper. Busy with time-saving preparations for the evening meal Mrs Park smiled and asked, "Did you sleep well last night?"

Charlotte attached a damper slice to the wire toasting rack and held it over the stove's fire. She turned the utensil over to brown the upper side before she answered. "No."

"Is something wrong, love?" The landlady stopped chopping the few vegetables on the table and waited for a response.

Roused by her instincts to keep her secrets safe, she apologised. "I'm sorry, Mrs Park. I had a bad day yesterday, and I brought my problems home with me." Charlotte sat at the table with the cup of tea and toast spread with homemade marmalade. She half expected the landlady to make some comment about the way she treated the sisters the day before.

"You owe my girls an apology. I believe you upset them when you came home." Hands on her hip, the woman was ready for a confrontation with her boarder.

Charlotte had no desire to discuss her behaviour with the woman. Eager to escape any further conversation, she tipped half her tea down the sink, added some water and gulped the liquid down. "So, I do. Excuse me, Mrs Park. I've got to rush off to work. I'll eat the toast on the run. I'll see you later." Charlotte sped from the woman's presence and rushed upstairs to freshen up before leaving the house.

Finally ready for the outside world, she headed downstairs and approached the door. A man's silhouette appeared through the panels. Dark insights of her imagination and past experience warned against re-action to fear. In an effort to gain control of herself, she took a deep breath; shook her shoulders, then reached for the door handle and opened the door to Michael's outreached arm. "Bloody hell, Michael. What are you doing here? You scared the life out of me." She shrugged off the sensation without another thought. *Why did the silhouette frighten me? A premonition perhaps or exhaustion.* Another Detective accompanied Michael and introduced himself as Carl Burghoff.

"Wasn't my intention. Charlie? May I come in?" He twirled the brim of his hat between his fingers. A nervous habit. "I considered your theory last night and decided to follow your suggestion, and here I am."

"I'll let Mrs Park know." Charlotte's ill-tempered mood lingered from her interaction with the twins. Michael's appearance at the door reminded her of their parting the night before. She could not rouse a cordial welcome no matter how hard she tried.

Michael's fingers moved faster on his hat brim. "Wait, you did ask me to check out this house."

Charlotte considered the need to talk with Michael on a professional level and managed to respond as politely as she could. "That was yesterday. I've changed my mind." She looked behind, half expecting to see Mrs Park at the kitchen doorway.

She whispered, "Michael, I can't talk here." Charlotte raised her voice. "Sorry, Michael, of course. Come in." The two detectives stepped over the threshold. "Wait here while I find Mrs Park."

Michael and Carl studied the entrance hall, especially the display cabinet full of curiosities as well as an uncut opal. The thread of opalescent colours intrigued Michael, who wondered why the rock was never cut for jewellery. A woman's voice jarred him from his thoughts.

One eyebrow arched high on her forehead as she spoke. "What do you want?"

Michael noticed the grimace on her face and suspicion in her eyes. Nervous tension strung her muscles taught while her fingers twitched inside the folds of her apron. Aware the woman was caught off guard, he purposely spoke in his most professional tone. "Are you Urtha Park?"

"I am. And again, I ask, what do you want?" Her eyes fleeted in all directions except at Michael.

"Relax, Mrs Park." Michael stood his ground and made no move less the movement be perceived as a threat. He introduced himself and his partner. "We are following up on the disappearance of a young woman by the name of Lailah O'Brien. We believe she resided at this address."

The sound of Carl's pencil scratching in his official notebook penetrated the silence.

"Disappeared? Now that's news to me." In a flash, the landlady's mood and outward appearance shifted from anxiety to pleasantness. Her change in manner did not convince the detectives she spoke the truth.

"Did you read the newspaper?" It was Michael's turn to raise an eyebrow.

"No, can't be bothered. The pages are full of doom and gloom." Her fingers in her apron continued to fold and unfold her apron front.

"You haven't answered my question, Mrs Park. Did Miss O'Brien rent a room in this boarding house?"

"Yes, she did."

Frustrated with the way in which the woman responded; Michael decided to ask one more question. "Did she leave anything behind that might help us in our search?"

"No, she didn't." Mrs Park crossed her arms.

Michael stifled a cough. "Would it be possible if we could have a look at her room?"

"I'm afraid I don't have the time to show you."

"We ask as a courtesy, Mrs Park. This was a spur of the moment decision to keep the case open."

"Sorry, detectives, the investigators at the time got a statement so you boys had better be on your way, then." With the front door handle already within reach, the woman pulled at the door handle and bade them a good day.

Outside, near the car, Carl commented, "Tough old biddy, that one, eh."

"Before we stir up too much trouble, I'll talk with Charlie and fill her in with my suspicions."

Chapter Eighteen

On Saturday nights, Charlotte met Magda outside Beberfalds before going home or to the Town Hall Dance. "Better not miss tonight's dance. I think your fellow has a crush on you." .

"And what fellow would that be, Magda?" Charlotte knew who she meant.

"You don't fool me, missy. That Detective Devlin never takes his eyes off you." Magda said as she tucked her arm inside Charlotte's. "Before we go to the Town Hall, let's go to the milk bar around the corner, order a milkshake, and check out the latest magazines."

Their pace quickened until they neared the door to the cafe. The bell above the door tinkered, alerting the owner of their presence. Dim lighting disguised shadowy forms in the back corner booth.

In an indistinguishable foreign accent, the owner suggested they seat themselves in the middle booth. "Light's a bit better there, girls."

"Do you have a copy of today's newspapers here?" Magda asked.

"You want to read the news?"

"Oh, no." Charlotte giggled. "My friend meant magazines."

Unaware of the time, they flipped through fashion articles. They giggled at some of the latest trends and the advertisements for new products to enhance female facial features.

"C'mon, no more dilly-dallying, Charlotte, else we'll be late for you know who."

"You're such a tease, Magda." Charlotte drained the last of her milkshake and slid from the booth to straighten her skirt. An uneasy feeling overwhelmed her as scents of fruits and florals drifted by. Nothing appalled her more than Divine 7. Charlotte noticed the lack of female presence in the café. She wobbled before she took a step.

"You okay, Charlotte?" The sudden change in the pallor of her friend's face raised concern.

"Yeah, just a shiver ran up my spine. What's that saying? Oh yes, someone walked over my grave." Her laughter mingled with the raucous voices outside, but the shiver remained until they stepped away from the shadows. Charlotte glanced back and saw nothing. The smell of Divine 7 still haunts her. Was death nearby? "Gosh, Magda, I can't explain what came over me." Charlotte crooked her arm over her friend's elbow. With a deep sigh to quell her agitation, she said aloud, "Let's go dancing."

Michael stood inside the entrance to the dance hall, patiently waiting for the girls to arrive. "Bit windy tonight, girls," he said while helping to remove their coats. The young man in the cloakroom passed over a ticket for later collection.

"Such a gentleman," Magda said, adding a subtle kiss on his cheek. "Look at that, red lipstick." She took her handkerchief from a pocket in her skirt and, with gentle strokes, dabbed at the mark. On tiptoes, she searched the dance floor for a glimpse of her American friend. "I've spotted him and his friends. Catch you later." She spun about and was out of sight in a heartbeat.

"Sorry about that, Michael. She didn't mean any harm. She – " before Charlotte could finish, Michael interrupted.

"Please don't apologise. She must be good company. She's so full of life." He watched Magda glide across the room toward the American soldiers.

Beneath the muted lights of the hall, couples swayed in slow rhythm to the music prior to the break. Nora arrived in time for the supper dance. One of Magda's American friends asked permission to escort her to supper. It was impolite for a girl to refuse. Charlotte understood more about the relationship between Michael and Nora. Although jealousy visited during the first meeting, Charlotte accepted the friendship Nora offered and began to enjoy the girl's company, especially her manner toward those around her.

When the last bar played, the lights blared bright. The signal for the patrons to leave. Couples meandered across the dance floor to gather up personal belongings and make arrangements for meetings or exchange goodbyes. Michael held Charlotte close as long as protocol permitted. No longer drowned by music, voices lifted to a higher pitch forcing Michael's lips against Charlotte's ears to convey his suggestion. "The wind outside has worsened; make sure you do up your buttons." Before he could change his mind, he asked her out to dinner on a night next week.

Magda boldly answered for her, "She's free Friday night, aren't you, love?"

"Good, Friday night it is!"

"That's done." Magda pulled Charlotte forward. "I'm sorry, darling Charlotte, but it's cold and raining; we have to leave, and it's hard to see in this light."

Worried for their safety, Michael said, "I'd be more than happy to escort you ladies, home, or at least get you a taxi." He had his hands in his coat pockets to ward off the chill in his fingers.

"Thanks, but the bus stop is not far away. Besides, since you organised patrols for this area, we feel safe." Magda held Charlotte's hand and led her off the steps into the crowd moving along the pavement.

They dodged the couples strolling four abreast. Some seemed to want the night to go on forever. Charlotte wished the same. The plight of the missing girls was far from her thoughts. She felt light-headed and happy for a change. "Why did you drag me off so fast? I thought he wanted to kiss me goodnight, Magda."

"Treat 'em mean to keep 'em keen, my mother taught me. You'll be fine, Charlie. He's smitten." Magda changed the subject and chatted about saving to buy new clothes and new shoes. "Red ones, I think. I might wear them one Saturday night."

"That I look forward to." Charlotte studied her reflection in the misted window. She wondered why her passion for the resolution of the disappearances waned. Nobody will interfere or distract me from my goal.

"Atta' a girl. And Michael?"

"Enough. Time for that later."

Magda tugged on the bell cord for the driver to pull up at the next stop. The girls edged their way past passengers in the aisle to step off the bus. A fresh attitude and a brisk walk in the night air filled Charlotte with optimism to discover both the abductor and the whereabouts of the missing girls.

Magda's voice broke through her thoughts. "Hope the kettle is still full. A cup of cocoa is what we need."

"I agree wholeheartedly."

Magda tucked her arm inside Charlotte's as they walked along the path toward the few steps to the porch. The front door was locked after eight pm. Magda retrieved the front door key from the stump under the front porch. "I so hate these panels by the door," Magda said as she closed and locked the door before they removed their coats.

"Sorry, Magda, do you mind if I take a raincheck on the cocoa and toddle off to bed?"

"Of course, I mind, but I understand. Good night, Charlie. Sleep well, and don't let the bedbugs bite." Magda headed for the kitchen to make herself a hot cocoa. "I think I'll take the drink upstairs with me."

"Good idea. Goodnight." Charlotte said with her foot on the first step. After securing her bedroom door, she pulled fresh pyjamas from a drawer and changed for bed. Charlotte's weariness claimed her as soon as her head touched the pillow.

Her friendship with Michael recently blossomed into something deeper. They often shared a meal in a cosy restaurant and a couple of evenings at his home. The boarding house was off-limits at mealtime for male visitors, however, morning or afternoon tea in the parlour on weekends was acceptable. Unbeknown to others in the boarding house, their afternoon teas related to police matters and not social encounters. They took advantage of the time watching the boarders and in particular Mrs Park and her daughters.

Two young women recently parted company with the dour Mrs Park. According to Charlie, the after-hours departures hinted at foul play. Mrs Park grasped the opportunities to garner information. The couple's conversations were far from divulging any investigation matters. The landlady served tea and cake to observe their interactions. Disappointed though curious, she hovered about the room. Michael was strict about sharing information with journalists, but he trusted Charlotte. She, too, was careful with titbits she managed to salvage from colleagues.

Chapter Nineteen

S tale odours of alcohol inside the hotel's private bar mingled with recycled nicotine agitated Charlotte's sense of smell. The place was ideal for conversations, not meant for the police. Here Brian and she could talk freely about probable evidence. The patronage, Charlotte noted, consisted of well-suited men, high fashioned companions and working-class men who mingled without fuss or conversation except to nudge past one another to order drinks.

Two hours before closing and already the public bar was full of men weaving in and out of dimly lit spaces. Fist fights broke out between drunken men. Burley barmen dropped the offenders straight into the gutter outside. Dodgy characters conducted whispered conversations within the serene private bar. Charlotte relished the opportunity to eavesdrop on these individuals, some of whom were the masterminds of controlled illegal affairs of the city.

The Ladies' Lounge offered little reprieve from the bar scene. A place where women of dubious character wandered in or loitered near the washrooms for a chance to pick up paying customers. Charlotte wandered into the Ladies Lounge on her return from the lavatory when a jab in her back unsteadied her grip. Charlotte spun on her heels to face a troubled soul who made no eye contact.

"Sorry Miss didn't mean to bump into you. Not paying attention." The painted face of the young woman paled in comparison to her pursed ruby red lips. Rouge of some sort outlined her hollow cheeks. A fake, moth damaged fur cape wrapped her upper torso in a manner like a mangy fox. Charlotte's quick glance at the muddy shoes and torn dress unleashed compassion.

"What's your name?" Charlotte asked.

"Elly, Miss. I'm sorry." She dropped her purse on the floor, unleashing its contents.

"Let me help." Charlotte crouched to pick up scattered bits.

"Never mind. I'll do it." The girl scooped up her belongings and stuffed them back inside, then clipped the purse closed.

Charlotte suggested the girl freshen up in the wash room.

"Don't want to go anywhere alone at the moment, please, Miss. Two men tried to grab me off the street. I slipped on the wet pavement and managed to break free." Tears streamed down her powdered cheeks. Charlotte's instincts kicked up a gear.

"Sit over there." Charlotte indicated a chair with its back against the wall. Charlotte added. "Wait here; I'll be back!" Elly submitted to the command with her hands clasped tight in a ball upon her lap. Her jittery eyes darted about the room. A customer shared a joke with Brian in the alcove. Not the right time to suggest Brian check on the waif in the Ladies' Lounge. She believed Elly would be safe with female patrons in the room.

Most of the women and men in the lounge ignored Elly. She was not of their calibre. Her dishevelled appearance was out of place amidst the glamourous ladies sipping on their champagnes or cocktails. The gentleman in their fine suits glanced sideways and spoke above whispers loud enough for Elly's ears. She felt uncomfortable seated in the corner with no means of escape. Was she safe here? She flashed her tongue at those who glanced her way. "Only a child." She heard someone say. "Yes, but she could make some good money if she played her cards right." A couple of the gaudily dressed ladies giggled and nudged each other.

Elly was about to leave when a side door to the room opened. Her skin prickled with fear. She tried to run, but her body refused to move. The corner of the room held her captive. Elly's eyes pleaded for help from those who ridiculed her. They turned their backs and left the room leaving her alone with the beasts who earlier attempted to snatch her off the street. Trying to fend off four strong men left her caught against the body of one whose leather coast reeked of rose and citrus. Odd, she thought, as the jab of fine steel pierced her skin. She fainted. Elly was gone in minutes.

In the meantime, Charlotte had joined Brian and his joker friend, but the man didn't get the hint she wanted to be alone with Brian. Any discussion about the girl in the Ladies Lounge remained closed.

"Last drinks." The call from the bartender warned the patrons the bar was closing at 6pm sharp.

"I've got something to tell you, Brian," Charlotte whispered. Brian looked inquisitively at his colleague. "Yeah, while you and your fucking mate were laughing, I literally bumped into a young woman who luckily had escaped the clutches of some men."

"Jesus, Charlotte, why didn't you say so." Brian moved away from the alcove. "Is she here now?"

"I've got her tucked safely in the corner of the ladies' room." Charlotte was already on the move between the two areas. "Follow me." The room across the hall was empty. So, too the corner where she left Elly. "Bugger!" she shouted.

"What's the matter with you?"

"Heaps." She snapped. "I can't believe she's gone."

"You said she was safe."

"I thought she was. I left the girl here about half an hour ago. She told me some men attempted to kidnap her off the street." Charlotte thumped her hands against the wall and kicked a chair over. "I can only hope she left of her own accord."

"Perhaps not." Brian bent to retrieve a dainty necklace from the floor. A silver heart with a ruby stone inset dangled from the broken chain. "Christ!" exclaimed Charlotte. She slumped into the nearest chair.

"This is Kings Cross, Charlotte; nobody sees anything or knows anything. The general rule is to look after number one." He ambled over and placed a hand on her shoulder in a caring manner. "C'mon, Miss Tyrell, we can look around. Give me a brief description." Armed with a brief description of Elly, Brian went to the front of the pub while Charlotte checked the washroom areas. *Gone. Vanished. Another one, Charlie girl, and you left her alone.*

The proprietors, David and Joan, wanted to close up after the last of the customers rolled out the door. Charlotte and Brian hovered near the entrance; their eyes peeled for any sign of the girl.

"We could do with a drink, Joan, before we head out, if that's okay with you," Brian asked.

"Why not love? I could do with one myself." David hugged his wife and pecked her on the cheek.

"We'd be breaking the law, David," Charlotte stated.

"Not if we have one or two upstairs. C'mon, sweetheart, give in." He pleaded with his wife. You like to have a drink on a Friday night." David said, "After all, our Brian's a friend."

"Our Brian?" Charlotte queried.

"Don't worry about that, love," Joan added. "They're cousins of sorts, and I don't ask. Get it?" Joan followed with a grin and a wink with one eye. "I know nothing."

"Oh, I see." Charlotte raised her palms high.

The women giggled. Conspiracy was not new to the crime reporter.

"You take our guests up, Joan; I'll bring the drinks. What'll it be, folks?" He held aside the swing door to the bar. "Shout's on me."

"Rum no ice," said Charlotte.

"Johnnie Walker on the rocks for me, thanks."

"Righto, off you go with Joan, and I'll be there in two ticks of the clock."

Chapter Twenty

Three floors up, Brian, out of breath, remarked on the fitness of the other two. Concern for Elly's status negated Charlotte's usual quick wit. "We've more to worry about than comparing abilities."

Rented rooms available on the second floor assigned a tidy sum for David and Joan's coffers. Local prostitutes rented five of the rooms. "I evicted one woman for services in her room." Joan noticed looks on the faces of her guests and said, "We like to think we give these girls a chance at normality. And, no, we don't act as their pimps. They pay the rent and behave for the benefit of having their own space."

David placed the tray of drinks on a sideboard. "Enough talking about this place. Let's have that drink."

"Do you know a young girl called Elly?" Charlotte asked. David exchanged a furtive glance with Joan.

Brian coughed. He noticed. "Well?"

"Yes. We do; why?" Joan wrung her hands in her lap, twisting her frock over to hide the action. David raised his glass to his lips. His eyes averted Charlotte.

Charlotte continued. "I helped her in the lounge tonight. Did either of you see her?" She avoided the temptation to gulp the contents of the glass in one swallow. *Slow, girl, slow, don't give the game away.*

A sharp anxious reply gushed from Joan. "I didn't."

Charlotte tasted tension in the room. Joan was adamant, and so was David. Eager to uncover their knowledge of Elly, she tilted her head to take a sip. A gulp might suffice to ease the ache in her soul. Soothed by the rum, she followed her instincts to ask another question. "What do you know about Elly? I met her tonight; she looked frightened. She said some men tried to kidnap her." Charlotte's eyes met Joan's.

Behind shifting eyes and twitching hands, lies slipped over Joan's tongue. "Nothing, we hardly know the girl. She comes in now and then to chat with some of the others, then disappears for days. Nobody knows where she goes or what she does between visits."

Charlotte knew from her experience with criminals when people lied. Their bodies underscored certain movements, such as the closing of eyelids when they spoke. Other indicators appeared, which alerted Charlotte, so she grabbed a chance.

"I'd like to speak to those 'others' tomorrow. Please arrange a visit, say ten o'clock in the morning. Time enough for them to dress." Without waiting for an answer, she beckoned Brian. "C'mon, finish that drink and let's go. Thanks for the late nightcap; see you both tomorrow." The last gulp of rum ran warm through her chest. David opened the door and led them downstairs and out the back into the alley.

"You've opened a can of worms, missy. Watch your back." David warned.

"Why?"

"No reason, but the back streets of Kings Cross aren't the safest of places in town." David was ready to close the door. "Oh, of course, you two write the news and don't read the papers." His belly laugh echoed up the empty lane. David bade them a safe travel home and closed the door. Street lights offered a glimmer of comfort to the two reporters on the main street.

"You sure got a way with people Miss Tyrell." He tried to lesson her worrisome mood. "I'll see you home, Charlotte." He worried for her welfare.

"Just see me on a bus would be great, thanks, Brian." Her words were soft enough to show appreciation, but thoughts of Elly occupied her mind.

The silence stretched between them like an overextended piece of elastic curling and unfurling. Each opened their mouth to speak but clamped their lips shut to maintain the tranquillity of the night. The time was late, and the last bus was due. Brian helped her step onto the bus and bade her good night. Empty of energy and flush with alcohol on an empty stomach, Charlotte reacted with a nod.

From the bus stop near her street, Charlotte trundled along, lost in thought. The dampness in the night air clung to her as thick as oil. Exposed hair beneath her hat stuck against her cheeks. Moisture trickled along her skin. Wet trouser hems stretched the fabric down past her heels to collect muddied residue in the cuffs. "Bloody weather. Why doesn't the rain fall somewhere else instead of all over me?" Her words drifted into the night along the empty street.

The boarding house loomed ahead. An eerie hush spread through the neighbourhood. Her pulse quickened. She glanced back. She rushed through the gate, along the path and loped up the stairs two at a time. Mrs Park stood at the open door. "I didn't expect you to be so late, Miss Tyrell." The words hissed like a poisonous snake.

Startled, Charlotte gasped. She clutched her chest. She took a moment to compose herself. She slurred her words. "Thank goodness you're up, Mrs Park; I don't have to bend over to get the key under the mat." The painted ghouls in the panels mocked Charlotte's attempt at politeness. "And you knew I'd be working late tonight."

"Ah. So I did." Charlotte saw the contempt in those dark eyes. The landlady's mood swung faster than a child on a swing. "For all it's worth, Charlotte, you do look like something a cat dragged in. Go upstairs and change out of those dirty clothes. I'll bring up a hot cocoa."

Charlotte's mouth dropped open. "Well, go on then, upstairs with you."

Not in the mood to argue with the woman, Charlotte surrendered and hung her overcoat on the spare hook on the stand. With each step, her slacks unleashed murky traces of water on the carpeted steps. Something to consider if sneaking in after curfew.

In an instant, her sixth sense evaporated the effects of the rum. Charlotte recalled Mrs Park's attire. *Dressed for coming in or going out?* A hasty about-turn on the stairwell proved her suspicion. The woman opened the display cabinet to place her special rock inside. Coming home. Charlotte remained on the stairwell until Mrs Park moved out of sight.

Hot water in the tub soothed her muscles. The smell of hair shampoo enticed sleep. The welcome cup of cocoa before bed summoned her from the tub. Mrs Park sat at the hall table where the first hint of morning light filtered through the French doors. No angelic face caught in the glow of dawn peered at Charlotte. Shadows distorted the woman's facial features. Her dark eyes divulged secrets packed tight and deep within her soul. *The eyes told all.*

Alarmed by her vision Charlotte looked closer at Mrs Park. Not fooled by the dressing gown, which partially covered the dress underneath, stockinged feet inside slippers, or the half cast hair net, Charlotte held her tongue. Questions could wait until tomorrow.

Chapter Twenty-One

Corruption and vice nestled with ease in Kings Cross after the Bohemian artisans and their muses and followers left the area searching for inspiration elsewhere. Beneath the winter sun, the homeless mingled with laggards of the previous night. Men, women and children extracted themselves from the gutters, alleys or doorways in a dreary search for transport or scraps of rotting food out of waste bins. The unbearable stench hung heavily in the air. Lost in their own assumptions of this planned meeting, Charlotte and Brian quickened their pace toward the hotel.

Apprehension burrowed through her confidence as they approached the entrance. Charlotte rolled her shoulders back and forth. *Shake off this mood.* Last night a frightened young woman entered her life. Questions about a link between all the disappearances concerned Charlotte. Sophie and Lailah lived at the boarding house whereas Elly described a physical assault on the street. Elly's appearance and her story about an attempted abduction roused Charlotte's investigative skills hence the request to meet the residents of the pub.

While the proprietor, David hung their coats behind the office door, his wife, Joan, approached the reporters. "All the ladies are in the lounge waiting for you. They're a bit put out by all this fuss."

Traces of stale tobacco lingered in the thick smoky haze clogging the hallway vents. Dirty floral-patterned carpet along the corridor muffled their footsteps. Wet spilled beer patches squelched beneath their shoes. Fly specks patterned the nicotine-stained walls. Piles of insect carcasses impeded light from the upturned ceiling shades. Paint peeled away in small sections from the ceiling and walls. Brian and Charlotte heard a woman's voice. "What's this all about? Why interview us? I need my beauty sleep."

Unrestrained whispers and giggles split the quiet inside the pub's walls. "Yeah, we all want to know?" Another voice reinforced the general consensus of the gathering.

Unified and bonded like sisters, they protected each other. With the thought forefront in her mind, Charlotte entered the room with Brian close behind. Eight women of various ages, grouped in twos and a threesome, except one who sat alone at the front. "Morning Joan. Can't thank you enough for your help."

Joan nodded then sat at the nearest table occupied by the lone woman, who was obviously the eldest of the group. City noise combined with cool fresh air charged through the open sash window. "Shut that fucking window!" A cry from a young girl. "That's a cold southerly blowin' in my face." A dark-haired woman slammed the window down.

Charlotte buried her surprise when Lily, Mrs Park's daughter, waltzed into the room to serve tea and biscuits from a tray that held an outrageous amount of milk and sugar. Black market, for sure. This was neither time nor place to check. She raised an eyebrow at Joan, who whispered, "Don't ask; I tell no lies."

The instant Charlotte asked if anyone knew Elly, argumentative discussion about who did and who didn't rose above the quiet murmurs of others. Brian nudged Charlotte in the upper arm to whisper, "the pot's stirred."

"So I see, but we need the ingredients," she whispered back. All eyes were aimed at the elder woman of the group. Mother hen, no doubt, Charlotte thought. To the woman who held the attention of all in the room, Charlotte asked for her name.

"Dot. What's it to you, Missy?" The sneer disturbed Charlotte and raised issues from her past. This woman carries her past and present in a soulless cage. Charlotte shuddered; internal conflict threatened to rip her apart. Photographs of mutilated bodies of women exposed Charlotte to the world of crime. Never forgotten, but still, the images surfaced, especially when during interviews such as now.

When he noticed her stance shift and pallor alter, Brian asked, "You all right, Charlie? Are you up to this?"

"All good, mate." She forced a smile of thanks

Dot sat at a table by the window, glaring at Charlotte. Amusement flickered in her eyes, but the sneer remained. Creases to the side of her dark eyes highlighted wasted years.

"Do you mind if I smoke?" Dot asked while her fingers caressed a pearl embossed cigarette case on the table beside a box of matches. The tick-tock rhythm of the clock resonated in the silence. The muffled sounds of the city retreated. Dot's weathered hands stretched over the case to withdraw a filtered cigarette. She tucked it in a holder between her lips. The strike of the match broke the silence. Sulphur disguised the pong of cheap perfumes. A flurry of movement in the back of the room caught her attention. "Brian, stop her from leaving."

Brian moved past the tables to request the woman remain in the room. When confronted, she said. "I need the lav."

"All right, off you go." Brian stepped aside, but the woman stumbled against his body on purpose to embarrass him in front of his colleague. The brush against his torso invited giggles and murmurs from the others.

Peeved with the slow progression of the interview, Charlotte raised her voice. "Enough of this pussy footing around, ladies! Does anyone here know Elly?" A hush preceded the constant shifting of bodies in seats. "Well? You, near the window. What's your name?"

Scared by the reporter's tone, the young girl said her name between hiccups. "Peg, Miss." Heads turned toward Peg, whose hiccups increased.

"Well, Peg, do you know Elly?"

Peg responded with a shake of her head. Charlotte waved her down and told her to get a drink. A voice from the back replied. "Ooh, now you're talking."

Eager to continue her day's work schedule, Joan shouted. "Enough! Behave, and let's get this over with. I have lots to do rather than sit here and watch these bloody games." Joan turned to Charlotte. "And you, are you satisfied that nobody here knows this girl, Elly?"

At first, Charlotte ignored the question and looked at Brian, who shrugged his shoulders. "To put this mildly, Joan, I believe one or more of you know Elly and are too afraid to come forward. I'll leave my card with each of you, and if you feel the need to convey any information, please phone." Brian passed her business card to each of the women. "We'll be off now. You've been more helpful than you realise." Charlotte gathered her purse and notebook and marched from the room with Brian not far behind.

Chapter Twenty-Two

The morning paper slammed hard on his desk. "What the hell is this?" Charlotte's temper escalated by Brian's supercilious grin. "A good story, that's what," Brian answered. Tempted to react to this unwarranted outburst, he counted to three before he spoke. "While you escaped to your comfort zone, I spent the rest of the night here."

"You stole my story, you arrogant, self-centred egotistical —"

"—Ahem." Rory's body frame towered between them. "Great work, both of you. Sales are up."

"Both of us? My name is not mentioned anywhere in this ...this... piece of ..."

"Calm down, Charlie. I made that decision, not Brian." Rory spoke with the authority of his position. Defeated for the moment, Charlotte sank into the nearest chair. The Editor laid a hand on her shoulder. "I know, the story belongs to you both, but if your name stays out of the news, you can go about this undercover business and work closely with Detective Devlin. After the police solve the missing girl case, you will get all the recognition you deserve." He looked at her sad face and vowed, "I promise."

She stood up and straightened her shoulders. "I wanted input into the article, especially about Elly, Brian. You didn't ask."

"Easy, Charlie," Brian said. To apologise, he reached for her hand.

She jerked away. "Don't touch me." She hauled herself out of the office. Her emotions swirled in anger and pity. Pity for herself and Elly and her wounded pride.

"Back to work, everyone. The show's over." Rory's ringmaster tone triggered staff to withdraw behind partitions. Hushed murmurs continued in corners.

Brian unfurled his long body to stand in front of Rory. "This headline belongs to Charlie." He slapped the newspaper at Rory's chest.

"I know." The front page opened with one turn of the folded crease. "Go after her. Sort her out and fix up whatever is going on between you two." Rory turned toward his office, where his medicinal purposed brandy bottle beckoned the seasoned drinker.

Winter clung to the city streets. Charlotte wove between shoppers trawling past window displays. Sprite on her feet, she dodged those laden with packages, flitting in and out of shops.

She yearned for somewhere quiet beneath a shady tree. The botanical gardens offered this, but she decided to visit Hyde Park. *Let's see where the girls disappeared.*

She sat on a wrought iron bench beside a sturdy upright trunk. The sigh of weathered leaves matched her mood. An older man ambled toward her. The sudden approach of a lean human creature in unkempt clothes stirred her fears. She dared not move, hoping he might pass by. Is *he someone to dread? Shake the thought out, girl.* She remained seated, alert and uneasy.

The bench seat creaked beneath his weight. "Hello, Miss. Miserable day, but your pretty face sure lifts a man's spirit."

To her amazement, the sound of his voice soothed her temperament. Her first instinct was to send him on his way, but a sense of mystery triggered a change in her mood. "Hello, to you, sir." Charlotte locked her fingers across her lap.

He made no effort to move away. "Name's Harold. How about you? What's your name?"

"Charlie, short for Charlotte." *Why am I talking with this stranger? Girls have disappeared from this neighbourhood. I know nothing about him. Stay alert.* She dared not make eye contact with him by keeping her focus on his feet. A fresh odour of spices and oranges emanated from his clothing in contrast to his unclean appearance. *That fucking smell.*

As if he read Charlotte's thoughts, he said. "Don't take too much notice of me, love; I'm harmless." He pulled two red apples from his canvas bag and offered one to her.

"No thanks." She replied.

Harold put the smaller apple back in his bag. "It's okay; you're safe with me. I know Mr Devlin and his friend Joe very well."

"B-b-but how?" she stammered.

"Too long a story today. I'll move along now, but it is nice to meet you." Harold stood up straight and slung his bag over one shoulder. "Be seeing you then." He said as he walked away toward the rail station.

Left wondering about the stranger and why he introduced himself to her, she remained seated in the park. She watched Harold wander away. His stride belied his appearance. *Who is he really? Does he know anything about the disappearances? He said he knows Michael and his friend.* Charlotte realised Harold might be helpful. Curiosity diverted her suspicious thoughts when she decided to follow Harold, but she lost sight of him within the crowd of pedestrians.

She left the park and headed for the cafe across the street before making her way to the Police Station. Michael was not in his office, so she asked the duty officer to write in the desk diary about a request to speak to Detective Devlin and added the word urgent to the note.

Too late in the day to go back to work, she caught the next bus home. She figured Michael might arrange a meeting with Harold if she asked nicely. Curious about Harold, she wondered if meeting the man was not accidental. Charlotte mentally tossed the why's and what if's until she stepped off the bus.

Chapter Twenty-Three

It's a fuckin' jigsaw. Charlotte's mind sorted through what little she knew about the disappearances. She strolled along the footpath churning the morning's meeting in search of answers. *Those women back at the hotel. Who do they think they are? One of their kind is missing, and they don't care. Or do they?*

She looked up and couldn't help but be amazed by the majestic height of the Jacaranda trees. Come Springtime, delicate blossoms will blanket the ground with fallen lilac blooms. In contrast, the boarding house with its dark secrets loomed ahead. She paused at the gate to gather her wits and untangle the links connecting the disappearances. Tread softly, my girl. Be careful.

Inside, she hung her coat on the rack in the entry hall when the kettle's shrill whistle ripped through the silent house like a steam train in a tunnel. A clink of china alerted Charlotte that someone was in the kitchen. A soft melodic hum lightened the atmosphere, but her entry altered the landlady's mood and her own. "I understand you know why I was at the hotel the other day."

Urtha Park stopped kneading the bread dough to wipe the sticky substance off her hands with a damp towel. "Pardon?"

"You know, don't you, Mrs Park?" Charlotte glared at the woman. "Don't lie; I saw Lily at the hotel."

"Now, don't go getting riled up with me, Missy. Lily does her job and does it well."

Urtha Park moved to the sideboard and returned to the table with two cups, saucers and a pot of tea. "What is it you want me to tell you? Lily is a good girl and does what she's told." The tea pouring ceremony was forgotten with the first tilt of the spout. "Here, have a cuppa and cheer up love. I'll give you the answers you want in a moment." Charlotte sat down opposite the woman.

"Lily told me about the meeting and how you fretted over a missing prostitute." A smirk appeared beneath her dark eyes. "How well did you know the girl?"

"Only met her on Friday night." Charlotte pulled the proffered teacup within reach.

"Why are you interested in the whereabouts of a young prostitute?"

Charlotte's skin prickled. She straightened her back. Her muscles tensed. *How did she know the girl was a prostitute? Rethink your next question.* To uncover the truth, she continued the spar. "I don't recall mentioning the girl was a prostitute, Mrs Park. Tell me what Lily told you."

"You can ask me yourself, Miss Tyrell." Lily walked into the room and sat beside her mother. "Hello Mummy." Urtha Park patted her daughter's hand to show affection.

Charlotte noted the action and deemed it void of a mother's tenderness. "What do you know about Elly?"

"Not much. She works the streets to make a bit of money. Hardly ever see her." A nervous edge to Lily's voice cautioned Charlotte. Faced with the task of unveiling whatever secrets these women share; Charlotte's soft tone quashed her usual abruptness. Charlotte asked if Lily had seen Elly the night she disappeared.

"Maybe I did, maybe I didn't." Lily wriggled on her seat, eager to put a stop to any further talk about Elly.

Charlotte seethed inside but managed to control the urge to shout. She stood up, rested her hands on the back of her chair and leaned toward Lily. "What's that supposed to mean? I saw you at the hotel the night Elly seemed to be in some sort of trouble."

Lily cowered and answered, "Hell, come to think of it, I did see her in the afternoon." She glanced at her mother. Mrs Park turned away; her lips pinched tight.

"Did you by any chance happen to notice the time you last saw her?" Charlotte struggled to keep her composure.

"I guess around the end of my shift." Lily twisted in her chair.

Charlotte leaned forward. "Did you think she looked upset or worried?"

Urtha Park intervened. "Why ask Lily about the girl? What has this got to do with her?"

Charlotte eased back, keeping her hands on the back of her chair. "Oh, you probably haven't heard that Elly may have run away or been abducted." Charlotte looked back at Lily, who averted eye contact. "I thought Lily might be able to help, but obviously not." Charlotte put her hands in her pockets. She believed she could coax more information out of Lily. "One more query, Lily, if you don't mind."

"If you must," Lily said as she placed her forearms on the tabletop.

"I was wondering if you noticed any strangers lurking out the back of the hotel."

Lily opened her mouth to reply, but Mrs Park interrupted, "We have better things to do, Miss Tyrell." Both women rose from the table. "Lily and I have duties to perform, including evening meal preparations. If you'll excuse us." Mrs Park casually moved forward and guided Charlotte from the kitchen.

The door softly closed behind Charlotte, who suspected the daughter knew more than she was letting on. Charlotte planned to speak to Michael about her suspicion that Lily may be involved in Elly's disappearance.

The parlour offered refuge until the other boarders arrived home. Seated in the wingback chair by the fire, Charlotte's mood dissolved under the spell of the hearth's fire. She had selected a book from the centre table, but the murder mystery lay unopened on her lap.

Through half-closed eyes, she watched the flames in the fireplace dance in the chimney's updraft. When the blaze burnt low, she added another short log. Hungry hot tongues spat sparks off the fresh wood into the black shaft. Mesmerized by the fiery dance, she leaned back to reflect on the events of the past few days.

"What's wrong with you?" Magda's voice broke through the quagmire in her mind. "You look downhearted. Has your new man dumped you?"

"Oh, Magda, it's worse than that." Charlotte shifted from her slouched position. Dying embers in the hearth flashed and disintegrated into ash. "The fire needs another log."

"What? You are mad?" She put her hand over her red lips to stifle a giggle.

"Of course, I'm not mad, stupid, maybe." Charlotte's lips pursed to say something else. Instead, she jumped up and grabbed Magda's hand. "Come. I need to talk to someone who will listen."

"Intriguing, I must say. Tell me more." Magda's eyes widened, and she allowed herself to be led from the comfort of the room. "Shhh. Not here." Like prowling leopards, they crept upstairs, avoiding the squeaking board. Magda had been inside her friend's room before and couldn't decide if the room was smaller than hers. However, the space was definitely neater and tidier.

"Here, sit on the bed, and I'll bring the chair over." Charlotte insisted.

"This is fun, Charlie; it reminds me of sharing secrets in the dormitory."

"Ha, if only this place inspired the same ideas to spend time sharing stories and jokes after dark." Charlotte placed the chair near the foot of the bed. "You're a dear friend Magda. Come to think of it, my only friend in this city." When Charlotte sat on the chair, she stretched her legs to cross her ankles.

Magda giggled. "Oh, and here I am, believing Michael Devlin was your best friend." The grin on her friend's face reflected everything Charlotte wanted in a friend. The best recipe for a strong friendship included a good sense of humour mixed with a certain amount of kindness and a good dose of compassion. Magda possessed all the ingredients.

"Tonight, I have something serious to tell you, and we don't have much time."

"Are you in trouble?" Magda's eyes reflected her concern.

"Nothing like that." Charlotte uncrossed her feet to curl her legs underneath her seat.

"Well? Spit it out, Charlie."

"Sorry, yes. There's another girl missing and most likely not reported to the police."

"Oh, my, another one."

"Yes, and I met her last night. She looked frightful in her muddied dress and shoes. And scared." Charlotte continuously gripped and released her hands.

"There are lots who look like that downtown. Nothing to worry about."

"Wait until you hear what happened."

"I'm all ears." Magda's eagerness prompted Charlotte to start at the beginning.

"Brian, my colleague, and myself went to a hotel in Kings Cross to try and listen to the local gossip in the bar."

"You got inside the Male Only area?" Magda's eyes sparkled with mischief.

"Sure did. Mind you, it did help that Brian knew the proprietors and I dressed like a man."

"Jesus, Charlie, I'm amazed." Magda slapped herself on the thigh. "And, you never asked me. You must be the first female to be inside a 'men only' area."

"I can't say if that's true. Anyway, I had no time to think of asking anyone else to join us." Dismay dulled the gleam in her friend's eyes. "I am a crime reporter, Magda. That's the reason we got inside."

"A crime reporter, but I thought you worked as a typist. Now I understand, Charlie."

"I'm glad you understand why, but you can't tell anyone what I do for a living. Promise."

Magda crossed her heart and fingers. "I swear."

"I bloody well know you swear. And worse than a trooper at time." Charlotte continued before Magda could respond. "This was our only chance to get any information about any of the missing girls."

"And did you?"

"No such luck until this frightened young woman rushed into the lounge. She claimed two men in dark coats tried to abduct her. She said she escaped when they all slipped on the wet road dodging an oncoming car. Her name is Elly, by the way."

"Pretty name. Go on."

This statement did not distract Charlotte. "Elly said the men lost their hold on her, and she managed to run inside the hotel, where she literally bumped into me on my way back from the rest room. I thought she'd be safe in the lounge, so I asked her to wait until I got Brian. After all, I had no authority to take a bedraggled female across the threshold into men only territory."

"Wait here, Charlie. I'll be back in a moment." Magda quietly left the room. The door clicked closed. She heard soft footsteps in the hallway, and before long, the handle on her door twisted and in spun Magda.

"I thought we might have a drink or two. Whatever takes our fancy." A bottle of Sherry held high over Magda's head begged to be poured into the two glasses she held in her other hand. "Sorry, no nibbles, will that worry you."

"Not on your life, Magda. Here put them on the bedside." Charlotte said as she scooped aside her personal items. "You can pour."

"Bottoms up, Charlie"

After a gentle clink of glasses, both women gulped down the contents. Charlotte wiped her lips with the hem of her cardigan. Magda used her blouse cuffs. "Needed that, Magda. Thanks."

Another tip of the bottle and both glasses were full of sherry. "Let's get comfortable before you continue." With that remark, both girls sat on opposite ends of the bed with their legs stretched out on top of the covers.

"You settled enough for me to continue" The sherry tasted sweet on Charlotte's lips.

"Yes, I'm ready to hear about this little escapade of yours."

Charlotte took a deep breath before she began. "I went to get Brian, who was caught up with an old friend telling joke after joke. I had to wait until the fellow left before I could tell Brian about the girl. We both entered the Ladies Lounge, but she was gone." Charlotte flopped against the pillow in defeat. "Everyone else had left by that time. I had nobody to ask what happened. Brian and I tried to look for her, but she had disappeared." She sipped her sherry to relish the flavour. Charlotte noticed Magda had emptied her glass. "I tell you, what happened the next day, when Brian and I returned, fucking screwed my head." Charlotte paused, waiting for another serving of sherry, which Magda supplied.

CHAPTER TWENTY-THREE

"I can't even imagine what might shock you, Miss Crime Reporter."

"Well fucking swallow this piece of news. Lily is the daytime housemaid where Elly disappeared."

"What? That's absurd; she wouldn't work in an iron lung."

"I agree, but now I'm suspicious of Lily and her interaction with the ladies at the hotel. Especially after this afternoon's conversation I had with our dear landlady and her daughter."

"What's next then?"

"I don't know; perhaps a visit to Michael might help."

"Be careful, Charlie. After what you told me, you might be next, which will not help anybody. Let's talk about it at the dinner table while Violet's there? On a lighter note, have another sherry."

"Excellent idea. Another drink might help the appetite."

A knock at the door silenced their exchange. Charlotte opened the door to find Kathleen waiting. "I just wanted you to know I saw Lily loitering in the hall near your room."

"Whatever for, I wonder?" Was Lily eavesdropping? While she pondered the significance of Lily's behaviour.

"Fancy a nip of sherry, Kathleen?" Magda asked in her usual flippant manner.

"Yes, please."

"Come in, Kathleen," Charlotte offered her chair.

Magda rescued the last glass from her room. Back in Charlotte's room, she held the bottle to the light. "Still enough for another couple of rounds, girls. No nibbles, though."

Kathleen reached for her handbag and offered a bar of chocolate. "Will this do?"

"I think you have our entrée under control" Magda's giggle shortened the length of the invisible string between friends.

"Now, what were we talking about, Magda?" Charlotte appealed to Magda's sharp wits.

"Was I talking about a Sherlock Holmes book titled *The Adventure of Unfathomable Silence?*"

"Oh yes, but I'd much rather talk about going to the Town Hall Dance." To confirm she understood, Magda put her fingertips against her lips.

"I can't make plans when my brain feels as thick as mud." Charlotte touched her temple and lips. Magda and Charlotte now shared a secret of their own.

"Too much chocolate, I think," Kathleen said. "We may have overdone it." All three burst out laughing.

The trio emptied the bottle of sherry between discussions regarding local news and where to shop for the latest fashion before the grandfather clock chimed the hour. "Gosh, we had better scurry downstairs; else, we won't be served." Kathleen picked up her handbag and made for the door. She turned around after stepping into the hall. "Thank you, Charlotte, and you too Magda. I've enjoyed this evening and hope we can do this again. My room next time."

"As long as you have chocolate," Laughter seeped throughout the upstairs area.

Charlotte locked her bedroom door before she turned to see Magda twirling through her doorway. "Life is bloody good, ain't it?"

"I'll let you know after dinner." Charlotte mumbled.

Magda, humming a soft tune, plodded ahead without a care in the world.

Charlotte had indulged in a few drinks earlier in the day with little food. She blamed the sherry for her thick tongue and dry mouth. Hunger gripes gurgled and rolled through her stomach. By the cooking aromas, she guessed, Mrs Park had baked a roast chicken. She headed for the dining room. Flush with alcohol, Charlotte wandered into the room as Mrs Park walked in carrying the first service tray.

"I'm sorry we're late." Magda snickered at Charlotte's attempt to be civil. Charlotte winked at her friend. Kathleen sauntered into the room without more than a hello. A smile spread wide across Charlotte's face when Kathleen mentioned she, too, had read *The Adventure of Unfathomable Silence*. To Charlotte, the clue was as plain as day. "I see by the table setting, the girls won't be joining us." *Well, at least the sherry and chocolate improved my state of mind. Pity my unsettled stomach rumbling.*

"Good," Magda said. "After those few glasses, I am as useless as a mule balancing on a tight rope."

Although they planned to discuss the disappearance of Elly at the dinner table in front of Violet and Lily, the absence of the twins was soon forgotten. The landlady's daughters were rarely seen apart inside the house. Charlotte knew another opportunity would present itself before the week ended.

Chapter Twenty-Four

"It's for you, Charlie." Brian held the telephone hand-set high in the air and waved it in her face.

"Who is it?" Charlotte asked.

"Didn't say." He turned back to his typewriter.

"Charlotte Tyrell here."

A muffled voice. "Get out of town!"

"What? Who is this?"

"Get out of town!" The caller disconnected the line.

Startled, she released the receiver as if it had burned her skin. She sunk into her chair and placed her hands over her face. Her muscles tensed. *What was that about? Why threaten me?*

Brian jumped with fright as the handset hit the wooden floor. Charlotte braced herself for a tirade of foul language, but it was a soft voice that asked. "You okay?"

"Give me a moment to collect myself." She dashed past desks toward the staff facilities at the end of the hall and ignored anyone who approached. Once inside a cubicle, she slid the bolt. She leaned against the door while her trained mind referred to mental exercises from her past association with a psychologist. Memories buried deep inside resurfaced. She closed her eyes to repeat her mantra. *Deep breaths - in - out. Release the demons to welcome clarity of thoughts.* Ten minutes passed before she exited.

Rory and Brian ceased their conversation as Charlotte neared her desk. Brian nodded agreement to whatever question Rory had posed. "I wonder who you two were talking about. Oh, let me guess; it's me."

Rory stood close enough to touch her shoulder. He reached out, but Charlotte ducked from his impending touch. In control of her emotions, and her voice resonating confidence. "I'm okay, Chief, truly. It was the caller who upset me when she told me to leave town." Her eyes searched for Brian for support. None came. He turned away.

"I'd like you both to come to my office."

Hemmed between the two men, Charlotte submitted. A desire to escape niggled at her, but the futile thought evaporated beneath her will to uncover the truth behind the threat. Always at ease in the chief's office, she sat in her usual place on the left side of Brian. Charlotte's concentration shifted from Rory's voice to the investigation of the disappearances and today's threat. Certain that the caller was female, she convinced herself of a possible connection between the two. The odour of cigar smoke infiltrated her thoughts, reminding her that she had drifted into her own headspace and not listening to her chief editor. She asked Rory to repeat what he had said.

Rory could only guess why she hadn't heard a word he said. He sucked on his cigar before he suggested Charlotte take some leave.

"Why? I can handle this." She looked at her boss with the expectation of agreement.

Rory pinched the cigar between his fingers and studied the glow at the tip. Ash dropped onto his blotter. He used the side of his hand to brush the mark off his desk. "It's like this Charlotte." He took a deep breath. "I won't have you risking yourself or others for the sake of getting a story, young lady."

"But—"

"—But nothing. I called Michael Devlin after Brian told me about the threat. I'm asking you to wait here and follow his instructions." One bushy eyebrow raised high on his forehead. "Is that clear, young lady? I am responsible for putting you in danger, and I will never forgive myself if something happens to you." Charlotte noticed his bushy eyebrows knot together as his temper flared. His puffy red face reminded her of a cartoon character. After all his huffing and puffing, she yielded to his demands.

Not a word passed between the trio. Charlotte broke the surge of nervous tension in the room. "Brian, I need a smoke. You got one? And Chief, how about a drink of some of that stuff you keep in your top drawer?" A sense of normality entered the room with the sound of her voice. She waited while Brian lit two cigarettes in his mouth. He passed one over. The long drag on the filter tip filled her lungs, and the exhale of smoke clouded her features. Ash dropped on her suit, which she brushed to the floor. Neither man showed surprise when Charlotte drained her glass and held it out for another before the men had raised their drinks. The bottle of brandy emptied within minutes. The room filled with clouds of smoke, and the ashtrays overflowed with butts before Michael arrived.

"Where is she?" he demanded. His voice carried through the walls. Michael's official voice made Charlotte shift in her chair and subconsciously trace her fingers through her hair.

Movement in the room pulled her back to reality as Brian opened the office door, and Rory pushed the window out. Air gushed in from both sides of Charlotte. The smoky haze drifted to the ceiling and melded into the nothingness of the atmosphere. She noted the change of mood and shivered. "Hello, Michael." Her quiet tone bewildered her. "Looks like I need your help."

"Certainly does, Charlie. I would like to take you down to the station for an official report. Do you feel up to that?"

She nodded in agreement. Strong hands helped her stand. Whose hands, she did not know. She heard Brian say he would get her coat, handbag and hat.

"Got a threatening call today, Michael, and I don't know why."

"I heard, Charlie, but let's wait until we get to the station. Here's Brian with your things."

With little effort on her part, Michael helped Charlotte put on her coat. She flung her handbag over her shoulder, and with a swift toss of her head her hat sat firmly in place. A police car with a constable standing at the rear passenger door was outside the building. He opened the door for Charlotte and Michael to sit together in the rear. Michael kept the conversation light during the short drive to the station.

Michael escorted Charlotte to an interview room. A female stenographer sat in the corner to take notes. Charlotte recognised the other detective as the one who visited the boarding house but couldn't remember his name at first. "Carl, is it?" She asked.

Surprised but pleased that someone recognised him, he smiled and acknowledged she got the name right.

Ever the gentleman, Michael asked if she'd like tea or coffee, and she elected for tea. The stenographer stepped outside the room to ask the guard in the corridor to bring a tea tray for four. The young woman announced, "Tea's on its way, Mr Devlin."

A knock on the door interrupted Charlotte's response to start the interview. Michael poured the tea for Charlotte and himself. Carl and the stenographer poured their own. The fragrance of the tea, mingled with the stench of stale cigar smoke, pushed her to frantically ask for the nearest restroom. Her stomach felt nauseous and unsettled, threatening to empty its contents. Michael allowed her to leave under escort with the female guard in the corridor.

In her absence, the detective confirmed the time of the call from the City News switchboard operator. Brian also explained Charlotte's reaction which prompted him to report the call to Rory. With the assurance that Charlotte felt better when she returned to the room, Michael started the interview. Charlotte expressed her concerns about the phone call along with the threat the caller passed over the phone.

Questions fired one after the other. Did she recognise the caller? Did she think the caller was male or female? Did she believe the call might be a hoax or a real threat.? Charlotte answered with a calmness that surprised even herself. Her responses were written in the detectives' notepads. The stenographer pencilled questions and answers in shorthand.

"Michael, the voice was definitely female, and yes, I have no doubt the caller meant what she said." Charlotte drained her cup before sharing her thoughts about a connection between the phone call and the disappearances. "Michael, I believe the missing girls and the threat may be linked."

Michael asked her to explain why.

"Gut feeling, that's all. I saw Elly before she disappeared. Her description of the incident where men tried to abduct her means that she saw them." Charlotte pressed her back against her seat. "Someone is trying to keep me out of the investigation. I'm not letting go despite feeling unwell." Contemplating the appropriate words, Charlotte removed her hat to run her long fingers through her hair. "I'm not doing this for the story, Michael." She leaned forward, resting her forearms on the desk to lace her fingers together. "I won't stop searching for the missing women because of a crank call." As she spoke, her eyes wandered aimlessly around the room. "I'm too involved to give up." Charlotte leaned heavily against the back of her chair with her feet firmly planted on the floor. "If you've finished, I'd like to start my so-called holidays."

After discussing the possibility of Charlotte being in serious danger, Michael agreed, on the condition he drive her home.

Arriving at the boarding house, Charlotte thanked him and tried to persuade him not to worry. Michael refused to heed her words. "You need someone you can trust to cover your back." He reached across her lap and opened the passenger door. "I guess I'm your man."

"I suppose you are, Michael. Maybe we can work together after all."

Michael pecked her on the cheek before she got out. "I'm here for you and those girls. Let's go find them. But first, I suggest we ignore the situation for the moment and go dancing at the Town Hall dance tomorrow night."

"Sounds good, I'll meet you there." Charlotte's smile belied her concern for the slow progress with the investigation.

Crimes in Sydney flourished, but none generated any evidence to instigate further enquiries about the missing women. The police had eased their searches but kept vigilant patrols at bus stop areas on Saturday nights. Charlotte knew the police needed more clues to pursue the case. *If solving the mystery is indeed up to me, then I will do just that.* She busied herself by browsing through her notes about the disappearances.

Chapter Twenty-Five

A reluctant Charlotte dressed for a night out at the Town Hall dance. With Magda out on a dinner date with one of the American sailors, Charlotte left the boarding house early to catch a bus. Nervous tension guided her to the back corner of the room where the dancers blocked her view of the entrance. She felt safe. "Ah, there you are." Michael touched her upper arm. "Come outside; we ought to talk about your work."

"My work? What about my work?" Charlotte pressed her tongue between her teeth, the only defiant act she could muster.

"Calm down, love, please." He pulled her into his arms. "Come, some fresh air might do us both good."

Charlotte agreed and allowed him to lead her by the hand to the edge of the front portico. Caught in a draft, she shivered without her coat. Michael slung his suit jacket across her shoulders. "That better?" He asked.

"Thank you, but you'll catch a cold." Charlotte snuggled up close to Michael.

"I've an idea," Michael spun her about. "Give me your cloakroom ticket to collect your coat so I can whisk you away to Nielsen Park where we can study the city lights."

"Do you think we could get something to eat on the way?" She was unable to decipher if the cramps she suffered were hunger pains or instincts curdling her gut. Without thinking, she blurted, "Please don't take too long, I don't want to be alone out here."

"Not like you to be scared, Charlie. What's up? That phone call obviously put you on edge." Michael half turned. He wrapped his arms about Charlotte's shoulders to pacify the fear percolating inside her.

"Never mind. I'll be all right. I'll step out from the shadows."

"Thatta girl' Won't be a minute." Confident she was safe in public; he went inside leaving her alone outside the building.

Movement over the low balustrade prompted her nerves to tighten and cramp. Dark shapes of men wearing trilbies moved away from the building's facade. The aroma of Divine7 cologne stirred thoughts of her mother. Baffled by its presence, she wondered why men might need to drench themselves in perfume. Within the minute, Michael returned with her coat interrupting her internal queries.

Michael mistook the pale colour in her face. "You must be cold, Charlie. Here let me help you into your coat."

Her eyes averted from his gaze. "Do you mind if we talk tomorrow? I much prefer to go home."

Disappointment changed his features. "I suppose so. Come, I'll drive you home."

What choice did she have? Those men in the shadows frightened her. Guilty of something for certain. Harmless - unknown. Not in the mood. Questions tumbled through her head, producing a make-believe headache for Michael's attention. He drove her home in silence. "I'll call for you at eight, Charlie and we'll talk about what upset you and if you have any fresh leads about the missing girls. We can go to Nielsen Park in the daylight and shoo away the gulls and watch the ferries go by."

"I'm sorry about my behaviour tonight. I can't explain how I feel."

"You need to sleep, love," He blew her a kiss after he restarted the motor.

Charlotte hastily returned the favour. "I'll be in fine spirits and ready to go to the park." He waited by the curb until she was inside the door, safe and sound, he hoped.

Chapter Twenty-Six

On Friday night, hostile southern winds attacked the city. Winter leaves torn from sturdy trees, attached to defenceless stockinged legs. Outer clothing, worn by nightlife seekers, trapped the shapes against the fabric. Hats whisked from heads, free as balloons, whizzed down lanes and alleys to be lost forever in the jumble of filthy drains and open bins.

Intoxicated and restless, Joe stumbled past tunnel dwellers to his own makeshift space. Unable to focus, he manoeuvred slow and unsteady toward his bed. His body unfurled in an ineffectual drop onto the comfort of a blanket and cardboard. *Bugger. Missed the bastard.* He rolled over to nestle atop his makeshift bed.

Nightmares flourished. Blue lights mesmerized him twice. Wingless angels hovered in the tunnel. One sneered at him. He closed his eyes. "Take me, please; I want to go." No response. When he found the courage to look, nothing. No blue lights, even the hum had died. No one there but himself, alone.

Alcoholic intoxication dragged him deep into unconsciousness until the morning clamour of neighbours filtered through his dreamlike state. Leaden limbs refused to move. A throb across his brow accentuated the sensation of a thick and furry tongue. His vision blurred, and his mouth was dry. *Death, come swift.*

Progress in activating all senses depended on his willingness to survive another day. A cure for the headache motivated the effort to rise. Joe raised himself with the utmost care by sliding his back up the tiled wall. The buttons on the flaps at the back of his coat grated his nerves as well as the shiny surface. *Jesus, what I need is the hair of the dog that bit me.* Each step through the tunnel to the street above bordered on precarious until he reached the streets above. Morning sunshine added to his discomfort by impeding his vision. He teetered along the sidewalk toward the shady trees in Hyde Park.

Harold bided his time on a park bench, waiting for Joe. "Here, lad, sit yourself down. I've got a cure for your misery."

Joe tilted his head towards Harold. "Thanks mate." Before he sat down, Joe released the agitation in his stomach behind a bush. "God, what I do to myself."

"The name's Harold, not God. You're messed up, my friend, and in dire need of help. Here, take this headache powder with a bit of water from the tap over there. You've got to look after your body, friend."

The tap stood at right angles beside a garden bed prepared for spring flowers. Joe envisioned himself amongst the seedlings crushing them flat in the soil beneath his body. *Body? Where? Whose? Mine?*

Someone else? Yes, an extra one last night or the other night. Those bloody lights. Later. Later.

One hand rested on the stake to counter his balance. The other released a flow of cold water from the tap. He flinched beneath the splash against his face. Stooped and wobbly without support, he used both hands to free the powder from its wrapper. The bitter tang on his tongue eased with a gulp of the cool liquid. His belly growled, eager to regurgitate the substance. *Got to sit before I fall.* Pliable as a rag doll, Joe sat beside Harold to moan about his existence. "What no commiserations from the sage?" Joe asked.

"C'mon lad, funniest piece of nonsense I ever heard. You're savvier about life than anyone I know." Harold leaned forward to feed crumbs to the pigeons swaggering about their feet. "Tucker is what you need, my friend, and a good bath."

"Sure do, mate, but my gut may explode on intake, and I don't smell any different to you."

"Spoken like a man." Harold guffawed back.

"How come I never see you in the tunnels, Harold? But I'm told you pass through. What's your purpose? Where do you go?"

"Shopping for fresh goods." Harold squirmed, uneasy with the direction of this conversation.

The throbbing ache behind Joe's eyes troubled him less than the evasive response. "Christ mate, there's no fresh goods in those holes, only angels of death walking in a blue haze."

"Ah, those beings." Harold retrieved a packet of cigarettes. "Have a smoke; calm your nerves."

"You know about these men?" Joe lit a cigarette from the packet in his shirt pocket. The first puff Joe inhaled instigated a coughing fit.

He suppressed the urge to further test his lung capacity. A thin film of smoke snaked upward. He snuffed out the cigarette between his thumb and forefinger before tucking it behind his ear.

"When did you last see them?" Harold changed the course of the conversation; he was more interested in what Joe knew.

"Last night, I think." "Yeah, last night – twice. Just another nightmare about Maddy, but not Maddy, someone else. Nothing to worry about in my drunken dreams."

With the ease of an athlete, Harold stood. Joe accepted the proffered hand. "Take care, Joe. We'll talk soon about your images."

Sweat banded in Joe's armpits and the small of his back. Midday sunshine tinged his face pink. Time to go grab a bite to eat. His stomach rumbled in approval. Cheap sandwiches and black tea are available near the station. Ham was scarce, but he relished the sweet cool meat substitute smothered in pickles. Patrons moved to other tables, leaving Joe alone by the window.

Street lights flickered on, a sign of day's end. *Is that how life ends? A flick of a switch. Maddy, Maddy, what happened, my love?* The persistent tapping against the windowpane shattered his reverie. He glanced sideways. Michael stood there. Joe beckoned him inside.

Michael's nose twitched as he sat down opposite his friend. "Jesus, Joe, you could do with a decent wash. Let me take you home and get you sorted. You look like..." He dared not say.

"Yeah, you don't say." Without a proper night's sleep, Joe didn't care what he smelled or looked like this morning. The previous night had been filled with the most haunting and disturbing dreams.

"C'mon, Joe, finish your tea and come back to my place." Michael removed his hat and placed it beside him on the bench seat.

Joe sniffed his armpit. "Jesus, I reckon I do need a decent bath and sleep." He gulped down his now cold tea and wiped his lips with the back of his hand.

Pedestrians sidestepped the pair as they walked to the station to collect Michael's private car. Joe buttoned his overcoat against the winter breeze. He pulled his woollen beanie from his coat pocket to push over his head. He laughed at the sight of bobbing pom poms on top of similar headcovers of passersby.

At the station, Michael asked Joe to wait outside while he collected his car keys. To his dismay, Joe was not waiting outside. Michael peered up and down the street, then spotted Joe on the other side. A wave of his hand brought Joe back to the station wall. "Christ, Joe, why'd wander off?"

"I didn't like the neighbourhood."

Out on the busy streets, Michael manoeuvred the sedan through the traffic toward his side of town.

Back at Michael's terrace house, Joe benefited from a hot bath, clean clothes and a decent meal. "Thanks, mate. Truly appreciate your help."

"The offer still stands, Joe; if you give up the drink, you can live here. Mates forever, if you remember our childhood oath."

"Where's my coat?" He asked to change the subject.

"In the wash getting all the muck off." A loud agitating noise came from the laundry room.

"Will it shrink?" His intention was to redirect Michael's focus.

"Probably. If it does, you can have mine. Well, have you considered living here?"

"Won't work. I like the comfort of the underground."

"Has your life come to this?"

"I'll be gone soon, mate. The trilby wearers are coming for me. They missed me last night." Michael raised an eyebrow in disbelief. Joe responded. "They'll be back. I know."

"For fuck's sake, stop talking nonsense and let me help."

Dirty dishes littered the kitchen table. The kettle whistled on the stovetop. Neither man exhibited the will to move until the machine required Michael's immediate attention. Joe remained seated, disconnected from reality. Sober, clean and well-fed. His thoughts drifted back to last night's nightmare. Unchecked tears traced lines down his cheeks. He remembered. The sneer on the face, a strange odour, and the girl he thought was Madelaine. "Another one is gone, Mick. Those bastards took another girl."

Chapter Twenty-Seven

At 4.05pm on Friday, Magda signed out from her workplace. Pedestrians eager to finish shopping scurried in all directions. She managed to reach the department store unscathed from the minefield of prams, toddlers and small groups of people. Not everyone obeyed the unwritten laws of traffic flow on footpaths.

Inside the store, Magda meandered past counters with displays of new post-war products for women and men. A saleslady proffered a perfume test. Magda allowed the woman to dab her skin with a spicy scent then toyed with the lady who expected a sale until another customer paused nearby. Magda took her leave when she noticed a placard suspended from the ceiling with Ladies Shoe Department printed in large letters.

The arrow directed Magda to the most beautiful pair of shoes. It was love at first sight. She asked the salesgirl for her size to try on. "Stunning colour of red, a perfect fit and ideal for dancing." She said to no one in particular. She pranced about the room, swirling to and fro. The price was on the high end of her budget, but she knew they would be hers within two paydays.

She spent each afternoon after work for the next fortnight admiring the shoes. She got to know the salesgirl well enough to call her by her first name. Arabella Tomkin and Magda became friendly enough to meet after the store closed. They chatted about their lives over cups of tea in the cafe near their bus stop. Magda learned about Arabella's parents, who doted on her. Arabella had pushed aside her desires to mix with others at social events. Mr & Mrs Tomkin welcomed their daughter's news of going to a dance. Her father's attempts to teach her how to waltz ignited laughter. Arabella described clearing a space in the living room for her parents to teach her to dance. At first, she was nervous, but her parents' performance on bare floors made it look easy. "One, two, three, four. Let the man lead you; he can see the other dancers, and your steps will be in time together. If you lead, there will be lots of bumping into others." The images triggered giggles.

Charlotte sometimes met the two girls at the bus stop with little time to spare for proper introductions. Monday night before the dance, Charlotte arrived on time to travel home with Magda. The trio discussed the upcoming dance and arranged for Arabella to meet them at the Town Hall on Saturday night. Charlotte's nose twitched at the scent of Divine7 Cologne. She hated that perfume.

Magda asked Arabella, "Do you think you will be safe until your bus arrives? Ours will leave before yours."

"Of course, don't be so silly. I've been doing this for over a year. Besides, there's no one about. Go! I'll be fine."

After showing their weekly pass to the driver, Magda and Charlotte chose seats in the middle on the side where Arabella stood. They put their faces to the window to peer through the reflective glass. Satisfied that she looked happy and safe, they waved goodbye, sat back, and relaxed. Charlotte broke the silence between them. "You must ask your friend to change her perfume."

"Whatever for? I love it. Can't afford her brand on my salary. Anyway, she gets a discount." Magda sounded huffy.

"I guess my nerves are tight as wire on a mast. Since Lailah, Sophie, Elly, and the other girl from the dance went missing, I hit the panic button without thinking. Divine7 Cologne seems to follow me everywhere I go, even outside my room. I hate the stuff. Sorry if I upset you." Charlotte smiled at her friend. An apprehensive air of dread threatened to stir past encounters with evil. Before she lost control of her anxiety, Magda nudged her in the ribs.

"Pull the bell; our stop is next." The bell cord was easy to reach. The loud clang of the signal bell alerted the driver to pull over. They waited until the bus moved on, then linked their arms and strode home at a brisk pace.

The unified click-clack of their heels on the street disturbed one or two dogs in the neighbourhood. They tiptoed through the pockmarked concrete hollows full of rain water. Their shoes would need drying out by the hearth. Their stockings would need washing before the next day. "Oh, give me the sunny state any day," mused Charlotte.

"What do you mean? Never rains in Queensland?" They giggled together. Best friends forever, Charlotte thought.

Chapter Twenty-Eight

"Another one reported missing, Sir!" The sergeant stood at Michael Devlin's desk with a copy of the morning's report. Michael raised his head. He closed an open file. The constable established the parents reported their daughter Arabella Tomkin absent on Monday morning.

The employer noted her card was punched at 5.30pm on Friday afternoon. Twenty-four hours wait is the normal procedure. Time enough for the girl to return home unharmed. The incident occurred within the time frame; therefore, the duty officer delayed the investigation.

The girl's parents demanded the officer verify her whereabouts on account of recent disturbances. To appease the worried parents, a constable went to the department store. The manager answered all the questions about the girl's habits and nature.

The typed account of the incident divulged further information. Staff at the store described a red-haired woman dressed in a council administration uniform. They noted she frequented the shoe department and befriended the victim. Further information about the unknown female included an approximate height of 5ft 6in, blue eyes, voluptuous, and last seen meeting with the victim outside the store.

"Let's find that woman then, Sergeant. I will go to *Mark's and Foy* to interview the staff." He swivelled his chair to face the window beside the framed photograph of the King and inhaled the stale air of his office. He had a few words to say to the King about the war and its forgotten men, but he kept them to himself.

His frown deepened. He massaged his forehead between forefinger and thumb in contemplation of an uncertain outcome. He hated the thought of additional statistics in forgotten records if the girls were not found safe and alive. He rose from his desk extended his arms, palms flat against the window frame, to shoulder his weight. His world was not at peace. He stepped back from the view of downtown Sydney.

Michael ignored the shuffle of the sergeant's stance. The tension in his voice spoke volumes. Another girl missing. Questions uprooted themselves in a maze of twisted shapes. Concern edged across Michael's brow while his gut knotted with tension. Within two weeks, young women had disappeared from the Hyde Park bus stop. He wondered if other disappearances might pass beneath the umbrella of the homeless and orphans.

Migrants arrived with regularity, as well as servicemen returning from overseas duty. Sydney forged ahead in growth. Crime increased in the underworld. Changes within the family structure disrupted ideals as well. Women gained paid employment against family values to the point of wearing trousers. To avoid family embarrassment or shame, pregnant young women were sent to distant relatives or placed in homes for single mothers. No matter what changed after the war, crime was perennial. His first task was with the constable, followed by a visit to the girl's place of employment.

His shift began the next morning. He hoped the city yielded to peace at least tonight. He needed a cup of something stronger than tea to ease the ache in his head. Joe most likely was out of rum. Maybe two bottles might suffice. *Here's to you, Joe.*

176

Chapter Twenty-Nine

Friday morning couldn't come fast enough for Magda as she planned to collect her red shoes before work. She phoned to let her supervisor know she would be late for work. Those new shoes would adorn her feet for the dance on Saturday night. She sashayed into the shoe department, looking about for Arabella. Another saleswoman greeted her. "Where is Arabella?" she asked.

"She's not here today, dear. May I help you?" The woman's manner matched the stiff starched white lace collar on her black dress. Her grey hair tied into a small bun at her nape was covered by a hair net. Her grey eyes were as dull as her voice.

She looked at the woman's name badge. "Please, Mrs Duncan, I often meet with Arabella here to look at those lovely red shoes, and I'm here to pick them up. She will be as excited as me. We spend time together over coffee or tea at the cafe before we go home." Magda never met anyone who could turn paler in an instant than this woman. Worried for Arabella, Magda asked, "Can you tell me where I might find her? Is she sick?"

"I'm afraid Miss, she didn't arrive home Saturday night. Her parents reported her missing on Sunday. I'm told the police are looking for her and have been asking when she was last seen." Mrs Duncan reached out to support Magda, whom she thought would faint. "Are you alright? Here, sit yourself down on the stool. I'll fetch a glass of water."

Magda could only nod in agreement. Her body swayed, and she thought she might topple to the floor if not for the woman's help. Customers looked her way, but none ventured close.

"Here you are." She placed the glass in Magda's hands. "Just sip the water." Magda took a couple of sips then passed the glass back to the woman. "I...I... might be able to help, I should talk with the police."

"I believe a detective and a constable are with the Manager arranging interviews with all the staff here, especially after I checked with her parents when she didn't show up for work." Mrs Duncan asked, "Would you like me to get the policeman?"

"Please do. I don't know if I can help, but I could try." *What happened after we left Arabella on Saturday night?*

Mrs Duncan approached the manager's secretary, asking if she could speak with the detective in with the manager. The supervisor's stance matched the straight creases in her box pleated skirt. The secretary knocked on the manager's door with the explanation the floor supervisor from the shoe department would like to speak with the detective.

Michael wondered why this woman needed to meet him now before the arrangements were finalised for staff interviews. The moment Michael heard about the customer's emotional breakdown over Miss Tomkin's disappearance, he knew he had to act. He excused himself and joined the woman to where she had left the customer.

He recognised her immediately. "Magda." Michael stepped near and squatted low in front of Magda. "Mrs Duncan here says you might have some information about Miss Tomkin. Are you steady enough to come upstairs to the office?" His gentle manner quietened her nerves.

She looked at him with a weakened smile while tears streaked her pale cheeks. "I think so?" she whispered.

"Let me help." Michael held one of her hands and placed the other under her elbow. She wavered. Her knees wobbled. He steadied her. "Take your time, Magda. My guess is that you might need some smelling salts."

"Good guess, detective, but no thanks." He guided her toward the lift.

The Manager's office was claustrophobic, with dark wood panels lining the walls. Dust covered bookshelves stood floor to ceiling on one side of the room. A huge oak desk covered more space than the large man seated behind it. His hair was thin and white. She wondered how he fitted in his chair. He looked too round. When he stood up from his desk his stomach preceded him as he walked over to greet them.

Under any other circumstance, Magda would have laughed at the sight. The manager turned a chair away from the desk.

Michael eased her to the seat. The manager took his leave. "I will be outside, should you need anything, Detective Devlin."

"Thank you, sir. My apologies for the inconvenience imposed on your time." He sat opposite Magda and waited for her to speak.

"What's happened, Michael. I just learned that Arabella is missing!" She retrieved a handkerchief from her pocket.

"Yes, it's true, I'm afraid. She didn't make it home Saturday night. Her distraught parents reported her missing on Sunday." He tilted up her chin. "I was coming to see you and Charlie. Miss Tomkin's mother mentioned you and her daughter had recently befriended one another. Is that true?"

At first, she hesitated to answer, but the words flowed as soon as she opened her mouth. He listened to Magda talk about her new friend. Michael pinpointed Magda and Charlotte as the last persons to see Arabella Tomkin.

"God, Michael. Charlie and I left her alone at the bus stop. We didn't see anyone loitering about. We should have waited. What's happened?"

"We don't know yet, Magda. I can't tell you anything except we intend to find her."

Chapter Thirty

Magda and Charlotte kept similar routines, starting with breakfast together. Mrs Park timed this mealtime to avoid suspicion of the herbal additive. "Since the morning is cold, I'll serve porridge in individual bowls from the kitchen."

"Thanks Mrs Park, you make the most delicious porridge," replied Magda.

"Then I expect empty bowls, Magda. What about you, Charlotte?"

"Oh, that's fine, Mrs Park. I'm happy with whatever you plan." Charlotte's face hid behind the morning's newspaper.

"If you come into town early, let me know. We could go out for tea and scones." Magda's casual comment caught a slight hint of eagerness from her breakfast companion.

"That would be nice. I'll let you know."

Mrs Park kept the phials of ground powder in her apron pocket. At night she hid the phials in her bedroom beside Sophie's empty container and two others for Magda and Charlotte. Sophie had been an easy target, but the landlady reckoned the two intelligent girls in the parlour might prove difficult to manage. Each morning neither Magda nor Charlie noticed the addition of herbs to their meal.

After three days of consuming the herbs, Magda's nausea attacked. She took to her bed when the cramps began. The timing of the symptoms worried the landlady. She had administered the dosages with utmost care. "I'll phone for a taxi and get you to the doctor as quickly as I can, Magda." Charlotte helped Mrs Park get Magda to the entry hall and waited until the car arrived to collect the women.

"I hope you are feeling better by the time I get home, Magda."

"I'll be fine, thanks, Charlotte," she said in a weakened voice.

Charlotte watched as the car drove away before going back inside. She had enough time to meet the bus. As she turned away from the front door, she stopped short. Lily and Violet stood at the foot of the stairs. They weren't about minutes ago. "Good morning, girls. Where have you been? You've missed the fuss."

Lily asked, "Why? What's been happening?"

Charlotte peered in the mirror to place her hat in the right position. She spoke to the girls' reflections. "Your mother has taken Magda to the doctor; she's sick." After a swipe of lipstick across her lips, she smacked them together, stepped back, and turned to face the sisters.

"Oh!" They said in unison.

Charlotte failed to see the knowing smiles between the sisters when she glanced at her watch. "Sorry, got to run or I'll miss the bus. Let Kathleen know, please." She left the girls in the same spot at the bottom of the stairs.

Violet moved toward the kitchen. "Mummy's at it again, Lily."

Kathleen entered the dining room expecting to see the others. "Where is everyone?" She asked Violet and Lily, who walked past with their breakfast tray.

"Oh, you missed the excitement. We have to get our own porridge this morning as Mummy took Magda to the Doctor. It was urgent; the poor girl's ill or something."

"And Charlotte helped before rushing off to catch a bus as soon as Mummy and Magda left," Lily added.

"Oh, my, I hope she gets better."

In the kitchen, Kathleen made toast and jam as the porridge looked unpalatable. Both girls glared in astonishment when she entered the dining room without porridge. It was later in the morning before they could talk without being overheard. "How is Mummy going to get Kathleen sick if she doesn't eat what she prepares?"

"Lily darling, one way or another, Mummy will add a special something to her meals. Let's go out before she brings Magda back home."

"Where shall we go?" Excited at the prospect of an adventure into the city, Lily clapped her hands like a child.

"Botanical gardens! The fresh air will do us good. Lily, grab our hats and coats. Better stick a pin in the hats. The wind's picked up."

Chapter Thirty-One

Magda needed help getting out of the taxi at the doctor's rooms. Severe cramps twisted her muscles in all directions. Mrs Park struggled to keep them both steady on their feet. The nurse led them to an examination room. Mrs Park worried she would have to explain to Sacrof if anything went haywire. Sacrof, her one and only sibling, knew nothing about mercy.

The nurse assured the patient and her aide that the doctor was with another and they needed to wait.

Doctor Zagrobbe acknowledged Mrs Park and his new patient. He requested the nurse to stay and help the patient undress in preparation for a full examination. He sat at his desk, asking Mrs Park questions. "Yes, Magda mentioned she was feeling nauseous this morning."

She nodded yes to his written note. 'Have you given her the powdered herbs?' She held up three fingers to imply three doses. "Hmmm..." Before he could ask further questions, the nurse advised the patient was ready. "Perhaps Miss Blakely can talk for herself now." He stepped into the curtained area and asked her age and when she last had her monthly flow.

Magda moaned. "This pain is different, doctor," she continued to clutch her lower abdomen. He explained she needed an internal examination to determine if her female organs were not compromised by any growths. Mrs Park sat at the doctor's desk, listening to the conversation behind the privacy curtain. She knew the exact reason for the procedure. Magda may be a suitable host for her brother's plans. "There, all done. Nurse, help the young lady get dressed."

Magda moved from behind the curtain, and the nurse left the threesome seated in the room. The doctor's calm and assuring voice emphasised his patient needed further tests to investigate a small ovarian growth. While he spoke, he opened a locked drawer to pull out a 4oz size bottle from which he measured a dose of a dark liquid for Magda to swallow. Without question, Magda swallowed a dose of the liquid, which tasted worse than it smelled, hoping the doctor's advice hit the mark and put a stop to the unbearable cramps. "There, your cramps should subside by tea-time. If not, take another dose." The doctor gave the bottle to Mrs Park with written instructions to keep it locked away. Mrs Park understood and placed the bottle in her handbag.

Mrs Park patted Magda's hand. "That's good news, eh, Magda" Magda did not reply.

"Miss Blakely, please wait outside in the waiting room while I tend to Mrs Park's appointment."

"You right to wait, love? I won't be long." The landlady rose from her seat and escorted her charge to the waiting room. "I'll be back after my consultation." The woman turned her back and entered the doctor's room.

Dr Zegrobbe sat behind his desk. "Congratulations, Mrs Park. This one is a beauty. Timing's right. Bring her back in a week to start her program."

"Are you that sure, doctor?"

"You doubt me? How dare you!"

Mrs Park backed down by his tone and insinuation. "I...I didn't mean that; I thought it would take longer."

"Get her home. I have a practice to run." He jumped out of his chair. Moving past the woman, he said, "I'll let Sacrof know of this. And if there are any changes, let me know immediately. The cramps may stop, but we tell the patient on the next visit that the growth has enlarged. The next step begins the process for Sacrof's grand plan."

Mrs Park exited the consultation room with Dr Zegrobbe in tow. "Off you go, then see me in a week and keep a close watch on my patient."

Magda failed to discern any hidden agenda between her landlady and the doctor behind the closed door. Severe cramps distracted her from any conversations in or near the waiting room. The taxi arrived shortly after the receptionist phoned for a car. As she rose from her seat, Magda struggled to steady herself, and, with Mrs Park's help, managed to get home and upstairs. Thankful for the privacy of her room and appreciating Mrs Park's attention when she brought in a cup of hot tea, sleep soon followed.

In the evening, a light tapping on her door stirred Magda. "Who is it?"

"It's me, Charlie. Can I come in?"

"Please do."

After switching on the bed lamp, Charlotte pulled the chair closer to the bed. "Sorry if I woke you. Mrs Park sent me up with your medicine which she went to great pains to measure, although I don't know why she has to keep the stuff under lock and key." Charlotte smiled at her friend, who reminded her of a lost child she once saw. Ignoring the vision, she added, "I'm not exactly empty-handed. I put a tray with soup and toast on the table in the corridor. Shall I bring it in?"

"Please."

"What did the doctor say, Magda?" Charlotte was curious about the sudden cramp attack.

"He said little. He gave me a complete examination. It appears I have a growth on one ovary." Magda raised herself up to sit on the edge of her bed. "Oh, he did give me some medicine for the cramps. The doctor gave me a dose before we left."

"Some good news, hopefully, the cramps will ease. You're so young, Magda, and it's good that the growth has been found early. Drink the soup, and I'll give you your medicine before I leave you to rest." Few words passed between the two friends while Magda sipped at the soup and downed the foul-tasting medicine. Charlotte extended sleep tight wishes and suggested that her friend ring the bell on the side table if she needed anything.

"Thanks, good night, Charlie."

Magda's condition improved by the next afternoon. She made her way downstairs to join the others for tea. Mrs Park rose from her chair to offer help. "Feeling better, love?" she asked, knowing that the antidote had worked its magic.

"Much better, thanks, Mrs Park, bit wobbly though, and still got a bit of a headache." Magda sat nearest to the fire.

Charlotte swapped places with Kathleen to be closer to Magda. "I'm so pleased you are better. Good sign, don't you think?"

"I guess so."

"The doctor will have you fixed up in no time, dear. He knows what he is doing." Mrs Park spoke with confidence.

Lily nudged Violet's knee under the card table. Violet turned her head toward her sister, flashing a discerning smile. The term 'fixing up' held different connotations for them and their mother, whose involvement in their uncle's plans remained secret from the boarders.

Silence bathed the dining room while the evening meal was served. Kathleen left before desert to visit friends in Newcastle and wouldn't be home until the weekend. Magda convalesced in her room and waited for Lily to bring a tray with the evening meal.

Lily returned to the dinner table and giggled. Violet understood why and joined in. Mrs Park squared her eyes on Violet, fully aware why the twins were amused. "Will you two stop sniggering?"

Charlotte took to her room after checking on Magda and leaving the tray of half-eaten food on the hall table. Lonely but not alone, she thought. Her friend needed rest. Michael was busy, and she had no leads on the abductions. Charlotte berated herself for her non-performance as a crime reporter. Back home, she knew a lot of town people who were happy to talk with her. Here in Sydney, people shied away from any discussion about the news or whenever called upon as a witness.

Magda managed to return to work within a couple of days.

At work Charlotte filled her days writing about crime in Sydney, Shipping news and social events. Nevertheless, the missing girls remained foremost in her mind. A week passed with little contact between herself and Michael. Their intention to meet up after crime scenes or news conferences was consistently hindered by their demanding work schedules. Michael cancelled their Sunday afternoon picnic early in the morning. Work, he told her.

The next morning at breakfast Mrs Park served Charlotte first. "Eat up, my girl; you'll be fine in a couple of days."

"What! I'm not ill!" Yet before the spoon of porridge passed her lips, she cupped her hand over her mouth and without excusing herself, she rushed for the downstairs bathroom.

"Oh dear. Mummy, she's not well." Aware of her mother's role in Charlotte's condition, she passed the obvious statement.

The landlady rolled her eyes. "She'll be seeing the doctor today. Now, shoo you two and get on with your day. I've little time to waste over idle chit chat."

Charlotte's cramp attack coincided with Magda's follow-up appointment. Mrs Park convinced Charlotte to visit at the same time. Charlotte agreed. Mrs Park telephoned the rooms to request an appointment in addition to Magda's scheduled time. The receptionist confirmed the doctor could see Charlotte at 9.00am.

The taxi with its three passengers stopped outside Dr Zegrobbe's practice ten minutes early. A fresh attack of cramps pierced through Charlotte's thighs and lower stomach, causing her to gasp. Mrs Park entwined her arm through the crook of Charlotte's elbow to guide her up the few steps. Magda followed the two women into the visitor's waiting room.

After completing the endless paperwork, Dr Zegrobbe entered and asked for Charlotte first. She answered each question the doctor asked. Her menstrual cycle had never caused concern; she believed she was in good health and admitted to liking a few social alcoholic drinks after work. The only exception was the unexpected cramp attack before breakfast.

The doctor spoke with Magda next. Her test results indicated she had a fallopian cyst which caused the cramps and uncomfortable sensations in her mid-section. The doctor suggested minor surgery to remove the growth. Magda had no idea that the doctor deceitfully read a fake report. He knew her body had more to offer and had been chosen for a greater need.

"Miss Blakely, allow me to make an appointment for you to visit a gynaecologist who will determine the next step to remove the growth." Magda fished a handkerchief from her purse to wipe away a tear. "Don't look so worried; this is a common problem and easily dealt with by a professional." Without further discussion, Magda agreed and exited the room as soon as she dressed.

Mrs Park stepped into the consulting room under the guise of a follow-up appointment. Too concerned with their own thoughts and discomfort, neither of the landlady's charges suspected any wrongdoing. With another boarder in pain, Mrs Park requested a second bottle of the antidote.

The taxi arrived within five minutes. Mrs Park squeezed herself between her now important boarders on the back seat. She chatted non-stop about nothing in particular. Sitting either side of the tubby old lady proved uncomfortable for Charlotte and Magda. As the vehicle turned corners, her body tilted dependent on left or right movement.

Mrs Park had spread her legs on either side of the hump over the driveshaft, causing the hem of her skirt to rise, but she wouldn't release her grip on her handbag.

This action puzzled Charlotte. *What precious item was stowed inside the purse that required knuckles to turn white? Did she carry wads of cash?* Nothing she thought of made any sense to Charlotte. She brushed aside these paranoid thoughts. Her instincts pushed hard against that decision. Michael's image drifted behind her closed eyes. Could she be in love? She believed she might be, but at the moment, Charlotte's only desire was to be alone in her room to think.

In the comfort of her room Charlotte revived shortly after another swallow of the awful mixture. Before afternoon tea, she entered the kitchen, aiming to quiz Mrs Park on recent events, including the supposed premonition of Charlotte becoming ill.

Caught unawares that Charlotte was up and about and, in her presence, Mrs Park busied herself mixing ingredients for a fruit cake. The noise from the electric mixer enabled the woman to gain a pittance of composure. "Charlotte, you startled me." Mrs Park turned the mixer off as if pretending she had not heard or seen her boarder enter.

Speaking with a quietness that stunned herself, Charlotte asked how the landlady knew of her illness prior to the stomach cramps.

The landlady's response reintroduced suspicion. "Just a good guess, I suppose."

Recollections of what happened at the doctor's rooms struck like lightning, "By the way, Mrs Park, I'm curious to know why you smiled when the doctor announced I was suffering the same illness as Magda?"

Mrs Park retorted defensively, "Was I love?"

"Yes, and I am wondering why."

To gather her wits, Mrs Park reeled and coughed to disguise her tone. "I was happy that your discomfort could be treatable same as Magda's." Mrs Park continued to measure and weigh each ingredient according to the recipe. "If you have the same problem as dear Magda, Dr Zegrobbe assured you that your health will improve under his supervision." The woman paused mid adding a measured ingredient to the bowl. "Why do you ask?"

The woman's fake air of concentration deterred Charlotte from soliciting information with tactless questions. Unconvinced of Mrs Park's sincerity and to garner a smidgeon of trust, Charlotte replied, "Oh, I guess I'm not my usual self, but I wonder why the twins and Kathleen aren't suffering the same affliction."

Mrs Park shrugged her shoulders, raised both eyebrows and turned her lips down to imply she had no idea. The woman began to busy herself and turned on the mixer to add flour in tiny amounts blocking further discussion.

Charlotte left the kitchen to enter the parlour, where she found Magda resting on a verandah seat in front of the open French doors. Midday sunlight highlighted Magda's unkempt halo of red curls. "Afternoon Magda"

Chapter Thirty-Two

Regeneration of the Zeronian bloodline remained core to the survival of the alien race. New generations to merge with the human world. Magda was chosen as the first for the latest method. Sacrof wanted his own cells blended with the beautiful woman and her friend Charlotte if the plan succeeded.

Anaesthetic held Magda in a deep sleep. Sacrof and two Trilbies waited in seclusion behind the panelled walls. They entered the room when the doctor released the lever. "She is ready." He stepped aside and said nothing more until asked. Sacrof signalled the Trilbies to carry her down into the tunnels. He never looked at the doctor but asked, "How long do we have?"

"Long enough, Sacrof. Your men carry a sedative if needed."

The gateway opened with Sacrof's opal keystone – one of a few that the emperor had collected over the past few years. Aged elders retained their talismans longer than necessary rather than relinquishing the keys to a protégé for safekeeping. Sacrof's spies located the weak elders and disposed of those men in ways that appeared to be deaths by misfortune. No one dared question the methods used against those untimely deaths. Everyone feared the emperor's wrath.

Kidnapped and taken unconscious to the laboratory, Magda underwent a procedure of implanting an embryo. The scientists used her eggs and sperm from Sacrof. Magda roused when the effects of the anaesthetic began to wear off. She felt strange and heard voices she did not recognise. "Quick, she stirs. Give her another dose!" Influenced by an uncontrollable flying sensation, her eyelids drooped. "That's better; she's in a deep sleep. You have enough time now to return her to the other surgical theatre."

In a drunken state, Joe's nightmares pulled him into another world. Still, his eyes alerted him to light and his ears to unfamiliar sounds. Silhouettes passed a short distance from where he lay invisible to anyone who chanced to look his way. Joe's bedding, like a mound of discarded rags, accorded his protection in the shadows.

Chapter Thirty-Three

Magda checked and rechecked her day count on the calendar. What she couldn't define was - when and how. She had refrained from any form of intimacy with men since her father's rejection. An unexpected pregnancy in her early teenage years changed her way of life. An aunt, her mother's sister, provided a home until the birth of Magda's baby on the condition the child be given up for adoption after the birth.

Her current symptoms did not reveal answers. *So, when? Think. Pick a date. Work backwards.* She started with the first of the month. The first week in June held nothing of importance. The second week was nothing of importance. The outline of events revealed a disturbing thought. She got ill toward the end of June and consequent visits to the doctor. *What happened in those rooms?*

No time to confront the doctor. It was more urgent to visit the Chinese woman in her little shop for a special concoction of herbs. She cried at the thought of losing another. She sniffled and dabbed away at her tears. This was different. Someone had violated her body without consent. *Why?*

The shop was not difficult to find in the heart of Kings Cross. Red and gold characters emblazoned the glass windows. Laden with a variety of jars and packets of dried foods, the shelves reached floor to ceiling. A bell over the door tinkled when Magda entered. An aged, almost skeletal woman bent at the shoulders shuffled through a beaded curtain that sounded like old bones creaking. The woman drew near. "You need help, Miss?" she asked. She wore a traditional costume of golden braid over her tiny frame.

Magda identified the Asian pattern of dragons, lions and large winged birds and wished she could fly away from her troubles. "You look sad, Lady." She stretched her withered arm to touch Magda's belly. Her scrawny fingers caressed her stomach. "I understand." The shopkeeper turned away without explanation, leaving Magda in front of rows of herbs. Uncomfortable with her misfortune, she rolled her hands around the swell beneath her waistline.

The beaded curtain rattled as the woman left the room and again as she re-entered. She handed Magda a package. "Take two teaspoons of this in a glass of milk, and all will disappear in short time." Her words were mournful and carried grief. "I know too much sometimes. Be careful, Missy. Danger follows you. You're not safe."

As the ten-pound note changed hands, the woman's gnarled fingers grasped Magda's. The touch delivered a slight shiver through her body. She pulled her hand away and ran from the shop. The voice followed, "Be careful, Missy, be careful."

Magda arrived home early. Not a soul about. She went straight to her room. Her personal strength ebbed and flowed. She struggled with her decision. Convoluted shadows at her feet unhinged her so much that she bumped the lampshade on the bedside cabinet. The glow from the exposed bulb warped the gloominess into a wild frenzy of lace patterns. Dark imaginary tendrils wrapped around her, squeezing until she was out of breath. She pinched herself. The apparitions vanished when she straightened the lamp. She went to the kitchen for a glass of cold milk. Local supplies had started to increase after the severe drought broke. She poured out a glassful and made her way to the stairwell. Mrs Park arrived as Magda reached the bottom step.

An inquisitive glare with an eyebrow raised, Urtha asked, "Afternoon, dear, you're home early. Are you ill?"

"No, Mrs Park. Work finished early today, so I thought I might catch up on some reading. I'll see you at dinner." Once inside her room, she locked the door. She set the glass of milk on the bedside table and plonked herself at the foot of her bed, where her handbag hung over the bedpost. She retrieved the packet of herbs from the brown paper bag and placed it beside the glass.

Despondent, she sat for some time, gathering the courage to drink the concoction. She picked up the packet to sniff the contents. The dried leaves reminded her of the smell of dense bush after a summer shower. *How can something so sweet destroy the innocent? But I have no choice.* She deliberated for a few minutes before crossing the threshold of indecision. The contents dissolved in the milk turning it black. As black as my soul. She swallowed the mixture in two gulps. She dry retched. She lay back on her pillow in the position of the dead. Hands crossed across her chest. Eyes closed.

She never asked the old lady what would happen; she already knew. The cramps began and her lower abdomen contracted with pain.

What's done is done. She tensed before a surge of excruciating pain in her lower abdomen racked through her body. Muscles expelled the adhesion to her womb. She removed her clothes and got some towels from her private bathroom. *No one needs to know.* The ordeal was swift; the deed was done.

She wrapped the greyish matter in an old newspaper for disposal in the incinerator. Her crying turned to sobs. Perspiration mixed with tears. Anger welled with the knowledge that someone tampered with her body. She concluded the doctor was involved. Too weak to move, and full of grief, she lay on her bed. In an attempt to calm herself down, she curled up, but her body refused to offer any comfort.

After dinner, Mrs Park prepared a tray to take to her now special boarder. *Poor dear, the treatment can be quite bothersome.* A knock at the door preceded Mrs Park's voice. "You all right, love? You've not come down for dinner."

Magda could not disguise the pain in her voice. "I'm fine, Mrs Park."

Mrs Park placed the tray on the hall table outside the door. She unlocked the door with her master key. Aghast at the sight before her, she barged in. On her bed, Magda twisted in pain. Blood covered the bedding. "What have you done? You silly, silly girl?"

Between bouts of pain, Magda screamed at her intruder, "Get out of my room! Get out!" Charlotte heard her friend yelling. She opened her door. "Is everything okay. What's wrong with Magda, Mrs Park."

Mrs Park played down the situation. "It's all right, Charlotte, nothing to worry about. Magda and I need to sort out the rent payments. "Off you go now. Scoot. Don't concern yourself." Mrs Park hovered outside Magda's door until she heard Charlotte close the front door. Certain that no one else was home, Mrs Park went to her private quarters and with a glass of water and a tin of phials. One of which contained sedatives. She held the glass of water laced with drugs to Magda's lips. "Drink. It will ease the pain. Don't worry, I'm getting the doctor."

"Is Charlie home?" Magda's lips quivered. She desperately wanted to talk to her friend before the worst happened.

"She's already left. Drink, please, Magda." Once again, the glass of drugs was offered. Fear prevented Magda from lashing out. *I'm bleeding to death. My punishment. Sweet Mary, what have I done?*

Mrs Park waited until she heard Magda's rhythmic breathing as she drifted into a drugged sleep. *Sacrof will hear of this, but first the doctor.* She locked Magda's door from the outside.

The doctor arrived and, after examination and diagnosis, determined Magda would survive. As he left the house, he said, "This is not good. You must let Sacrof know, Urtha."

"I know." Mrs Park whispered as a shroud of fear enveloped her form. Sharing this news with her brother suggested his angry temperament to rally and lash out at anyone near, even her.

After the doctor left, Mrs Park busied herself to visit her brother. Satisfied that Magda relaxed completely, Urtha fiddled with the opal in her pocket as she waited for her taxi. Duty to her brother ensured a loyalty beyond comprehension. A duty she knew as life-threatening for her and her daughters. *That stupid girl's fault. I know the danger of Sacrof's anger.* She harboured no doubt that her brother would deliver severe punishment to the girl for her sin.

Chapter Thirty-Four

Friday night arrived with a mixture of sadness and joy for Magda. She was free of the unwanted burden but troubled by her decision. A meeting with Detective Devlin was scheduled for tomorrow morning at ten sharp. She missed Arabella, especially now that she owned the red dancing shoes, but her friend was gone, and nobody knew where.

Magda slid her stockinged feet between the leather uppers and innersoles. No rainfall for a couple of days gifted a chance to wear the shoes to break them in. Immersed in a sense of self-awareness, Magda stepped onto the footpath outside the building. She was looking forward to meeting Charlotte after work. Hope the shoes tread well on the dance floor after manoeuvring the cracks in the footpath. She waited for the city tram to Beberfalds.

As she alighted from the tram, she tripped over a passenger's outstretched leg. She fell through the opening doorway and landed hard. Bystanders edged away from the incident. Magda saw the uncertainty in their manner. She waved them away when she got up from the pavement.

A man leaned forward and said, "Here, let me help! I'm a doctor." And to the anxious driver, "You have traffic backed up behind you. Don't wait. I'll take her to my surgery and attend to her cuts and scratches." The conductor stepped out the back of the tram to speak to the doctor but was politely dismissed. "I've got your tram number, so don't worry. If there's any concern, I'll contact your supervisor." Satisfied with the man's assurance, the conductor instructed the driver to continue the run. Nobody doubted the man's credentials. He looked the part with a small medical bag in his hand.

Magda managed to balance on both feet thanks to the doctor's insistence that her pride hurt and nothing more. Prepared in advance, Sacrof waited until his cohort gripped the girl's hands. Magda jerked as she felt a jab in her neck. "Relax" - the last word heard before she collapsed. A dizzy sensation embraced her; her body sagged into the man posing as a doctor. Sacrof caught her. Pedestrians avoided the trio, but one dared to ask if everything was all right.

Sacrof's response brought a shrug from the enquirer. "Drunk again, mate. Hold on tight, dear, and we'll get you home." The threesome proceeded along the footpath in the opposite direction to the stranger, who went his own way without a backward glance.

Drugged, immobile and unaware of her surroundings or the opening at the back wall, Magda was carried through the underground by her abductors. A savage headache, compounded with her inability to move, shocked her senses mid recovery. Fear choked her. Panic increased her heartbeat and worsened when she realised, she was bound to a chair which rendered her helpless. A blindfold restricted her sight. She sensed someone near and spat in their direction. Bluffing was not her forte but a verbal attack, her only defence. "I told everyone about your scheme. The police know!"

Her captors dismissed her pleas. "Enough! You have jeopardized everything we worked toward for the survival of our people. You have put yourself and Zerona at risk! We will deal with you later."

A rush of cold air swept across her legs as a door opened and then slammed shut. Scared, she struggled. Tears moistened her blindfold. The textured fabric shrank against her eyelids. Its rough materials stank. Her hands bound firm to the back of the chair thwarted any effort for freedom.

Sacrof ordered two men to prepare for another crossing. He wanted the other one brought over tonight. "First, I deal with the horrid creature bound inside the chamber. The one whom we planned to bear my child; but chose to destroy my unborn. The child of the future is dead as she soon will be." Sacrof marched with purpose toward the chamber.

When Sacrof re-entered the room, Magda sensed his nearness. Magda ceased attempts to loosen the bindings. Her sense of hearing increased. Panic gripped her soul. Evil swept close. She inhaled pungent body odour. Lost in the dark behind her blindfold, movements inside the room terrorised her mind.

She tensed from the sensation of foul breath against her cheeks. Muscles in her neck contracted. Her hair was wrenched so hard she screamed. A razor-sharp blade slashed her long locks, lessening the weight of her tresses. Uneven chunks fell, caressing her shoulders before snaking across her red shoes. Her mind envisioned the act. Not a sound from the intruder. She knew her hair had been hacked away by the lightness on her scalp. Magda shuddered.

A man's voice deepened her fear, "You didn't look after yourself. You destroyed my child, but I have your reproductive cells, and another shall be chosen to bear my child. As for you - you cannot be trusted; therefore, you no longer matter."

Magda flinched as each nerve pulsed and tensed. Blood pumped through her heart at triple the normal rate. Her stomach churned, about to explode. Death whispered. She smelled her own fear. Her tongue was dry. To and fro, she twisted her head to follow the sounds of her evasive predator. Sacrof edged close, behind her, beside her; her mind played tricks. His hideous laughter resonated. One slice of the blade. In a whisper, her body succumbed to death's chilling embrace.

Tossed through the portal, her carcass lay twisted and exposed. Drops of blood formed a semicircle. A voice fractured Joe's nightmares. "A halo for a fallen angel."

The sound of someone near stirred Joe from his nightmare. Through bleary eyes, Joe saw a woman's body near his bed. He blinked and shook his head, hoping the image before him was a dream and he would wake. "Jesus, Mary and Joseph!" he cursed aloud. His inner voice bellowed *Get the fuck out, mate! You might be next!* Shaken and hung-over, he struggled to his feet, determined to get as far away as possible. He left his belongings behind.

Evacuate! Evacuate! Incoming! His mind returned to the battlegrounds. He staggered into the early morning light, ready to fight. He saw Harold and leaned closer, "Quick, round up the troops; the enemy's arrived."

Caught off guard, Harold appeased his friend. "Okay mate. Wait here, and I'll get the boys."

Joe grabbed Harold by the shoulders and pulled him back. "No, I'll get Michael and his boys. They'll know what to do. It's not for your troops."

"Okay, mate, if you think so. Are you sure you haven't had a nightmare?"

"Damn right, I'm sure. Yeah!" Joe slurred. "Except..." He covered his face with both hands to will away the vision of a twisted, bloodied body. A few steps to his right stood the nearest public phone box.

Joe's odd change of behaviour baffled Harold. "I'm here if you need me, Joe. Going nowhere today."

Joe fumbled in his pockets for coins, then decided to make use of reverse charges. Michael accepted payment for his friend. The arranged signal of 'Mayday, Mayday' came through the line. "Okay, mate, I'll be there in a jiffy. Wait outside the main entrance."

"Ain't going nowhere, Mick. This is real. You've got to see it yourself." Joe hung up and staggered backwards out the door. He paced back and forth across the entrance. People weaved about without any sense of direction except to steer away from Joe. He reeked of moldy clothes, booze and tobacco. Somehow, he remained unaware of his surroundings bar the crooked path he wove. "God help me, there's a dead girl in the tunnel." Nobody stopped to listen.

Chapter Thirty-Five

"Pedestrians instinctively cleared a path for the two police officers and plainclothes detective to exit their vehicle. Joe beckoned the trio to follow him on to the station. Michael opened his mouth to ask Joe a question. "Not now, mate. Grab your torches. You gotta see the body first." Gasps and whispers from the curious bystanders prompted Michael and his escorts to follow Joe into the tunnels. Guided by torchlight, Joe's pace quickened to short of running. He stopped a few steps shy of the spot where the body had been unceremoniously dumped. "I can't look at her." Joe slumped to the tunnel floor. "She's just a couple of yards ahead."

Michael understood. He left one of his men with Joe. Anxious not to disturb any clues that might support Joe's claims of a body, Michael and the other policeman crept forward with utmost care. Their eyes darted around, trying to make out the details of their surroundings in the limited light of their torch beams. Michael yelled at Joe. "You bastard, Joe. Your nightmares are starting to confuse you or the alcohol has finally muddled your brain." Michael rubbed the back of his head. "There's nothing here, Joe."

Joe leapt to his feet. He strode over to his friend. "What the fuck are you talking about? I saw her, Mick." Shivers ran up his spine. "Where's she gone." His face paled. He began to question himself before his mind cleared. "She was there." He pointed to the pool of blood on the floor and the scattered spots extending up the nearest wall.

Michael crouched low and touched a droplet. "Feels like blood."

"Somebody tossed her out of the lights, Mick, I swear." Joe put his hands in his pockets. He rocked back and forth. His lowered his voice. "The splatters around her head reminded me of a halo. And, her hair had been hacked away, too." Joe raised his voice. "She couldn't have got up and walked. She was dead." He shook his head in disbelief. "Those fuckin' lights disappeared by the time her body hit the floor." Joe's voice trembled. His body began to violently shake. "You don't believe me, do you?"

"Just a minute, Joe, stop jumping to conclusions. Let me look around first." When he shone his torch further away, he noticed a pair of ladies' shoes lying askance on the floor. "I believe you, Joe." He rose and looked at Joe. "I'm guessing these don't belong to you."

Joe glared at his friend. "Fuck off."

"I'll get forensics down here." Michael sensed fear rise within his friend. "In the meantime, I'll have these two, stay here, while you and I go to the station."

At first, Joe refused to go. "If it's a statement you want, I can give you one here, Mick. I don't want to go anywhere near a cop shop." Joe glared at his friend. "I know what I saw. Even I can't explain how a dead girl can get up and walk out of here."

After convincing Joe to leave with him they left the tunnel and drove back to the police station. "We'll sort this out when we get a report back, Joe." Coded messages over the two-way radio prevented any conversation between the two men.

Joe sensed trouble ahead. *Fuck this world.*

CHAPTER THIRTY-SIX

Beberfelds Corner proved an ideal place for people to congregate after work. Eager to attend the dance, Charlotte waited for Magda. Charlotte's demanding workload meant that they often missed crossing paths at home. Impatient to be at the Town Hall before the dance started, Charlotte shuffled from one foot to the other. Her mind shifted from studying everyone walking past to recollections of meeting Michael and his childhood friend Nora.

Nora was pretty, fair-skinned, with blue eyes and blonde hair. She had curves in all the right places. Sometimes the drab winter overcoats unkindly hid the shapes of female forms. Once inside the town hall, dancing was the first priority, especially with the introduction of new dance steps.

Magda and Charlotte bonded in the first week of Charlotte's arrival a month ago. Their personalities were as different as chalk and cheese. Magda was outgoing, and some would call her a risk-taker, whereas

Charlotte was quiet and shy and often mistaken as a snob. This was far from the truth. Her past had nothing to do with her future. But her memories of losing both parents in a car accident on the Minden range evoked a few tears at times. The car accident was the result of a sneezing attack whilst driving. Her father lost control, and the vehicle flipped and rolled down into a gully, ending upside down in a creek. Both occupants were trapped inside. The investigator stated unconscious by that time. It took a long time to get over the shock.

She shook off her memories. The past cannot be changed, but the future invited fresh challenges mixed with exciting times. Thank goodness I met Magda, who was fun, happy and could cheer up anyone except the mean and nasty twins. These traits were truly embedded in their personalities. Charlotte wondered about the family gene pool. When Charlotte and Magda talked about the twins, Magda had one answer. "They will drag you into their world of doom and gloom, Charlotte. Keep your distance."

Charlotte shook herself out of her reverie to the sound of the Town Hall Clock. She counted seven chimes. A cold evening chill moved through her body. She shivered as if something sinister touched her soul. No sign of Magda. Charlotte no longer felt the urge to be at the dance. She hadn't been feeling well lately, and Michael would have to wait.

On her way home, her thoughts turned to worry. Maybe there was an accident. Perhaps I should go to the Town Hall in case she went there because she was running late. A state of uneasiness settled heavily on Charlotte. All the 'what if' scenarios poured through her mind on her way home. The porch light illuminated the front steps while the hall lamp welcomed latecomers. Front doors closed at curfew exactly at midnight. Mrs Park's rock was not in the cabinet. A sign she was out. *God knows where.* Mrs Park appeared to care for her boarders like a mother hen.

Rational thoughts crisscrossed her mind. Charlotte consoled herself that Magda might have joined other friends for an all-night party for the sailors. Magda could explain herself in the morning.

Charlotte usually slept late on weekends, but the urgency to ascertain whether Magda had arrived home safely compelled her to an early rise. The winter sun did not promise a perfect Sunday or the following days. Charlotte checked her friend's room and found that Magda hadn't returned home. A quick phone call to Michael to alert him of her friend's absence. He suggested they meet at the Police Station, where she could file a missing person's claim.

The week turned sour without any clues of Magda's whereabouts. No messages for Charlotte, whose intuition sensed foul play. Interviews at the mayoral office left the police with no alternative but to deem Magda a missing person. She confronted Mrs Park a few days later. "Where's Magda? What do you know?"

Charlotte's anger unsettled the landlady, who coiled like a snake ready to strike. The woman's eyes narrowed to resist the challenge from the strong-willed woman who stood within arm's reach. Mrs Park counter attacked. "Calm down, missy, Magda was behind with rent, and I asked her to leave. Apparently, she left in a hurry last week before settling her account. You heard her the night she demanded I get out of her room."

"I don't believe you. We were supposed to meet on Saturday night, and she didn't show up. She hasn't been home since that morning."

"I have no other explanation, dear." Mrs Park controlled her emotions. She couldn't divulge anything. "Perhaps she didn't want you to know." She reached for Charlotte and gently patted the back of her hand, "It's all right pet. I'm sure when she's settled, she'll drop you a line." Charlotte withdrew from the touch and pretended to relax.

Charlotte feigned her reaction to cease further conversation. *Lies Lies. Michael will find her.* Charlotte dared not think dead.

Chapter Thirty-Seven

The supervisor in the Mayoral's office became concerned for Magda's welfare after three days. Magda worked within the local council and was highly regarded as she was working on new strategies for town planning. Her enthusiasm and input impressed her superiors; hence her absence the fear for her safety was arguably cause for concern.

The supervisor knew Magda had recently moved to Sydney and apparently had no spare time to make new friends. Her address at Mrs Park's Boarding House for Young Women in Kings Cross raised anyone's concern about the safety of young women in the unsavoury suburb. Magda failed to notify the office of any leave. With no reasonable report for her absence, her immediate supervisor contacted the boarding house.

The conversation with the landlady made no sense to the woman. Magda had taken leave for medical reasons and was expected back at work. Mrs Park said that Magda left owing rent and denied any knowledge of a set of keys when told the office keys had not been returned.

An uneasy feeling washed through the supervisor while talking with Mrs Park. She tried to brush the emotion aside, but the thought of something untoward happening to Magda kept niggling away at her thoughts. Detective Devlin, who was in charge of an investigation into recent missing girls, visited the Mayoral offices recently. Staff confirmed that none of the members had seen or heard from Magda for about a week. Small talk across desktops related to one question – where was she?

Chapter Thirty-Eight

Charlotte presented herself at the local Police Station to add to Magda's missing person file. Mrs Parks lied when asked about her boarder. On Friday night, as Charlotte passed by Magda and Mrs Park near the kitchen, Charlotte witnessed rent money change hands along with a receipt.

"Magda would have made contact by now," she told the interviewing officer. "Maybe she had an accident or was taken to a hospital somewhere in the city."

The officer asked if there was any reason for this assumption. "Yes, Magda had been unwell for a couple of weeks." Poised to write a statement, Charlotte fumbled with the pen, and it rolled toward the interviewer.

The officer's quick reflex returned the pen. The interview continued, "Do you know if the lady in question - Miss Magda Blakely attended a doctor's surgery?"

"Yes, the same one I attend. Dr Zegrobbe's rooms near St James' Station. The doctor thought she had a tummy upset," Charlotte added. "Oh, and I was unwell myself." Charlotte remembered the new shoes, "I remember her new shoes! She had bought herself a new pair of red shoes on the day she didn't turn up." Charlotte tapped her fingers on the counter. "We planned to go to the Town Hall dance that night."

The duty officer was unaware of the red shoes found amid blood splatters in one of the underground tunnels.

"Will you please let Detective Devlin know I am here?" she asked.

"He'll be in tomorrow, Miss Tyrell. I'll see that he gets your report."

Charlotte bade a goodnight, although her mood kept her in poor spirits.

"Goodnight, Miss Tyrell, I'm sure everything is all right, and your friend will eventually turn up." He closed the file and put it aside.

The following morning Charlotte arrived for work. On the bus, all the unimaginable 'what ifs' thrashed about in her head, but none offered resolution.

"Do you think she has met with foul play, Charlotte?" Brian asked.

"I hope not," replied a despondent Charlotte. "Why would you even think that, Brian?"

"C'mon Charlie, given the events of the past months or even earlier, we can't discount another abduction." Brian spun his body to the side to converse with his colleague face to face. "It's the only conclusion at this point." He offered a clean handkerchief from his top drawer to soak up her tears.

"Thank you." She said as she wiped her eyes. "I just don't want to believe she is gone."

Chapter Thirty-Nine

They stepped into the morning sunshine without any fuss. Michael inhaled the crisp air to discharge the tunnel's musty odours from his lungs. "Another wintry day." Joe fidgeted all the way to the Police Station. If he could, he would have avoided another run-in with the law, especially the wallopers of the Hyde Park precinct.

The promise of bacon and eggs and a hot bath after signing a statement lifted Joe's spirits. As the men barged through the entrance toward the duty sergeant's desk, Joe's mood altered. His nicotine-stained fingers reached for cigarettes to calm the tremors surging through his nervous system.

Joe listened to Michael's explanation of the night before and the need for a witnessed statement from Joe. Infuriated by the smirk on the officer's face, Joe clenched his fists, ready to pounce. Michael's voice sliced through the madness in Joe's mind. "Calm down mate. You'll cause more trouble than you and I can handle." Joe accepted a lit cigarette from his friend. "Now, sit down while I find someone to assist you with your statement."

Amused by the story of the blue flashing light and disappearing body in the tunnel, the sergeant said to no one in particular, "Whatever will they think of next?"

The previous night's bailed detainees filled the front area to capacity. A detective, discussing the recent disappearance of a young woman with a constable, ambled past Michael, who interrupted the conversation. "I have some information you need."

"What did you say? Information? Mick, have you got a lead?" asked Detective Bernard Smith.

Joe butted in, "Yep! We sure do!"

In a more polite voice, Michael asked, "Could we discuss this in my office, Bernard? And get the Chief Inspector on the double."

Joe and Michael entered the room with a tall arched window overlooking the busy street below. Michael stood in front of the window, waiting for Bernard and the Chief. Joe arranged three chairs in a semicircle within the space in front of the desk. The senior officer walked straight to Michael's chair in an act of superiority. Bernard sat on one seat closest to the view while Michael chose the middle one in front of his senior officer, leaving Joe to the one in the corner.

"Well, who's first?" asked the Chief.

Joe described the entire events of the previous night minus a time frame. He hated watches; he hated time as it snuffed away his youth and shortened his life.

Michael added his part, including the discovery of the red shoes.

Bernard suggested he and his superior step out of the room. In the hall Bernard offered a suggestion. "Perhaps this man Moody knows more than he's telling. I believe I need to question him again."

"Don't understand why you would suggest a follow-up." He tucked and refolded his shirt cuff. "Besides, I know Detective Devlin keeps an eye on the derro." As an afterthought, the Chief added, "An odd pair, I reckon, eh, Bernard?"

"The boys say the same about any of us," they both laughed at the thought.

"We have to let him go, for the time being, Bernard. Get your gear and take the Moody fellow and Devlin to the site to establish a crime was committed in the tunnel. The derro is probably suffering from delusions and looking for sympathy."

Bernard added that the fellow's military background and mental status should be thoroughly checked. "You know, Sir, both men are highly capable of killing someone, and more than likely have weapons of their own, especially Mick's mate. Word on the street is that he was a sniper during the war and sunk into the pits of despair since his return."

"All the more reason to check out his service records, then we can make an informed decision."

"Then you agree that he is our prime suspect!" Detective Smith beamed with confidence.

"We'll know more when we check out the scene of the alleged crime or if it has been a prank."

Two Detectives, one Chief Inspector, one homeless war vet, and two constables entered the tunnels where Joe slept at night. Joe shuddered. "Easy Joe," Michael's assurance missed its target. The red shoes lay with a broken heel as if they had been tossed aside and discarded. On closer examination, Bernard noticed the pair of bright red shoes with scuff marks and little wear on their soles contrasted with darker spots splayed in a semicircle. A policeman whispered, "Do you think that's blood?"

Detective Smith replied. "Could be."

Bernard ordered Michael and Joe to stay where they were and not move. The inspection warranted a closer investigation. When Bernard knelt down, he could see small tufts of red hair inside and outside the semicircle. The policemen followed the trail of blood, but to their amazement, the traces ceased abruptly at the back wall.

The puzzle widens. Bernard was positive the marks would lead to a body. Joe was now their number one suspect. Was Joe guilty of a serious crime, or was it all contrived to seek attention from authorities? Time to hash out the evidence before pointing the finger. "Justice will be served," Bernard whispered.

Chapter Forty

Back at headquarters, Michael and a colleague, Carl Burghoff, decided to visit the Boarding House for Girls. Magda's room being their main point of interest.

Confronted by the two detectives she had met before, Mrs Park's huffy mood worsened. As per police procedure, they showed their name badges. Michael spoke first. "A friendly chat with you, Mrs Park, if you don't mind. We understand you are the landlady of these premises. Is that correct?"

"Yes, why? Has something happened to one of my girls?"

"We'd like to ask you a few questions about one of your boarders, may we come in?"

"Of course, Detective Devlin. Do come in." She opened the door to its full extent. "Please wipe your shoes on the mat. You can hang your hats and coats over on the hooks." Carl shuffled his feet across the mat. Michael repeated the process.

Agitated and wary of the unannounced visit, Mrs Park stood aside while they settled themselves. She hid her hands beneath the drape of her apron front and accompanied them into the parlour. In an attempt to remove herself from the room to gather her thoughts, she asked if she could arrange for some light refreshments.

"No, thank you." Michael drew her attention while his offsider wandered about the room. "We understand, Miss Magda Blakely resided at this address. Is that correct?"

The muscles on her face tightened. "Yes."

"May we inspect her room?" The question caught the woman off guard. Michael observed the shift in her composure as if he had touched a nerve.

Rehearsed words escaped. "There's a new boarder in that room, and I'm afraid it's inconvenient today." Mrs Park tried to sway them to leave and not bother her girls.

Michael's voice remained steady and assertive. "With respect Mrs Park, your boarder won't mind if we politely ask."

"Please don't tell me you are investigating a murder!" Mrs Park bit her tongue.

Startled at first, his suspicions increased. "Murder. Who said anything about murder?" The detective's determination heralded a softer approach to his request.

The landlady chided herself for her thoughtless reaction. To compose herself, Mrs Park took a deep breath and asked, "You lot don't normally check out a room of a young and foolish girl, unless something has happened, do you?"

Michael watched the woman's eyes dart in all directions. Her response for his reason to look at Magda's room tweaked his instincts. "Not always, Mrs Park, and hopefully not this time." Impatient, he asked. "Now, if it's all right with you, we're here to inspect Magda Blakely's room."

Mrs Park's attempts to disguise her emotional fear failed. "If you must, it's upstairs first door on the right; follow me." Slight changes in mannerisms, gestures and voice tones alerted the skilled observer. Michael and Carl climbed the stairs behind Mrs Park. The house remained quiet.

The landlady tapped on a door on the upper floor. "Patricia, dear, are you in?"

A petite young woman opened the door. Behind the plump landlady, two gentlemen produced police identification badges. Michael breached the silence. "Sorry to disturb you, Miss, we only want a quick look at this room. Unfortunately, the previous occupant of this room has disappeared."

"Oh dear! Please, come in. Do you think she is one of the missing girls?"

"Yes, she didn't show up for work —

Mrs Park interjected. "—You need to talk with her sailor friend. I'm sure he knows where she's gone. Left in the middle of the night, she did."

Nonplussed by the outburst, Michael asked the landlady to wait in the hall. "We'll let you know if we need you."

Mrs Park grunted and stood her ground in contempt of the request. "Out! Mrs Park! Or I'll forget I'm a gentleman." Michael slammed the door behind her. "Our apologies Miss; we won't be long; just a quick inspection." Michael entered the private bathroom leaving his colleague to look around the bedroom.

When he found a twisted packet of dried leaves stashed behind the cistern. He signalled Carl to join him. They closed the door. Careful not to touch the packet, Michael secreted the evidence into his breast pocket after showing it to Carl. "This is enough evidence to investigate Magda Blakely's disappearance." He whispered. He placed two fingers to his lips. "We keep this to ourselves." Back in the bedroom, the detectives thanked the boarder for the inconvenience. Michael turned the doorknob to leave, with Carl behind him. "One question Miss. Did you notice anything out of place when you moved in?"

"Nothing, Sir. I moved into a clean room."

Mrs Park heard and breathed with relief. She'd disposed of all of the evidence the night Magda met her fate.

Before leaving, Michael asked to see the past and present tenant register. Mrs Park proved difficult and reluctant to produce her books. Michael warned Mrs Park of his intention to confiscate registry books and rent receipts.

"Whatever for?" On the defensive, her tone was abrupt. "Your warrant doesn't cover the entire premises, detective. Make sure you have the correct paperwork if you return."

Not as co-operative as earlier. Maybe Charlie's right about this house. Michael's eyes roved around the walls near the entrance. As the men retrieved their coats and hats, Charlotte stepped onto the porch with a handful of freshly picked flowers from the garden. "Ah there you are, Charlotte, please see these gentlemen off the premises." Mrs Park headed back to the kitchen, Michael spoke loud enough for Mrs Park to hear, "Dinner tomorrow night at my place, Charlotte?" It was a question more than a statement. He winked at Charlotte. "I know you still miss Magda but would you like to go dancing on Saturday night? It's been ages since you had some fun. I'm sure you'd enjoy some time out."

"I'll think about the dance, but dinner sounds nice."

His lips caressed her cheek as he left. He smiled when she blushed. "I'll look after you. See you tomorrow night after work, bye."

Michael shouted loud enough for his voice to travel through the entrance. "Thanks again for your help, Mrs Park. Have your books ready for our next visit." He ordered rather than requested. Michael and Carl stormed out of the boarding house with plans to request a search warrant.

"Murder, who said anything about murder?" Carl repeated when he got into the driver's seat. No explanation covered Magda's disappearance, with only her shoes recovered.

"You all right, Mick?' Carl asked. 'Want to talk about what's eating at you."

"Not now, Carl."

"I hear you." Carl turned his attention back to parking the car.

"Organize the warrant first up, Carl."

Chapter Forty-One

She watched him walk to his car and waited until he drove away. She felt good for the first time since...she dared not recall. Tears formed and flowed. She quickly wiped her face before anyone saw her. She closed the front door behind her as she returned to the entry hall. Mrs Park's voice startled her. She stood in the kitchen doorway.

"He's gone then, has he?"

Charlotte's senses reeled at the tone as if the woman wished he had gone for good. Before she answered, she inhaled slowly, "Yes, Mrs Park, the house is back to normal. No men on site."

"Well in that case, I'll get dinner ready. You're such a dear, Charlotte. I'm off to visit my brother later."

Charlotte scaled the stairs two at a time. Once she entered her room, she settled onto her bed, clutching her pillow for added comfort. Afternoon shadows snaking across the floor, disturbed her senses. Troubled by the illusion, she lay atop the bedcover to shut out the gloomy performance.

She woke with a fright. Her nostrils prickled, and she caught a faint whiff of Divine7. Her heartbeat increased. She trembled. She took stock of her surroundings, aware of hushed voices in the attic room. She decided to lie on the floor close to the air vent.

The conversation was audible. The smell of Divine7 cologne was stronger at the vent. It was a man's voice. "Urtha, we can't take this girl yet. It's too soon. Keep your attention on the reporter. She is too close. Everything else is going to plan. Your people owe you. Remember your mission Urtha." A door closed above. *Whose room are they in? If so, why?*

Four chimes from the grandfather clock alerted her to pre-dinner drinks. The aroma of Divine7 oozed into her room, so she opened her window. She glanced down into the back garden and saw two men wearing trilbies loitering by the path. She covered her mouth with her hand and stepped away. In her haste, she knocked her vase off the ledge. Afraid to move in case they noticed. She decided to invent an excuse for Mrs Park that the curtain had caught on the vase and pulled it out of the window. She could lie. She wondered if her voice might betray her. *Say nothing about the vase and pretend it happened before I woke up. God, who were those strangers? Who was the man talking to the landlady? Does their presence have anything to do with Lailah, Sophie and Magda? How safe are we? How safe am I?*

Chapter Forty-Two

Michael and Carl returned the next day with a warrant to search the premises and asked to speak with Charlotte if she was home. Filled with indignation, Mrs. Park reacted strongly to their return. "This is a respectable boarding house. What impression do you think my neighbours will have? Why do you want to see Charlotte? Has she done something wrong?"

"Nothing to worry yourself about, Mrs Park. Charlotte sometimes helps with police investigations."

Carl noticed two young women lurking between the kitchen door and entry hall. "Boarders, Mrs Park?" Carl asked.

"No, my daughters, Lily and Violet." Mrs Park scowled at Lily and Violet, who slunk back behind the kitchen door.

Carl turned back into police investigator mode. "Mrs Park, if you don't mind, we're here to look at your tenant registers?"

She shrugged her shoulders. "There's none to show you. A regrettable incident occurred here yesterday."

"What incident?" Michael's temper flared.

"Anything to help your inquiry, gentlemen, but there's nothing left." She paused to stir the soup simmering on the stove.

"And why is that?" Michael noticed the smug expression sweep across the woman's face.

"The only explanation I can give is the swaggie I employed misunderstood my instructions to tidy the cellar." Defiance straightened the woman's spine.

Carl interjected before Michael responded. A shiny mark on the top shelf of the display cabinet caught his attention. "Mrs Park, what's missing here?"

"Missing? Why? Nothing!" She stumbled over her words, wary of the detective's questions.

Carl pointed to the dust-free spot on the shelf. "There!"

"Oh! That's not missing; I have it in my pocket. Family heirloom, you know. It's a valuable opal." She fumbled in her pocket to retrieve a stone. "I like to have it close for the positive energy it releases."

Mrs Park inhaled slowly to regain her wits before suggesting the detectives follow her to the kitchen where she unlocked the cellar door. Descending the stairs the detectives expected to find registry books and suitcases as Charlotte described. The smell of fresh paint altered their mood. *Bugger! Too late! We need those rent records and registry books!*

In the nearly empty room, Michael saw only a small collection of unwanted furniture, old paint cans, and labelled rusty metal sea trunks stored against a wall. Nothing in the cellar depicted the imagery of Charlotte's description of the cellar. She and Magda described the room with rows of labelled suitcases stored on shelves and registry books archived in neat rows. What Charlotte expressed about the cellar was not open for discussion. Michael turned to Mrs Park.

She masked her gleeful expression. The clean-up proved successful. Nothing left behind.

Fresh paint on the floor disguised traces of shelving and boxes. The air was redolent with the scent of citrus fruits. Anger hardened Michael's tone, "You look at the incinerator, Carl. See if there's something we can salvage from this mess. Come, Mrs Park, back to the kitchen. I want to see Miss Tyrell if she's home."

Back in the hub of the house, he watched the old lady fuss over keys to lock the cellar door. He wondered why she kept the door locked. The basement odours were forgotten when cooking smells reminded him of his early breakfast. When Carl came back with bad news, the strain to withhold his anger muted any hunger pains.

Carl had checked the garden incinerator. He scraped ash from the furnace. "Couldn't find any paper, locks or leather to show evidence tampering." Carl shook his head side to side. "Nothing, boss. Nothing. Whatever burnt in that incinerator is gone."

Chapter Forty-Three

"Mrs Park," Michael spoke her name with venom on his tongue. "If I find that you have been party to the destruction of evidence, you will pay for your involvement. Do you understand?"

Mrs Park stammered, "But...but...I...I... explained what happened."

"I don't care what you told me. I am investigating serious crimes, and crucial evidence is no longer available. Now, if Miss Charlotte Tyrell is at home, have one of your daughters ask her to come down." Florid with anger, he strode into the parlour with Carl right behind him.

Mrs Park nervously asked Violet and Lily to fetch Charlotte. The two girls raced from the kitchen doorway, and bounded up the stairs.

Charlotte turned her door lock and spun about to face the wearisome pair.

Lily fired the first question. "The police want you downstairs?"

Before Charlotte could answer, Violet interrupted, "What have you done?"

Lily's nerves got the better of her. "What do you know?"

Their behaviour was no less than a rabble of reporters expecting answers to the scoop of the century. Charlotte had other ideas. "Now, girls, let me see. Maybe they should talk to you. You both sneak around the house at all hours of the night. You whisper secrets to each other. Do you want me to go on?"

"No." An emphatic reply was spoken in unison. Fear linked their little fingers together in unison.

The landlady looked nervous when she greeted her downstairs. "Ah, Charlotte, Detective Devlin and his partner are waiting in the parlour for you. Would you like me to chaperone you, dear?"

"God no, Mrs Park." Charlotte contained her laughter.

Through their investigation regarding the dried herbs from Magda's room, Michael and Carl learned of Magda's pregnancy and ensuing abortion. "Did she tell you the father's name?"

"What! That's the question of the year, Michael. I didn't know she was pregnant. Magda was ill with bouts of vomiting for a couple of weeks. She seemed better after Mrs Park took her to visit Dr Zagrobbe. Her ill health generated the doctor's concern. He requested further tests. I believe all this happened in his rooms." Charlotte dabbed at her tears. "Something's wrong, and I mean seriously wrong, for her to disappear."

"Mrs Park." Michael called as he opened the parlour door. In her haste to move away, the woman tripped over the curled rug but she managed to reach for the sideboard to gain her balance.

"Yes, Mr Devlin." her voice quavered. Her hands shook in unison. Caught eavesdropping, she recovered her composure so fast that anyone but Michael might have missed it

"Tea for all, please."

"Righto."

He left the parlour door ajar before suggesting they all take a break and wait for Mrs Park to return with the tea. Michael hated this part of any enquiry, especially now with Charlotte. She got under his skin in a nice way. *If I could wrap her in my arms and take her away from all this, I would.* A noticeable silence broke beneath the sound of Carl's pencil scratches on his notepad. Notes he'll evaluate back at headquarters.

"May I come in?" Mrs Park asked. Steam rose from the spout of a teapot. The woman placed the tray on the sideboard for each person to attend to their own specifics of sugar and milk. Michael neglected to ask the woman to leave.

"Let's continue, please. Charlotte, what arrangements did you and Miss Blakely make for the dance?" Charlotte retold the events. The two girls planned to meet after work at Beberfelds' corner. "Magda never arrived. She did say she might be late. She'd bought a new pair of shoes to wear at the Town Hall dance. I waited for over an hour, then came back home." Charlotte knotted her fingers together. "She was excited about buying new shoes. I looked forward to a night out. We enjoyed our Saturday night in the city."

"Do you know what the shoes looked like?" Michael relied on Carl to take note of the conversation. The pencil scratching continued.

"Is that important?" She held her cup of tea mid-air.

"Yes!" both men replied in unison.

Urtha Park's eyes widened; she faked a cough to disguise her gasp. No one noticed.

Charlotte's teacup rattled; her grip wavered. As she placed it on the saucer, she turned her head to the right as if looking for help. Her eyes met Michael's. "I didn't get to see them. I do know she planned to collect them and wear them to the dance." Charlotte's lips quivered. "All I know is that her new shoes were red, with high round heels." Her words broke between sighs. "A new style without ankle straps. She wanted that pair more than anything else." Tears trickled past her nose. She wiped them away.

Michael asked Charlotte to go with them to the station for further questioning.

"Excuse me! Why? I have told you all I know. Michael, why is this necessary?"

He didn't answer. "Mrs Park, we need you to come as well."

Urtha Park required more than polite persuasion. "What have I got to do with this. The silly girl didn't leave a note or anything. Go ask the boys she met at the dance."

Michael's temper nettled, "We could do this the hard way, Mrs Park, if you prefer! Help her with her coat, Carl."

"I'll get my own, thank you."

"Carl, wait for Mrs Park. I'll take Charlotte out," Michael spoke softly to Charlotte, "Something's not quite adding up."

A shiver snaked along her spine. Each nerve twitched beneath the sensation. "I sense it too."

"Let's analyse your journalistic instincts, shall we?"

Charlotte nibbled on dried ginger to quell a sudden burst of nausea. Anxious and nervous, she puzzled over all the questions. The house was a wonderful residence, and the girls were good company. *Oh, Magda! Will we find out what happened to you?*

Inside police headquarters, Charlotte was escorted to Michael's office and Mrs Park to an interview room. The two detectives stood in the corridor. "All the evidence falls short of requirements to support our theories, Carl."

"Right. Who do you want me to interview, the old hag or your girlfriend?" Carl asked.

Humorous undertones lifted the corners of Michael's mouth. "I'll take Miss Tyrell; you've got the landlady. Let's go."

Mrs Park bluffed her way through the fact that she'd ordered the destruction of records in the basement. "Like I already told you, Detective. A drifter came by and asked if there were any odd jobs, and as I had stored old newspapers in the basement, I got him to burn them. I didn't know he included the books as well until you came looking for them. I didn't get his name. I gave him a hot meal and two pounds, and he was on his way." Carl got as much as he could from Mrs Park and let her go after an hour or so.

Charlotte and Michael had a lot more to discuss. Charlotte gave as much information as she could. By the time the interview ended, afternoon rays indicated a colourful sunset.

Michael cautioned her not to leave town. When he realised she was tired and hungry, he concluded the session. He offered to drive her, but she knew that a ride on public transport would settle her down.

Mrs Park was not at home. Kathleen waited for Charlotte to return home. "Mrs Park left a flask of hot cocoa for us. She reckoned you would need some after today's ordeal and asked me to stay up and have one with you. She worries about you, Charlotte, and so do I."

Charlotte didn't want a fuss, so she did not resist the offer. "Ok, I could do with some company. Hot cocoa sounds great."

"There may be a fruit cake in the larder we can nibble on."

They washed and dried their dishes and said goodnight at the top of the stairs. Kathleen's door was on the right of Charlotte's. A long day was over, and she needed sleep. *Am I next? Don't be silly!* Her intuition shook every nerve in her body until she yielded to slumber.

Chapter Forty-Four

Aphone call from Doctor Zegrobbe panicked Mrs Park. "It's time for the reporter to see me. Make an appointment for Friday." The phone conversation was one way. The doctor hung up before she had a chance to postpone the date. Mrs Park confronted Charlotte at the entrance before she had a chance to close the door. "The doctor wants to see you on Friday. I've made an appointment for 4.00pm." Before Charlotte could respond, the landlady added, "The doctor said it was urgent he sees you." Mrs Park left Charlotte standing near the coat rack.

Charlotte raised her voice "Mrs Park, I have an important meeting on Friday."

Mrs Park half turned about and studied her own reflection in the mirror on the hall stand. "Cancel it; your doctor's visit is your first priority. It is your health under consideration after all, not your career."

Irate with the old woman, Charlotte stepped toward her landlady, but Lily and Violet announced their presence from the parlour. "Mummy, what's all the shouting about?" asked one of the twins, Charlotte's temper eased off to answer, "Nothing that concerns you two." Mrs Park's head dipped a nod, then stormed off toward the kitchen. Worried her temper might ignite at the dinner table, Charlotte elected to stay in her room away from the household tenants.

At 4.00pm sharp on Friday afternoon, Charlotte entered the doctor's chambers, where a visiting gynaecologist happened to be in attendance. Mrs Park sat in the waiting room to escort her charge home. Charlotte understood why the doctor said it was urgent to visit. She wished Mrs Park was more thoughtful and not make appointments on her behalf. Before her examination, the specialist recommended a mild sedative before she undressed. He explained the drug would take a few minutes to relax the pelvic floor muscles. She remained seated in the patient's chair and accepted the tablet without hesitation, not fully aware of the effects this particular drug imposed. An attempt to stand failed. She slumped into the chair with her head lolled to one side. Mrs Park was invited into the room. Aghast at the sight of Charlotte, Mrs Park demanded to know if the two men had killed her. Dr Zegrobbe ordered the woman to return to her home, and they would have Charlotte back in her room by the morning, after the procedure. "Are you taking her across to Zerona?"

"We certainly will take her over for participation in Sacrof's plans. Our operating theatre is ready for this patient. Everything is going to plan."

The front office staff had finished for the day, so Mrs Park used the phone in the reception to arrange for a taxi pick up. She left Charlotte in the hands of her brother's scientists.

Crime continued in the city day and night. Michael finished after midnight on Friday night. Too tired to drive home, he grabbed a spare bottle of rum from his office cabinet and decided to visit Joe in the tunnels. Michael's footsteps echoed in the deserted street as he headed for St James Rail Station. He needed company tonight, and Joe might be the right person to sit with and discuss his problems. He couldn't figure out why he wanted to see Joe tonight. Joe might be drunk and not listen to anything. Michael entered the abandoned tunnels in search of Joe. He passed the sleeping homeless bedded down in the only safe environment they knew.

Michael reached Joe's spot in the shadows and woke his friend, who was muttering in his sleep. "Jesus Christ, mate, you fuckin' scared me. I thought my time was up." Joe unfolded himself from his covers and sat up as best he could. "What the fuck are you doing here?" Joe's impolite manner raised a cheeky grin from his friend.

"I thought you might need a friend. So here I am." Michael offered the bottle of rum to Joe, who snatched it before Michael changed his mind. "Sorry, that's a lie. I need a friend, and I picked you."

Joe opened the bottle. "Here." He handed the bottle back to Michael. "Sounds like you probably should be drinking this, not me."

Michael gulped a mouthful.

"Okay, okay, leave some for me." Joe reached out for the rum. In the dimness of torchlight, they sat in silence, sharing the rum until the bottle was empty.

A humming sound interrupted Michael as he started to share his problems. A swirl of blue lights covered the blank wall. The moving colours across the blank tunnel wall mesmerised Michael for a moment. Too afraid to move; he and Joe had nowhere to go. With their backs against the wall, they flattened themselves on the grimy floor, desperate to remain inconspicuous. In a low voice, Michael requested Joe switch off the torch.

Three men wearing trilbies and dark clothes appeared from nowhere through the blue miasma. One man carried what looked like a drugged or deceased female over his shoulder. "Is that a woman?" The noise of the intruders' heels on concrete floors muffled the soft whispers passing between Michael and Joe. "Told you so. Angels of Death, I call them."

Joe's memories pushed his mind back to a time when he lay in a muddy ditch dispersing enemy snipers. His shaky fingers couldn't budge the switch. He stashed the lit torch beneath the protective layers of cardboard between the floor and his blankets. When his friend tapped hard on his shoulder blade, Joe sharpened his wits as best he could. Even though Joe doubted he had the stamina to help rescue the unfortunate victim. They both leaped out of the shadows and caught the strangers by surprise. To defend himself, one stranger callously dropped the limp body off his shoulder. As her body hit the floor, her coat swept dust into choking swirls. Not a sound escaped her mouth. All three defenders ignored the woman and continued to fend off their attackers. The brutal strength of the trio overpowered Joe and Michael's amateurish attempts to nab the abductors.

In his inebriated state, Joe's fists missed striking any of the oddly clothed men. As Joe stumbled into the wall, he tripped the closest figure. Misjudging his aim, Michael managed to topple another during an altercation. While in the midst of grabbing and rolling about like clowns in a circus ring, Michael and Joe suffered the most hits. The strangers were as skilled as world champion boxers using deft movements of ducking and weaving against an opponent. The two alcohol affected men began a downward spiral from pain. Each punch they received began to swell and restrict muscle movement. Cuts and swollen marks near their eyes affected their vision. Unaware that one of the strangers had backed into a corner away from the melee, Joe and Michael continued to fight with what remained of their wits and strength. Within seconds the fading lights regenerated.

Joe and Michael lined up to rush forward concurrent with the discharge of a weapon in a hand of the man by the wall. Electric pulses fired into Joe and Michael, who collapsed in severe pain as their muscles hardened like stone. Unable to move, they watched the three strangers leave the tunnel through myriads of vibrating iridescent blue lights. For whatever reason, Joe's Trilbies left the woman behind.

In excruciating pain and discomfort, Joe and Michael roused from their temporary paralysis. The stiffness of their bodies delayed any reactions to halt the hasty retreat of their adversaries. Blueness eased into grey before the tunnel hurled back into soft shadows. The first to get his bearings, Michael struggled to a crawling position. Each movement punished his body further as he edged on all fours toward the female body lying askew in the dirt.

Able to move his limbs, Joe fumbled for his torch and was amazed the battery hadn't failed. The single light penetrated the darkness. The yellow beam fixed on Michael in the shadows. "Here, Mick, I'll roll her over."

The movement left the torch slightly out of reach. Michael inched sideways to pick the torch up. "Can't see her face yet, but she's breathing."

Another hint of light grew stronger after Joe managed to light the kerosene lamp. Joe sat against the wall and mumbled, "Hell. What was that all about?" He scratched at his head.

Michael peered at the woman's face. "Charlotte?" The sight of her face sent shock waves through his body. He checked her pulse. "She's alive, thank God!"

She started to rouse from the drugs. Her eyelids blinked. She licked her lips. "Michael, is that you?"

"Sure is, love." He pecked her forehead. "Stay put. I'll get you a drink of some sort."

"Where am I?" Her eyes drifted toward Joe. "And who the bloody hell are you?"

Michael turned to face his friend, who had moved to the end of the wall; oblivious to Michael's statement. "Joe, are you okay?"

"Yeah, sure. You need to look at this, mate." Joe continued to wipe his hand over the carved symbols.

Michael insisted Charlotte remain prostrate on the floor until he checked out what Joe was fussing about. Unsteady legs stumbled with each step forward. The mysterious hieroglyphic patterns of a fish, water, and sun etched deep across a tile face bewildered both men.

"This is the spot where that fellow put his thick hand before the lights grew brighter." Joe couldn't stop caressing the symbols until the signs became embedded in his mind. He promised himself to unearth their meanings or use.

Michael watched Joe meld into the wall, almost invisible. He knew better than to disturb his mate.

Joe coughed. "Tell me! Did you see the same thing as me?" He dragged his hand across the top of his head to rest the palm on the nape of his neck.

"Yes! I did, but right now, we have another puzzle to solve." Michael's brow knitted with concern lines.

"Did I hear you say her name?" Joe asked and stood beside his friend.

"Yeah, it's Charlotte, the one I want to marry. This is the girl I met at the dance. I told you about her. Don't you remember?"

"What the fuck did those men want with her?"

"How the hell should I know? And I don't think she knows either." Michael looked back at Charlotte who drifted in and out of a consciousness. He asked for Joe's last bottle of rum to give some to Charlotte. "Make yourself useful and go out to the street and call for an ambulance"

Michael's agitation annoyed Joe. Joe lit a cigarette, inhaled deep, inducing an uncontrollable cough, then spat out phlegm as a result.

Charlotte stirred.

"Christ, Joe why can't you do as I asked?"

"See, she's breathing normally now and no visible signs of breaks and blood. She'll be all right." Joe unscrewed the top. "Wanna drink? You'll have to use the bottle; my crystal glasses are all packed away!" His comment eased the tension.

Off duty and on a so-called social visit, Michael accepted the bottle and passed it over to Charlotte, who wiped the bottleneck before it touched her lips. Michael took a swig himself. The liquid oozed down his throat, where the warmth of the alcohol spread inside his chest. He passed the bottle back to Joe. Joe gulped a mouthful before resealing the cap.

Groans emerged from Charlotte, trying to move. Michael held her down by the shoulder. "Don't move, Charlie, in case you've broken a bone or two. You need to be careful."

"What are you talking about?" Her head hurt. "I think I bumped my head."

"You sure did, Miss," Joe spoke from the shadows. She tilted her head to the side, and he smiled back at her. "I'm a friendly." He said, raising his hands to gesture a surrender. "Michael will vouch for me."

She looked back at Michael. "Help me sit up." He placed his arms beneath her back and supported her to a sitting position. Her rumpled dress caught up beneath her thighs. He gently pulled at the hem to cover her legs. "Ooh, A thunderous headache is looming!" She ran her hands over her head and felt a small bump on the side above an ear.

"If that's all you got, you're damn lucky, Miss." Joe's remark got her immediate attention.

Confused, she spoke in short bursts. Her eyes widened with fear. "What's happened, Michael? Why am I here? How did I get here?"

He tried to dispel her fears. "It's all right, we got to you before..." he drifted off mid-sentence. He changed tactics. "Do you remember anything from early this morning?" his words failed to soothe her.

"Like what?" To disguise her quickening pulse, she picked at imaginary fluff on her clothing. The headache intensified, threatening to block her common sense. She would not surrender to the need for relief until she got answers. *After two months, all I know is that he's a detective. Nothing else except for a couple of dinner dates and meetings at the Town Hall. He's mentioned his friend in the tunnels. Can he be trusted?* She watched Michael open his mouth to speak, then close it again. She wanted to ask why he was stalling. Frustrated, she stated, "Well? I'm waiting!"

"Okay. Let's start with how your day began and what happened right up to this point." His detective skills rose. His notebook would be a distraction. He wanted to watch her facial expressions. "Joe, come over and listen; I need your ears." Under silent protest, Joe sat by Charlotte, opposite Michael. "Let's hear your side of the story."

Joe reeked of all sorts of smells. Hygiene was lacking in this quarter. Charlotte pinched her nose when Joe sat close. Her voice was quiet. "Nothing but the usual morning shuffles out the boarding house. An afternoon appointment at the doctor for test results and, if need be, arrange times for further tests. An ordinary morning on all counts except the appointment."

Her narration continued. She and Mrs Park arrived a few minutes before schedule where a nurse escorted her into an examination room. "The doctor told me he had to do a thorough examination. A nurse held a syringe with some drug in the tube meant to calm my nerves." She rubbed her forehead with both hands, hoping the gesture would release her memory. "Strange, Michael. That's all I remember until I saw you and heard this man's voice." Charlotte nodded toward Joe.

"That's okay, Charlotte; you're safe now." He sat with his back against the wall with his arms loosely over his bent knees.

Charlotte pitched her voice.

"You keep saying that. Safe from what? You're scaring me!" Her breath quickened.

Michael recalled the fight to rescue a woman from three abductors. In the spur of the moment, Joe and he had decided to be heroes. Further explanation revealed the intruders went back to where they came from, leaving their prize behind. "You, Charlotte, were their victim."

Michael worried she might hyperventilate. "Trust me, please. Let's get you to the hospital."

He signalled for Joe to step forward. "We'll tell you more after you've been checked by a medical officer." Michael bent over. "I'll help you up if you feel strong enough to walk." Joe, too, stood up in preparation in case she lost her balance. He was a little unsteady himself.

"Here, let me help." Michael lifted Charlotte to her feet. "Easy goes."

Unclear of her whereabouts, though Michael had told her a little about her abduction She wondered if she could she trust him when she hardly knew him. Nothing he told her made sense. An earlier relationship tested her faith in men. Her career came first, and she survived the breakup. Heartbroken by someone who declared his love shattered her dreams of married life. Sometimes her anger got the better of her, and she lashed out at anyone who got too close. *Could a relationship with Michael be any different?* Charlotte controlled her temper until logic surpassed her instincts.

Time on her own in her own space was her foremost thought. No need to make the situation worse while I am in their hands in these damn tunnels. She could play their game and pretend to believe the ridiculous story. In the dim light, Charlotte's headache worsened. She closed her eyes blocking out any visible of a fight on the men's faces. "Thanks," Charlotte wobbled and reached for Michael. She rubbed her thighs and backside to subdue the surges of pain.

"By the way, you did land hard and probably have a few blue and purple spots. Let's get you up to street level and get you to the hospital emergency. If we don't move now, we may get caught in the early morning rush on the platform."

Chapter Forty-Five

A rush of air in the exit tunnel preceded a squeal of metal brakes on metal rails. "For fuck's sake, you'd think the bastards could run late one day." Joe threw his arms high in despair. "It's peak hour, and the bloody platform will be crawling with early morning starters."

"You forget Joe, our business is to meld with alighting passengers to the street." Michael pulled Charlotte closer to his frame to protect her from the crush of bodies. "Stay close, Charlie. I'll get you through this mob."

To hell with trust and logical thoughts. Providence brought a chance to escape by way of a burly man charging through the throng toward the trio. Charlotte leaned into the man who stumbled, swore and shifted aside. The action loosened Michael's grip. Swept towards the exit Charlotte disappeared from sight amid a swell of humanity in motion of opposing directions. Michael, unsure if she had stepped into the departing train, asked Joe, "What do you reckon? Did she get on that train?"

"Don't think so, but if she got caught in the rush, she'd be on the street already." Joe scanned all directions.

Michael stretched to full height and bumped an old lady who staggered and toppled onto her knees. He helped her gain her feet and edged her to the side of the stairwell handrail. He faced the wall and not the crowd to assure the woman was uninjured. Within the bustle of commuters, Charlotte passed by unnoticed. By the time Michael turned back to peer up the stairs, Charlotte had left the main entrance and entered a public phone box on the other side of the street. Empty pockets except for a scarf forced her to reverse charges to Brian's office. Expecting to speak with an informant who usually reversed the charges, he accepted the request. Surprise turned to consternation when Charlotte's panting voice pleaded for help and to meet him in St Mary's by the 8th Station of the Cross, where Jesus meets the women of Jerusalem. He had no idea but left in a hurry.

Joe lagged behind Michael who raced up the stairs two at a time into the morning sunshine. "I'm here and nowhere near fit enough for this foray of sudden exercise." Joe said as he arrived at the top of the stairs, gulping in the crisp morning air.

Frustrated, Michael looked at Joe. "Where could she be?"

Joe shrugged his shoulders. "Your guess is as good as mine." Stragglers, ignoring the men with bloodied faces, filed along the platform for the next train.

Aware of Joe's inadequacy to run, Michael suggested they split up. "She can't have gone far. I'll go up the street, and you check out Hyde Park."

Everyone looked the same to Joe at this hour of the morning. Dark winter wear completed the uniform of the day. Stylish hats, coiffed hairdos, and multi fashioned shoes distinguished women. From the back, one man's appearance matched those around him. Unfortunately for Joe, he couldn't remember what Charlotte was wearing. He recoiled at the thought. He had been close yet aware only of the blue light and the abductors.

Joe responded to Mick's whistle. A sound from their childhood. Mick pointed toward the cathedral at Charlotte in full flight up the stairs tying a red scarf over her hair.

An ambulance with a blaring siren coursed its way through the busy street. Traffic jammed in all directions. Before the vehicles started to move, Joe and Michael dodged in and out of stationary cars and buses. Michael grabbed at Joe as a tram crossed their path and dashed forward toward the Cathedral, unmindful of his surroundings. Homeless people meandered about the park. A constant parade in search of scraps in rubbish bins or half stubbed cigarettes on the ground. Living full time in the tunnels offered little for a fulfilling life. The rumble of passing trains underground disturbed the peace that he needed most of all.

Harold sat perched on a bench beneath an arbour. Any protection from the winter was better than none. Joe paused long enough to offer Harold his last cigarette in a last-ditch chance to catch his breath. Harold looked up at him. "Thanks, mate. Much appreciated." Joe didn't respond. His heart thumped in his chest; he was positive his lungs might burst. He pinched his side; a muscle spasm doubled him over. His head ached. His breathing was rapid. He wanted to return to the tunnel and forget everything.

"You okay, mate?" Mick shouted from the other end of the park.

"Yeah!" To Harold, he said, "Nothing a rum won't fix." Joe straightened up as best he could when he heard Michael's order to pick up the pace. With a great deal of false bravado, he willed his body to move. Charlotte disappeared into the cathedral. Joe and Michael entered and stopped to adjust to the dim interior. Incense hung thick in the air. Joe felt sick. He was glad of the cooling sensation of holy water on his forehead as he made the sign of the cross. His weight shifted to genuflect before the altar.

"No time for that, Joe," Michael whispered. He helped his friend to stand. "Can you see her?"

"Not yet. I'll go along the side aisle nearest the street in case she is hiding behind one of the pillars." Before Joe took one step, "What do we do now?" he whispered to Michael nodding at a Trilby character stealing along the aisle Joe had chosen to inspect. "Not exactly the place to force a confrontation."

With a boyish grin, Michael replied, "What we do best, fool. We need a distraction to flush her out. Remember when we used to joust as kids?"

Joe remembered their boyhood game of pretend fighting. "Who you calling a fool, you pompous bastard?" Their loud verbal abuses, flowered with foul language, distracted the churchgoers' attention to prayer.

"Hey! You two!" A priest bounded toward them. "Get out of here! This is a place of reverence and not for the likes of you." His arms waved them out the door.

Backing down the steps, Michael tugged at Joe's coat. "Quick! Let's get to the side of the cathedral before the cops arrive. If I'm caught in a melee with local parishioners, the chief will have my badge."

Michael and Joe ran across the road to the park opposite St Mary's side entrance and made their way to the far end. Shade on the western side of the tree offered an opportunity to hide from view. After a brief discussion between the friends, Michael would follow Charlotte while Joe followed the Trilby. Michael prayed that Charlotte left before the Trilby reacted.

Chapter Forty-Six

Overweight but able to draw on skills from his track and field days, Brian rushed to the cathedral in response to Charlotte's phone call. A poorly dressed woman wearing a red scarf stood beneath the 8th Station of the Cross. He looked around but couldn't see Charlie anywhere. The woman touched his shoulder and startled him, inviting a sharp retort. "It's me, Brian. Take me somewhere safe. I'm in danger." Charlotte shook from head to toe. "Don't ask questions; I haven't time. Just get me out of here."

Both turned toward the sound of angry voices at the entrance. The raucous behaviour of Michael and Joe startled Charlotte. Everyone in the cathedral turned their attention to the scuffle at the main entrance. Brian placed his left hand in the small of her back to calm her anxiety.

Surrounded by half-light from candles, they stood rigid in the pillar's shadow. Before panic struck her senses, Brian wrapped one arm around her shoulders. He took her elbow in the other to guide her outside, across the street, and into a nearby alley.

Michael recognised Brian and surmised Charlotte was the woman trotting close by the reporter heading for the closest laneway.

Joe waited as long as he could for the Trilby to appear. Joe struggled to maintain a regular pace. "Still under the influence and out of condition," he spoke aloud. Nobody heard. He stopped to catch his breath. Not more than one hundred metres away, Michael followed Charlotte and her companion a fellow he couldn't recognise from the cathedral. Muscles in Joe's body tightened while nerves locked sinews - he needed to catch up. *Bugger!* His body was unforgiving.

A cold marble wall offered Joe a solid base to lean against. Guilt moved him off the wall to walk toward the lane. A slight movement ahead distracted him. He caught a glimpse of the Trilby lurking in shadows beneath a fire escape. He saw the unmistakable flash of a handgun with a mounted silencer too late. The smell of gunfire residue triggered memories of death on a battlefield.

Safe in the alley, neither Charlotte nor Brian looked back nor heard Michael's approach or the man in the black trench coat with a Trilby low over his brow. Their panting concealed the soft pad of shiny black shoes on the wet surface.

"Catch... your... breath... Charlie." Brian said between pants.

Shaken and confused, she managed to nod in agreement. The bump on her head hurt as well as her thighs, where bruises began to throb. She jumped with fright at the sound of Michael's voice. Brian placed himself between Michael and Charlotte.

Undeterred, Michael shouted. "Charlie! What's with you?" His temper flared. "Why did you run away? We were taking you to emergency." He snapped at Brian, "and what the hell are you doing here?" His questions hung unanswered. Before Charlotte uttered a word, Brian gasped.

His body jerked, mouth wide open, a dark streak oozed from his head, staining his collar.

Joe's mind lapsed into a swirl of mud, bodies, smoke, and sounds of gunshots. He watched Brian slump to the ground in a crumpled heap with a head wound. Blood oozed and mingled with rivulets of rainwater escaping from nearby downpipes. Death pierced Joe's heart. It clenched his gut so hard his stomach yielded unsavoury contents. An upturned kerosene drum provided a seat.

Charlotte paled, unable to absorb the scene played out in front of her. She trembled; her legs weakened. Michael caught her before she fainted and held her close to prevent her from collapsing onto the grimy pavers. He could feel shudders sweep through her as he attempted to console her. He offered reassurance that she would be all right. Charlotte responded to his soft words and began to gain colour in her complexion. She made no attempt at release from the pressure of his arms or to lift her head from his chest. She felt safe for the first time in what seemed forever.

Renewed determination unnerved Joe, but he needed help to defeat his own demons. Now was not the time. He panted and displayed a brave front.

A tenant in the quarters above the lane phoned the police at the sound of a gunshot. The police arrived as well as an ambulance. An attendant and driver checked Charlotte for injuries. None worthy of note apart from the forehead bruise. They recommended a much-needed rest and follow up visit to her doctor later in the day.

Uniformed police scoured the scene of the crime for clues and witnesses. There were no clues, only three witnesses - a crime reporter, a detective and a returned veteran. Carl separated the trio to question them on an individual basis. They agreed to an escort to headquarters for more interviews.

Michael and Joe's statements corresponded with Charlotte's and, as the victim in this incident, related more information than the two men. To the interviewing officers, their stories were either well-rehearsed lies or true. Artful skills with weaponry attributed to either man. Both male witnesses attested that Michael pulled Charlotte back from the gunman's firing line.

Unfortunately, Brian fell within range.

Chapter Forty-Seven

Escorted home by late afternoon, Charlotte went straight to her room. Without consideration of the suspicious behaviour of the landlady and her daughters, Charlotte fell into bed. She rubbed her fingertips across the lump above her brow. Unusual for a fit and healthy young woman, Charlotte woke the next morning feeling queasy. She dismissed the symptoms as a result of yesterday's events.

All the boarders sat at the dining room table. Odours of bacon and scrambled eggs mingled with hot porridge turned her stomach. She rushed for the bathroom.

Mrs Park restrained her joy and excused herself to tend to Charlotte. "You all right, love?"

"Feel better now, thank you, I don't know what came over me," Charlotte answered in a croaky tone and leaned against the door until her stomach settled.

Mrs Park returned to the dining room. Her mind was filled with thoughts about the changes Charlotte would bring to Zerona. Charlotte's impending abduction was imminent, as the process of impregnation had already begun.

Joe was another matter - often detained for drunken behaviour, lewd language in public spaces and at times in a rage. His companions on the streets feared him and avoided him as best they could. Mischievous boys lit tuppeny bungers and watched him jump and hide in the gardens or behind bench seats. Little did they know crackers often sounded like gunfire and caused him further distress.

In Detective Devlin's absence, Carl shared his own accounts of the recent crimes. He and his colleagues named Joseph Moody as the perpetrator behind the abductions and murders since the incidents unfolded close to where he slept. Carl alleged Michael may have covered for Joe based on their close friendship. Everyone agreed with Carl's conclusions.

After the interviews, Carl presented the Chief Inspector at the station with a report naming Joseph Moody as a suspect. The senior officer spoke with the authority of his position. "I will inform Detective Devlin of our findings and remove him from the case. Am I clear?" All acknowledged the implication of Carl's address.

Chapter Forty-Eight

Morning light through breeze tossed lace curtains cast ethereal shapes across the floor. Tree branches caught in the winter breeze clawed against external walls. Charlotte stirred and stretched; her mother's words 'Get up, sleepyhead' buzzed in her head.

Showered and dressed, she made her way downstairs. The silence of the house begged her to tiptoe. Sunday morning bliss for the boarders was to sleep in late. Mrs Park flitted about the kitchen. Porridge bubbled in an old saucepan next to the steaming black kettle. Yesterday's home-baked damper was sliced for toast. Two trays set with condiments of homemade jam from the garden's fruit trees were ready for the dining room.

"Good morning." Charlotte's cheery salutation startled the woman whose hands were deep in a bowl of cake mixture.

"Oh, you scared me, love. You're up early today. Have you got plans?"

"Yes. I do, Mrs Park. Michael Devlin is calling for me around eight this morning." She saw the morning meal was ready and didn't want to wait for the others. "Do you mind if I eat here this morning?"

"Not at all, dearie. Sit here beside me." The landlady nodded toward a chair next to where she stood. Charlotte's back was against the window. She watched Mrs Park wipe her sticky hands on a wet cloth before spooning porridge into a bowl and pouring a mix of powdered milk and water from a ceramic jug.

"No sugar today, Charlotte. Hard to get with the shortages."

The thick lumpy porridge glued itself to the side of the bowl. The addition of powdered milk swilled on top of the gluggy mess. Charlotte consumed the warm mixture regardless. The ritual of spinning a teapot dressed in a colourful cosy amused her. The skirt of the cover flouncing up and down reminded her of Magda's flared petticoats.

Mrs Park noticed Charlotte's amused look and said, "Gives the leaves a chance to brew." *Mum used to say that. Am I homesick?* Charlotte purged that thought.

The landlady filled two cups with hot tea and then sat on a chair in front of the wood burner. The warmth from the kitchen fire spread throughout the room.

The brief moment of peace erupted into a vocal skirmish between Lily and Violet as they approached. "That's my dress, and I say you can't wear it."

Lily stuck her tongue out in rebuttal. "It's pretty on me and doesn't suit you."

Charlotte looked in the direction of the voices to see Lily waltz through the doorway. *God only knows why she thinks the dress is pretty.*

"Excuse yourselves, girls, and go and sit in the dining room. Breakfast is ready."

The sisters apologised in unison but left without giving Charlotte a chance to respond.

"Sorry about the interruption Charlotte. The heat here is steaming up my glasses." Mrs Park pulled a handkerchief from a pocket inside the apron to dab at her eyes. "Those two worry me an awful lot. I wonder when they'll find the courage to break free and make their own way in the outside world."

Charlotte nodded in agreement and sympathy. "They are old enough to move out, Mrs Park. Perhaps you should encourage them more."

The woman paled and snarled, "What would you know about the world, Missy?"

Charlotte didn't understand the sudden mood change and avoided further animosity. "Nothing, Mrs Park, nothing at all." She stood at the table, ready to leave. "I'll wait for Mr Devlin in my room. Oh, before I forget, I'll be home for dinner tonight." Charlotte spun about, leaving a stunned Mrs Park to get on with her duties.

Upstairs in her room, Charlotte recalled the conversation after the sisters left the kitchen. Mrs Park's mood swing happened at the mention of the phrase "outside world". A simple reference to what's beyond the front door. The grandfather clock swung into action and interrupted her thoughts. By the count of five clangs, she had locked her room and raced downstairs into the entrance by the last gong. The hands on the clock's intricate dial indicated eight o'clock. *Haven't been on a picnic for ages. Hope the weather holds out.*

A car's motor fell silent, followed by the sound of a door closing. She willed herself to breathe in anticipation of a doorbell ring. She opened the door to Michael, who tipped his hat in greeting. "You ready for a day out, Miss Tyrell?"

"I am indeed Mr Devlin." She pinned on her hat, wrapped a scarf about her neck and allowed Michael to help with her overcoat. To Charlotte's surprise, Mrs Park's reflection appeared in the hall mirror. Sourness shrouded her features. Charlotte ignored the glare and said, "I'm off, Mrs Park. I'll see you at dinner. Bye."

Michael closed the door behind them. When they neared his car, he advanced ahead to hold the passenger door open until she sat inside the vehicle. He was a careful driver and turned the corner onto the main road to Bondi Beach. "Have you seen the sights of the Eastern Suburbs, Charlie?"

"Haven't had time to explore. Been too busy." She studied his profile and blushed when he caught her out.

"Good, Nielsen Park, here we come."

It was a short drive past stately homes and tree-lined streets by the harbour. The park kissed a sandy beach in front of a kiosk filled with diners. Michael found a shady spot and set out the picnic in the middle of a tartan patterned rug. A gentle breeze swept across the waters. The backwash from a passing ferry slapped the sandy foreshore.

"What are your plans for the future, Charlie?" Michael asked. His thoughts in opposition to his actions. He really wanted to toss away the food and wrap her in his arms. His mind said otherwise.

"I suppose, like any young girl, I dreamt of marriage and family, but that all changed some time ago." Charlotte turned away. To change the subject, she pointed out the immigration ship leaving the harbour empty of its human cargo. "Do you think it's safe to travel overseas now?"

"It's not something I want to do. What about you, Charlie?"

She sighed. "A pipe dream, I suppose. Maybe when the world is in a better place."

"Repairing the damage from war takes time and money. Healing time for both survivors and families of lost ones is just as important."

"You are a thoughtful man, Michael. Any girl would be pleased to take you home to meet her father."

He noticed her eyes twinkled when she smiled. Michael put out the small platters of food and got two glasses ready for the rum. It was the only spirit left in his office since his last meeting with Joe.

Squawking seagulls took flight with their wings spread upward and curled at the tips. As they descended, their talons touched the grass, winged feathers folded against their bodies. They charged and pecked at one another for front position.

"Ignore them if you can, Charlie. They're a bloody nuisance." Michael waved his arms to shoo the birds away.

"Birds are fascinating to watch, don't you think?"

"Not pests like these."

Michael served them a shot of rum each with cheese and crusty bread. Next out of the basket came egg sandwiches, followed by Anzac biscuits. Michael lay on his back after he packed away the plates and the bottle. "Look, Charlie, see the cloud over the harbour heads - it looks like two dancing bears."

Charlotte joined him and disagreed. "No, it's not. I see an old hag dragging a sack behind her."

"Gruesome creature, aren't you?"

"Not usually; my skin prickles after lights out. My wild instincts imagine foul play inside the rooms at night. I am convinced that Mrs Park and possibly her daughters are withholding information. And, by the way, what about the suitcases and belongings Magda and I found in the cellar. Have you got an explanation?"

"Don't spoil today, Charlie. This is a day for your soul, not your mind." Michael leaned over and kissed her forehead and changed the subject. "Have you got a bathing suit?"

"What for? It's bloody winter, and the water is icy."

"Not now, but in summer. Can you swim?"

"Wait and see, but I did represent my high school." Memories of those competitions flooded her mind erasing the earlier macabre thoughts.

The afternoon sunset streaked the western sky in pinks and mauves across the harbour. Dusk preceded a drop in temperature. The day ended at the front door of the boarding house.

"Thanks, Michael; I loved the walk around the harbour shoreline."

"What? Didn't like the picnic?" He laughed as he pulled her close to kiss her.

Charlotte allowed their lips to touch and thrilled at the caress across her mouth. He released her and said, "Goodnight, Charlie; I might see you tomorrow at work."

"I'm sure you will." She waited at the door until he drove up the street. She gagged in the hallway. That bloody smell. I have to find out who wears Divine7 cologne.

Chapter Forty-Nine

Police were out in force in the city, particularly near the bus stop at Hyde Park. They searched for any morsel to connect Joe to the disappearances. Whoever committed these crimes left nothing behind, not even a footprint. Three young women had now disappeared. Plagued by thoughts, Michael sat at his desk to sift through the facts about the case.

Charlotte was anxious about the two girls from the boarding house and had raised her doubts with Michael. Charlotte had no proof but was suspicious of Mrs Park. Sophie and Magda left the boarding house under questionable circumstances. Magda was not behind with her rent, as stated by the arrogant Mrs Park. Charlotte was with her friend each time they paid rent. Michael told her she needed receipts and records of payments as proof. Something he and his colleague didn't find.

Michael shifted when his mind reflected on Joe's predicament. How well did a person get to know and understand another? Would there be signs of mental illness? What damage from time spent on battlefields causes someone like Joe to flip out. Should he have spent more time with his friend? They did rescue Charlotte from the faceless ones. Was Joe involved? He did make a mayday call when the first body turned up. Had he moved the corpse before Michael arrived? Nothing supported this line of thinking but the seed of doubt planted itself in his mind.

The constant drinking of alcohol changed Joe. He could become violent at the drop of a hat. His rants and raves in Hyde Park brought about a couple of nights in custody. Undeterred, he continued to get drunk. The rum helped him forget his old dreams and quietened his new nightmares. He wanted to be alone. He convinced himself that solitude was his Saviour. God didn't help those on the battlefields.

On his own, Joe didn't react until cornered near a bench seat. His arms flayed in the air, and then he would stand like a skilled boxer when anyone approached. A couple of the young constables have toppled beneath the full brunt of fists across their faces. Often a few stragglers heading for the tunnels would stop to coerce Joe. "Hit the bloody wallopers, Joe; give them the what for!" Joe was not the fighter he used to be. He was weak from alcohol and lacked physical training, and he soon tired.

When he arrived at the scene, Michael's first instruction was to move the sightseers away from the area. Joe performed like a madman as Michael neared. He stood near enough for Joe to hear his voice. "What are you doing, Joe? Have you gone mad?"

Joe turned his stance on the defensive. "Mate!"

"Do you think we could talk?" Michael spoke quietly to calm him down.

"What about, Mick?" Joe remained rigid.

Michael stepped closer.

"Don't take another step, Mick, else you will get the same treatment as the others, friend or not!"

Michael negotiated with Joe while some of the police got near enough to pounce. Flattened and handcuffed before he knew what happened, Joe cursed Michael.

"Take him to the station and lock him up."

Joe was hauled away but not without fuss. Another officer copped a kick in the shin.

"What's turned him, Carl?" Michael asked his colleague.

"Don't know. According to Harry, nobody saw Joe come out of the tunnel until tonight. He spent the whole day underground. The old man said it was unusual for Joe to miss the morning soup van."

"Well, something bit him on the arse!"

"Let him cool off for a half-hour, and I'll go talk to him." He worried for his friend. Joe was under constant watch in case he hurt himself. He fell asleep as soon as the door of the cell locked. Initially, the guard thought Joe had died until he heard the rhythmic snoring inside the cell.

Stirred out of a hazy sleep, Joe woke to see Michael leaning over. Joe's knuckles were raw, his clothes reeked of sweat, and he felt nauseous. He mumbled, "Where am I?"

"Safe, Joe. What's happened to you? I've never known you to be so violent."

Joe withdrew into the corner. "They're after us all." Several officers moved in and out of the cells with other detainees. Michael recently caught wind that the Senior Officer wanted to blame Joe for the abductions and the death of Chartotte's colleague. Careful to protect his own reputation, Micael denied he saw Joe's Trilbies when they rescued Charlotte. This wasn't the time or place to confirm the reality of his friend's visions.

"Who is Joe?"

Joe ran both hands through his hair. "Those fucking angels of death walking in the tunnels." He reached out to grab Michael's are. A guard rushed into the room.

"It's ok; he's not going to hurt me, are you, Joe?"

"Nope."

"Are these the same beings we talked about before?" Michael understood. "The same beings who tried to abscond with Charlotte."

"Yeah. You know who. The wingless angels of death who wear Trilbies."

When Joe confided about what he saw, he assumed his vision to be a nightmare. He was drunk, after all. Michael assured Joe that he was safe. Together they might make sense of what happened in the tunnels. He especially expected Joe to change his story about the mysterious Trilbies. Joe wasn't happy about the charges of causing a disturbance and striking police officers. He would remain in prison until his appearance before a magistrate at a later date.

CHAPTER FIFTY

The extra police presence in Hyde Park irritated the homeless, who gathered in small groups to bask in the afternoon sunshine. Silence preceded any approach by the constables whose purpose was to question the down and outs. Any response from these street-savvy people might generate leads to the whereabouts of the missing women.

At a short distance from the park's entrance, Joe sat close to old Harold on a bench seat.

Both men avoided eye contact. Harold moved away first toward the inner city, Joe walked away not long after. The solitude he found in the tunnels beckoned Joe back to the underground, away from the sun's warmth.

Recent turmoils stirred memories of Madelaine. Joe imagined Madelaine encased in a womb of blue lights with the Angels of Death. He cursed himself for believing in such nonsense.

He speculated these creatures of his imagination, haunted his nightmares. "Ah! Yes! The Trilbies! Bloody hell! Why me!" He shouted at nothing. His voice echoed in the void. No longer in a mood to analyse the puzzle, he opted to drown his sorrows and think no more. The hours melded together until a light hit him square in the face. "What the..." he exclaimed.

"...Settle down Joe; it's me, Nora. I'm worried about you. Are you okay? I thought you could do with a friend tonight."

He pushed the light away from his face. "Go away, Nora! Leave me alone!"

"Listen, Joe, Maddy was my best friend and close like a sister." She paused to swallow, "I would do anything to bring her back?"

"What good would that do? She's gone, without a trace. I read the police report."

"In that case, I'll sit with you awhile." Nora threw her scarf over the dirty floor before she lowered herself to sit. The tunnel resembled a giant broken down iron lung. The stale air she breathed lingered in her lungs. "Why do you choose to live in this squalor?" She waved her hands around his dusty domain.

"Leave me alone." He slurred with no patience for her condemnation of his lifestyle.

A soft humming noise distracted Nora. "What's that?"

"They're coming, Nora." He questioned whether to hide or offer himself to the intruders to spare Nora. No choice but to hide. "Quick." An unmistakable urgency in his garbled whisper warned Nora to obey. "Under this!" He wrapped his army blanket about them before she had a chance to object.

She stifled a sneeze. The space filled with swirling blue lights before three of Joe's Trilbies appeared from inside the colours - on a course toward the station platform. Nora whispered, "It's not a dream, after all, Joe, they are real."

Chapter Fifty-One

Nora laboured to breathe, but fear snared her in place. With difficulty, she ignored the stench of Joe's army blanket. When Joe tossed the cover aside, Nora jumped to her feet and gulped the stale tunnel air. She peered along the tunnel and, without thought, planned to follow the men who passed by.

Joe dusted himself down. "You still here, thought that scenario might have you running for the hills." He staggered when he waved an arm in her direction, his fist around the neck of the rum bottle. He raised it in salute. "Off you go then, little Miss Nora. What's keeping you here?" Still, under the influence, he made no sense of Nora's command to stay put while she chased after the three men. He shrugged his shoulders without a second thought for her safety but was grateful she left him alone.

He guzzled the rum as if his life depended on the substance. The rush in his throat caught in his chest. He gasped. "God, I love this stuff." Sleep returned to quieten his soul for a short while.

Nora quickened her pace to get to the rail platform in time to catch up with the three men. Fortune was on her side. The men had stopped to wait for a train to pull into the station before leaving the tunnel.

At the top of the tunnel entrance steps, Nora ascertained the men were not in her vision and hoped she wasn't too late. A sparse number of commuters hovered about the platform. She raced up the ramp to see the faceless men get into a taxi. The next vehicle moved forward, and before the driver stopped, she opened and closed the back door faster than a whip crack.

"Where to, lady?" His eyes on the rear vision mirror.

"Follow that car!" Excitement rippled through her body. *Always wanted to say that.*

Her expert driver manoeuvred through the traffic. The vehicle they followed pulled over in a quiet street outside a Boarding House in Kings Cross. "Park here. I want to see where they go."

"Clock's ticking, love." He relaxed in his seat, turned the interior light on to read the newspaper.

"Turn off the goddamn light." Nora shrunk low in the seat beneath the window line. The windows fogged with the difference between inside and outside temperature.

The night air turned crisp and chilly. Mellow tunes from the driver's radio circulated through the car. A soft glow on the dashboard highlighted the driver's profile. Reflections on the inside windows disguised any movement outside the confines of the car.

Not long after three men exited their cab, Nora's driver jerked and slumped across the steering wheel, activating the horn. She jumped with fright.

The passenger door closest to her seemed to fly open as if on its own accord. A painful sensation in her upper arm rushed through every muscle. Nora heard a female voice, "Dump him in the harbour and take her with you. Sacrof can deal with her."

Nora lost consciousness. One of the men dragged her out of the vehicle and tossed her over his shoulder. The other man shoved the taxi driver along the front seat to make room for himself behind the wheel. He started the motor when the others were ready to leave. Both cars headed toward North Head, where an isolated area provided the perfect place for a supposed suicide. They sat the driver behind the wheel and hooked his shoe on the accelerator. A small flame ignited the fuel drenched rag in the petrol tank as they pushed the car over the edge. The taxi exploded mid-air.

"Well done, boys. Let's get back to meet my brother in the tunnels."

A woman's voice grumbled about her difficulty walking through the tunnel. Joe stirred. Ah, Nora's back. He rolled his head to the side to chastise Nora instead he saw the intruders. He counted six people - three females, one of whom looked like Nora, and three Angels of Death. He surmised the complaints came from the older woman.

Unaware Joe lurked, ready to pounce; the small party stole through the shadows in single file. Two of the men carried a limp female over a shoulder.

They had no time to react when Joe struck the group head-on like a cannonball fired at close range. Joe lunged even though he was in no physical shape to take on the single file of intruders moving forward.

The unexpected leap of force behind Joe's body weight stunned them all, and like a train crash, everyone fell or stumbled to the floor with limbs flailing in attempts to get to their feet.

The comic book scene unravelled before him. He mentally pictured the baddies who keep their black hats on except this scenario was real. Lives were at risk. Amid a hazy mental state, he instinctively attacked without taking a moment to think. A sham hero in full battle rage lunged at the group. His only thought was to save the women like he and Mick had saved Charlotte.

Joe noted the older woman against the wall, crawling on hands and knees, looking for something. Joe was uppermost on the pile of bodies. His Trilbies squirmed beneath him as they attempted to recover. Both women were dropped to the floor. At first, Joe thought they were dead, but then he realised they were probably unconscious. Before he regained his footing, a sharp pang struck him between the shoulder blades. He hadn't heard a gunshot, perhaps a silencer. Pain of the highest degree navigated the length of his spine.

His senses swirled into a befuddled dream filled with sounds of slurred voices. A heavy boot kicked him in the middle of the back to push him over then weigh him down. The floor was cold against his cheekbone now flattened against the surface. Joe could not move. Every muscle along his back locked with spasms. The faceless ones stood tall above him. His one act of bravado had brought him undone.

A man's voice waffled through the haze. "Who else have you got here? We were expecting only one tonight."

"This one followed us to the Boarding House, Sir." The tallest of the Trilbies spoke.

The foot on Joe's ears squashed his cheek harder to the floor. He heard parts of the conversation.

"Our driver attempted...failed...We found her...outside...her driver was...disposed of...car...

cliffs...heads...exploded - no witnesses."

A curse exploding from the newcomer brought another boot into Joe's ribs.

"This one...useful...our cause...pretty." Stunted conversation between the old woman and the man he couldn't see.

"...no use for her. Leave him...I'll finish her off...human authorities will blame...dispose of two...same time."

Chapter Fifty-Two

Joe's immobile muscles and limbs maintained an unbearable pain. With limited vision, he recognised Nora. By the way her arm furled away from her shoulder, her collarbone had snapped. Her scream confirmed his suspicion. The tumble had pinned Nora's legs beneath one of the thugs who struggled to untangle himself from her twisted body. Incapable of helping his friend, Joe witnessed and acknowledged her pain. His interest in the other young woman fell short while he concentrated on Nora's predicament.

The other young woman remained unconscious, oblivious to any injuries or the unfolding scene. Nora tried in vain to release her legs. The pain tore at her nerves with each movement of her body.

Enraged and unable to move, Joe watched a peculiar looking man help the older woman off her knees. After straightening her attire, she stood behind the newcomer.

Yanked up by her hair, Nora pleaded, "Aagh! Please don't hurt me. I've done nothing. Please! Please! I beg you!"

"Silence!" The newcomer's glare brought Nora to submission. One of the Trilbies knelt over the unconscious young woman. The man asked, "The girl?"

"A bump on her head, but she'll be okay."

"Who's this then?" He nodded his head back to Nora. He removed his hands from beneath the many folds of his cape to reload a weapon.

The older woman whispered. "She followed us. I don't know how much she knows."

A sensation of dread rolled in Nora's head. In defence, she proffered, "I know nothing."

The questions came from the man who paralysed Joe. "Do you know where you are?"

She shook her head from side to side, unable to speak. Pain levels from the fracture increased. She tried to hold up her arm. Without a sling and hospital attention, the pain levels increased. She squeezed her eyes shut when a muscle spasm rippled across her back.

"We will find out everything you know, my dear." His tone shifted. "Tie her up!" He ordered. Mrs Park gasped. "Silence, sister. This has nothing to do with you."

"But..." Urtha angered her brother when she questioned his actions.

"Go! Before I put you in chains and drag you away to the outer rims of our borders." He glared at his sister, who collected the damaged rock dropped in the ruckus and made her way back to the rail platform. She would look another time for the broken piece of opal. She willed herself not to look back. She heard the first scream before a train rumbled overhead. Another few minutes, and the girl would no longer exist.

Regardless of the agony in her shoulder, they tied her hands behind her. Pain numbed her mind. Nora drifted into a semiconscious state. She did not hear the conversation around her. "What about him?" asked one of the Trilbies.

"This one we leave behind. Deemed a madman, insane, and alcoholic. We use him to keep our home safe." Sacrof kicked at Joe and laughed when his ribs cracked. "He'll be unable to move for a couple of hours. Drunk again if anyone comes looking for him."

Screams wake her, her screams. Sacrof grasped her broken collarbone. Bone protruded through her skin, where he squeezed the injured area. "Glad you could join us." He growled like an animal. His grip eased in case she fainted.

Fear engulfed her being. Her pain was now secondary to her fight for life. "Who are you? What do you want?"

"Why were you following my people?" He leaned over and wriggled the protrusion.

"Don't know what you mean!" She screeched between gasps. Another squeeze, and she almost passed out. Courage departed. Pain racked through her body. Tortuous pain ripped up and down her spine, followed by muscle spasms. She opened her eyes as a vice-like grip tightened around her neck. Death was imminent. A slow ordeal for an innocent.

Powerless, Joe watched this monster draw a dagger and place it against her cheek. The blade drew blood.

Sacrof relished torture and torment of his victims, especially the helpless. It had been a while since he experienced such pleasure.

Nora's nose broke under the slam of his fist. The tissue around her eyes swelled. "Just get it over with," she spat at him.

Joe closed his eyes as the blade sliced across her thin neck; it cut through the chain on her keepsake pendant. The pendant fell to the floor. Tears flowed from Joe's eyes. Death in the ugliest form accessed his memories. At that moment, evil entered his life. Fear spread like wildfire in his mind. *Am I next?* He brushed the notion aside. Nora was dead, and he met the executioner. A desire for vengeance deepened within. Effects of the electrical pulses began to wane. Joe heard the order from the leader of the group.

"Leave him alone and let human justice lay blame at his feet." Another kick at Joe's ribs.

"Bruise him around the knuckles and head. Tug at his clothes as if involved in a struggle."

Joe's body jerked with sudden movement when he surfaced from his insentient state, alone with Nora's twisted and broken body; her throat slashed ear to ear. Her face was severely damaged. Puffy tissue did not disguise the broken jaw, missing teeth, or the many slashes across her skin. Her hands and feet remained bound.

A swollen eye blurred his vision, and body muscles twitched. The stench in the tunnel incurred battlefield memories of the foul odours of death. He managed to roll away from the murderous scene. A ruthless churning emptied his stomach of its watery contents until his abdominal muscles cramped tight. He tormented himself for his inability to save her. Revenge - his new motto.

One tiny drop on his tongue fell from his bottle of rum. He talked himself into lighting a cigarette but fumbled with the open packet only to have the contents tumble into a dark red puddle. He managed to save one. After several strikes of a match, he sucked slow on the filter for the first drag. As a result, his stomach fought the invasion of nicotine into his lungs. The calm sensation did not happen at first, but his mind won the battle between coughing and spluttering fits. Every detail of Nora's death etched deep inside his memory.

Michael, I need you. The effort to stand devoured remnants of energy. Something on the floor near his feet caught his attention. A stream of light from a nearby air vent highlighted a piece of rock. Encouraged by the distraction, Joe crawled over to inspect the bright object. The broken stone measured about two inches wide with jagged edges. He considered the shard might be a piece of the bigger rock the old lady placed over the symbols on the wall. He remembered the old woman on her hands and knees, looking for something. *This perhaps.* He sidled up the wall and used it for support to edge along. About three steps away, he touched symbols carved into rock past the last wall tile.

He placed the stone against the symbols, not understanding their use. He withdrew the stone from the wall the instant a tiny blue light appeared. "Bloody Jesus, Mary, and Joseph!" He made the sign of the cross. Astonished by the power he now held. *Hide the rock. Tell no one. Vengeance can wait.*

Chapter Fifty-Three

Painful movements hindered Joe's progress out of the tunnels into the street. The early morning fog hung heavy on the city. Visibility was poor, but Joe knew his way to the phone box. His clear voice across the telephone line, "Mayday! Mick, Mayday! Bring your bloody people with you. No time to waste. I'll be outside St James Station." Joe hung up before Michael asked any questions. No time to listen to Michael's chatter about help for returned servicemen

Joe blamed the old boys' brigade, whose mindset belonged in the dark ages. *Men should be able to handle the tough as well as the good times. Useless waste of time.* Like many others denied help after the war, Joe sought isolation in the abandoned tunnels beneath St James Rail Station. To anyone who might listen, he criticised old desk jockeys who planned attacks without sound knowledge of ground conditions. He described places and times when Friendly and enemy bullets and bombs rained on young men. *Kids, in fact. What madness is war when the fight for freedom sacrifices thousands of lives? Will the next generation be any different? May the mistakes of the last war never happen again.*

Memories, albeit far from good ones, helped Joe avoid the present. Shame-filled tears pushed down his bruised cheeks. Salt stung in open cuts, a reminder of his guilt. Guilt possessed him for surviving when mates lay dying or dead beside him. He jerked back to the present.

Joe wondered if Nora's body remained in the tunnel and not disappear like the last one. The other one wasn't left behind. Just her shoes. He shuddered. *Could I be guilty?* Drunk as usual. This thought strengthened a desire for more rum, but he had none. The bottle was empty. *Return to Nora in case she's been taken.* In a way, he hoped she had. No, of course not.

He lived but not Nora. Joe's guilt spread to anger. Mortified by his weak attempt to pull Nora away from the Trilbies, he vowed revenge. A promise was made to rectify his life and revert to the wisdom and strength of a soldier. *Oh, God, can I do this?*

Rain followed the fog by the time Michael got to Hyde Park, where he spotted Harold "G'day, Harry. You seen Joe? Supposed to meet him outside the station, but I don't see any sign of him."

"Yes, I saw him not long ago; he was pacing the sidewalk. He didn't see me. He looked sick or something; he must have gone back down the tunnel Lots of rumbles and noise down there last night." The backlash of air from passing trains sounded like a woman's screams. None of us left our beds."

That last statement registered alarm. Michael knew Joe was in trouble. He rushed off toward St James' tunnels and Joe.

Chapter Fifty-Four

The editor of the newspaper received a call from a contact. Charlotte heard the tap on the glass panel and responded to his hand gestures. Rory pressed the speaker button to allow Charlotte to listen to the conversation.

"Murder in the tunnels," her boss said and added, "More likely a couple of derelicts riling up one another until one of them breaks." Before the handset rested in its cradle, Rory Calhoun gave his star reporter instructions. "Be a good 'journo', Charlie and cover the story ASAP. I will hold the front-page print as long as I can." At the shrill rings of the black desk phone, he waved her out of his office without a second glance.

Charlotte called to the photographer. "Get your gear and follow me. Police have a murder victim in the abandoned tunnels." She grabbed her bag and coat, ready for the photographer, who rushed between desks with his camera bag over one shoulder.

Excited by the fact the story would cover the front page news, she jumped at the chance to be first on the scene. The prospect of returning to the tunnels quickened her heartbeat. Charlotte had pulled the night shift for the first time. Her mouth was dry. She licked her lips as she rushed to St James station to report on the incident.

Hopes for a good story overshadowed her unwillingness to return to the tunnels. The place where Michael and Joe allegedly executed her rescue. The aftermath of her escape on the platform resulted in Brian's death. Michael and Joe believed the shooter meant to cause her harm. *It doesn't matter; Brian's dead. But why?* Her desire for the story outweighed a compulsion to retreat.

Charlotte arrived at the entrance to the tunnels, where Michael barked orders at the constables and detectives. "Cordon off access to the tunnel. I don't want anyone down there until I say so. Is that clear?"

Poised with pencil and notepad, she asked with the aplomb of an investigative journalist. "Hey, Michael. Why all the men? You usually don't have this many on an investigation. Was it a fight between a couple of the homeless or something else?"

Startled to see her amid the clamour of sirens and heavy boots on the pavement, he shouted, "Jesus, don't sneak up on a man like that." The rain had stopped, but gutters, full of debris washed along by torrents of muddy water, overflowed. "Why are you here after what you have been through? I expected you to cover the fashion and garden parties' pages." He squared his body with hers to look her straight in the eyes. His hands were on his hips in a show of authority.

She was none too pleased to hear anyone belittle her work, especially someone she liked. She glared at him. "Bloody funny, old man! I'm here to do my job!"

"Sorry. Didn't mean to offend. You'll get a story, no doubt. All I can say is that there's a body where we think Magda disappeared." Michael withheld the victim's name.

"Where Magda disappeared?" She mouthed the words. She couldn't speak. Despair returned at the mention of her friend. Charlotte sensed a shift in his manner and ascertained that perhaps he held back more information for her scoop.

Michael answered her question before she uttered the words. "Yes, Charlie. I've seen the body. Joe was there. Joe will be arrested for murder."

Charlotte caught her breath. "Surely not. He's your friend. Isn't it a bit early to determine guilt? A suspect or witness at least." Surprised by her outburst to defend Joe, she bit her bottom lip. A change of pallor to Michael's skin unleashed sadness in his eyes. She withdrew a desire to be near him, to comfort him. After her experience in the tunnel, suspicion reared at times to challenge her instincts. Whenever these thoughts surfaced, Charlotte struggled to convince herself of Michael and Joe's claim of innocence.

"Not sure, I don't want to believe it, but it's more than a coincidence. Besides, it's the same spot." He turned to enter the tunnels.

Charlotte grabbed his arm. "Do you know who the victim is?"

Michael half turned in response, "Nora. It's Nora's body, mangled and bruised, on the floor beside Joe's bed."

Charlotte's pencil snapped in half under the force of her grip. "Are you sure?"

Shocked by the scene before him, the last thing he needed was to share an intimate moment with Charlie. Two of his childhood friends were here, one dead, the other a witness. To connect the word guilty with his thoughts undermined all he shared with Joe. He knew he could trust the man with his life, so why would he doubt his word. Charlotte can't be here with all this mess. "Nora's dead." He emphasised dead to convince himself to admit the battered, twisted body belonged to innocent Nora. His temper flared. "Why the bloody hell would I say otherwise? I don't want you here! You got your story! Go! Write up the news and take your camera boy with you." She reeled, hurt by his angry tone.

Her assistant held her steady.

"You know the girl. Charlotte?" he whispered.

She straightened her stance and retrieved another pencil. "Yes, but we are still going down there. We'll follow at a slight distance. Remove the lens cap and get as many photos as possible."

Detective Carl Burghoff entered the area, forcing Charlotte to step aside. She didn't get a chance to ask Michael more questions.

Out of sight, Charlotte and the photographer followed the police along the tunnel. With Carl in tow, Michael led the way, directing the uniformed men toward the space where Joe sat huddled against the wall. The City News photographer moved amongst the constables to get a shot of Joe and the body. Charlotte edged forward, although her heart beat faster than normal. She breathed in the stale air. A pungent stench reached the newcomers before the death images revealed an unimaginable horror. Camera flashes exposed the scene in gory detail. Michael ordered two men to escort the photographer out of the tunnel. Charlotte hid inside a hollow built into the wall. The space was dusty, and cobwebs clung to her hair, but she had a job to do. The public had a right to know what happened in their city. Everything she learned raced inside her head. Her heart told a different story, but she was not giving up her right to a headline. Belief in her abilities as a reporter overshadowed her fears.

Driven to succeed, she advanced further into the tunnel, closer to the body. She couldn't tell if it was Nora. Perhaps Michael was mistaken. She recognized Joe. A policeman stood guard over him. Her spine tingled. She questioned her motives for her presence. She got her story, but her instincts denied Michael's statement that 'Joe is the killer'.

Concerned about Joe's injuries, Charlotte asked herself questions - why hadn't he left the scene if he was guilty? How did he coerce Nora into the tunnels? Where is the murder weapon? Why aren't his knuckles damaged from battering Nora? Her questions scrambled into a gigantic puzzle that perplexed her mind. She was afraid for Joe and didn't understand why.

Something was amiss. She wanted to find out now, not later, if Michael had the answers.

Nerves along the nape of her neck prickled. The memory of when Michael and Joe found her in the tunnel had been erased. She trembled. Maybe he is a killer. For now, she was a journalist at work and brave enough to follow the police into the unknown. She bit hard on the inside of her cheek. She tasted blood and recoiled at the message racing through her mind. Maybe Michael's presence that night saved me. Perhaps Joe had intended to kill me.

Out of sight of Michael and other policemen, she edged out of the hollow and inched her way to the murder scene. Charlotte brushed hard to rid herself of the sticky threads, and whatever creature may have tagged along. Once out of the shadows and into a gloomy light, the death scene tugged her interest to find out more.

Harsh bulbs on portable stands exposed the lifeless shape of Nora. Charlotte screamed when unhinged memories of another time and place surged in her mind. A time when a murderer trapped her inside her Ipswich home. If her neighbour had not phoned the police to report an intruder at Charlotte's back door, she would have been his next victim.

"Get her out of here!" Michael shouted to no one in particular. Charlotte turned and scurried back through the tunnel. Not far behind the group, she paused. She ran the tip of her tongue across the spot where her teeth had drawn blood.

Something niggled at her. She looked at her palms, searching for answers. She rubbed her nose where it itched at the tip. "What are you trying to tell me" Her question aimed at the ceiling as if some spirit hovered above. She rubbed her nose with the back of her hand to stop the twitch. Did she smell something other than death? Her sweaty palms revealed nothing. She bent her head down and put her wrist close to her face to check the time. The whiff of perfume teased her nostrils. She slapped her palms together. She knew the answer and shuddered. Divine7 Cologne aromas lingered in the tunnel and lessened the stench of death.

Chapter Fifty-Five

Joe sat slumped over like a rag doll with his arms wrapped around his knees. Nora's body lay sprawled across the floor, her throat cut and her body bruised and swollen. Charlotte watched a short distance away as the officers approached Joe. "There will have to be an autopsy. Do you know who she is?"

"Yes! she is...er was my friend, Nora Peters. Known her since we were kids, sir." Joe answered with the realisation that any mention of Nora was past tense. He started to mumble, "I should have done more." He didn't appear to be aware of the nearness of the uniformed men until Michael touched him on the shoulder. He looked up at Michael. "Joe, I am taking you into custody for Nora's murder." Handcuffs snapped securely around Joe's wrists.

Before Charlotte moved away, she saw the constables haul Joe to his feet. His shouts resonated deep inside the tunnels. "What the fuck, Mick? You know I didn't do it. Look for the Trilbies! You know who the fuck they are! Look for the lights in the wall!" No one listened. She stepped aside to let the group pass. Joe turned his head toward Charlotte.

"You believe me, don't you?" His question disturbed her.

"Let it go, mate; you're as guilty as hell." One of the men stated.

She indicated she did with a nod of her head, but her heart remained indifferent. She reckoned his ordeal had weakened his internal strength.

"Wait!" he demanded. "I need a doctor! I'm injured." Any movement was slow and painful. His shouts of innocence reverberated off tiled walls. Pushed and half dragged without consideration for his wellbeing, he continued to yell.

The inspector walked near the body and asked the others to stay clear. He ordered Michael to leave the tunnel while he looked around. Michael protested. The officer above Carl took control of the situation and dismissed Michael pending an inquiry, or he face immediate arrest. Carl followed several sets of prints leading into and from – his only description – nowhere.

"Get the department photographer here," Carl ordered. "And after he's done, arrange the body transfer to the morgue. Move it!" The last order intended for the two officers staring at the body did not create a stir of movement. He lost his patience. "Now!" The two constables left the scene and radioed the call through to headquarters. They waited on the kerbside outside the station entrance for the police photographer to arrive with the body van.

It didn't take long for Carl to arrive at a conclusion. Joe had to be the perpetrator unless Michael Devlin knew different. What a fantasy the homeless drunk wove about Angels of Death and taking other young women. In consideration of Joseph Moody's reputation, Carl had reason to charge the man with murder with the first instance, the reporter in the alley, and the disappearance of the redhead as well as this young woman. Convinced of Joe's guilt. Carl left after the body was removed.

Charlotte and her photographer hid until the tunnel was empty of all personnel except for a couple of constables looking for a weapon and other evidence. The bells of the Town Hall clock were silent between the quarter-hour. She glanced at her watch. Plenty of time to catch the print run. The photos will be ready with my story for front-page news tomorrow.

Earlier, Michael followed his senior officer's orders and left the tunnels. Conscience stricken; Michael joined the homeless in Hyde Park rather than head home. At least the locals would leave him alone while he considered his next step. His motives not to substantiate his friend's statement shamed Michael. "Howdy Mick," Harold's voice penetrated the detective's darkening thoughts. The soulful tone put Michael on guard. "G'day."

"What's happening over there?" Harold shifted his arms off his knees and folded them across his chest. "The police are in a bit of a frenzy, so what brings you here and not with your kind?"

Prepared to leave in a hurry, Michael eased his body to balance on the edge of the park seat. "A murder, mate. A dreadful, horrible murder." Tears turned to sobs. "Joe has been arrested for the abductions and murder of that reporter and also for tonight's victim, our friend Nora Peters." Michael wanted to scream to release the torment. The image of Joe sitting dumbstruck near Nora's disfigured body rushed through his mind. A sudden awareness struck him. "I'll thank you for not sharing this moment with anyone Harold. I'm back on the job." Michael rushed off, leaving Harold to ponder what happened to cause the change of heart. Harold was a patient man and positive Michael would share his findings when the time was right.

Before the day ended, Michael phoned Charlotte's workplace. "Will you come to my place after work please? I'll explain when you get here. I need your help. It's about Joe's arrest."

"Dear God, Mick, I thought they would let him go."

"I'll explain it to you when you get here."

Charlotte arrived at the address. Michael's solemn expression and bloodshot eyes indicated a lack of sleep since the morning's events. He grasped Charlotte in a tight embrace then wept. He walked her through the doorway into the living area. The room was in a mess. It didn't take long to piece together that Michael notified the police. "Believe me, Charlotte; I had no choice in the matter. Joe needs protection; I fear for his life. There is something else you need to know; please sit down. This isn't easy." Michael looked around the room, avoiding Charlotte's worried face. He would rather be anywhere else but here in this room right now. "Charlotte, that was Nora's body in the tunnel, and I believe in Joe's innocence. Carl overlooked pieces of crucial evidence important to Joe's case. Joe's clothes and bedding were not covered in blood. A thorough investigation would prove Joe as a witness, not a murderer. Nora's blood was on the opposite side of the tunnel. Splatters were visible on the ceiling and wall behind her. The gash at her throat done from behind would have stained the killer's clothes."

"What do you want me to do?"

"Mention this in your newspaper." Michael twisted his fingers in and out of fist shapes.

"The police will charge Joe with murder based on the fact that he was in the vicinity of the murder." Michael paced back and forth. "Proof! That's what I need. Find a weapon."

Chapter Fifty-Six

Nora's body was finally released to the family. Michael took it upon himself to make all the arrangements for the funeral. Wrought with grief Nora's mother, Mrs Peters, struggled with the knowledge that someone she watched growing up turned out to be a killer. "Michael, you've all known each other since childhood. Is he truly guilty?"

"I know, but Joe is not the same man we knew before the war. Time on the battlefield altered his perspective on reality. I have doubts myself, and I want to believe his innocence, but the evidence puts him at the crime scene. Losing Maddy did not help his mental state either."

"You lost her too, Michael," she said.

"Yes, I did. Their future was all mapped out. She was the light of his life, and he expected to get married and start a family when he returned. Unfortunately, her disappearance snuffed his drive for life. It's a lonely life on the streets, but his weakness for alcohol became his excuse." Hunched in his seat, elbows on his knees, he placed his head in his hands. Life, these past few weeks, turned into an actual horror tale. He withheld his knowledge of the lights and Joe's visions. He knew they existed, but he protected himself from ridicule. He was a police officer first and foremost.

"I'm too old for this. No parent should bury a child. I hope he gets what he deserves." Tears streaked her powdered face.

He changed the topic. "The requiem service is scheduled for Friday at eleven in the morning in St Mary's Cathedral. A choir from her old school will sing the hymns."

"Thank you, Michael; you are the son I never had."

Michael retreated from the house and made his way home. His mind was filled with images of Nora. His pent-up emotions erupted with thoughts of her violent end. The phone rang four times before he could muster himself to answer the call. "Hello," he said.

"Michael, it's Charlotte; I wondered if we might meet somewhere later."

He sucked in a breath before he answered, "Not tonight; I need to be alone."

"I understand, Michael. If you do want company, please call. I'm considering leaving Sydney. I'll see you at the funeral. Bye."

"Bye." Michael placed the receiver on its cradle and began to pace the floor. He wasn't sure if he heard correctly. Charlotte leaving? Was it love or professional protection for Charlotte that distracted his thoughts? Considering the events of the past weeks, he struggled to define the emotion. He knew for certain he would miss her, but could he keep her in Sydney? He needed to discuss her decision. Tonight was not the time.

Friday was a time for final goodbyes to a friend whose demise tore at his heart and scarred his soul. He was determined to stand by Joe above everything else. He knew Joe inside and out, and he knew him incapable of such a despicable act of violence even in battle. *Or was he? Do I truly know him? I just have to get through today.*

At least a hundred people entered the cathedral, and most signed the visitors' book. Charlotte sat beside Michael and held his hand. Mrs Peters sat closest to the centre aisle. Her white lace handkerchief dabbed away tears. Michael thought she would need help through all this and put an arm around her. She turned and smiled, unable to speak. At the conclusion of the mass, the congregation spilled out into the street. The internment was a private affair with a small group of close friends and family at the cemetery to lay Nora to rest.

Muffled sobs disturbed the quiet of the graveyard as the sombre faced men lowered the coffin. "Ashes to ashes, dust to dust." Those few words echoed in Michael's head. He looked around at the friends and relatives gathered for the last moments. *Joe should be here.* He turned to Charlotte and, in a low voice, said, "I don't believe Joe could do this to Nora." He knew Joe was not mentally unbalanced. His sin was that of a disillusioned soldier who suffered from battle fatigue.

Charlotte heard him speak but could not decipher his words. She felt afraid. Her body tensed. Her senses reeled. The feeling was unimaginable. A faint odour wafted toward her. It was strange that the Divine7 essence rode the outdoor breeze. She was in mortal danger. She trembled beside Michael. Her eyes darted about, but she saw nothing but shady trees and gravestones.

At first, he thought her tremors were part of the pressure of the moment. His gaze stretched beyond the mourners, where a stranger lurked in the shadows. He wondered who he was and if he should know him. He glared at the strange man dressed in long robes. The man moved away accompanied by a man wearing a trilby. "My God!" he exclaimed, then found himself the centre of attention. His outburst was accepted as part of his grief. He knew otherwise. He pulled Charlotte closer. She was ashen. He did not want to alarm her, so he remained quiet.

"Charlotte, we need to talk as soon as this is over." He clasped Charlotte's hand tighter to protect her at all costs. He was puzzled why he should see the mysterious Trilbies in the cemetery. He wanted to follow them, but he knew that would be futile in a graveyard full of monuments and thickets of bush. "I believe you are in danger."

Alarmed at Michael's tone, she stammered a whisper. "Christ, Michael, don't scare me." Charlotte turned her head toward his shoulder and, in doing so, knocked her hat askew. She deftly adjusted the fit before she whispered. "Not now, please. Later."

"Are you going back to the Peters' place?" Michael asked. "It's important I tell you what's happening around you."

"Like what, Michael." Her voice acidic and her tone fractious, she altered her stance away from Michael. Charlotte meant to show anger to hide her true feelings from this man. Too much happened over the past three months to nurture herself. Mourners nearby glared in her direction.

He bent his head to her level. "I don't think you understand how vulnerable you are when you go off on your own."

"I'm a big girl, Michael, and quite capable of looking after myself." She pulled her gloved hand away from his grip. She pinched the sides of her clutch purse.

"Oh sure, like when we found you in the tunnel and rescued you, if you remember."

"How dare you, I don't trust you anymore." To widen the gap between their bodies, "I have no recollection whatsoever of events that left me alone with you and your so called friend in an abandoned tunnel."

Before Charlotte edged away, she whispered. "And one of you is charged with this girl's murder." Embarrassed by the stern stares from family members and mourners, she moved to the back of the gathering.

Michael did not follow. *Fucking women. Why doesn't she understand I'm grieving the loss of a dear friend. I owe it to Nora to be here. To say goodbye.*

Once the coffin was lowered, and mourners began to leave, Michael scoured the cemetery for Charlotte. He found her standing in front of the left wing of the nearest tombstone angel. His irritation melted when he noticed how forlorn she looked compared to the compassionate features of the stone angel.

Although wary of the Trilbies lurking inside the perimeter of the graveyard, empathy surfaced when he caught up to Charlotte. He apologised for his behaviour and wrapped an arm around her waist to hold her even closer to save her from any impending threat. As a good detective, he perceived the Trilbies haven't finished the job and are planning something... *they are near.*

Chapter Fifty-Seven

Headlines on newsstands where paperboys shouted – 'Tunnel Murder Trial Starts Today'. Charlotte's article made front-page news. For some reason, her anticipated elation remained hidden even though Joe's mental state and living standards shook her belief in the man's innocence. The press section in the courtroom filled when the doors opened. Charlotte sat on the end seat in preparation to escape back to the newsroom with an update for the late edition.

When he approached the press section, Michael said to Charlotte, "I'll get him a good lawyer and help as much as I can. We need to find some evidence to free Joe."

"I'm working with your lot from a journalistic point of view. I have been investigating Mrs Park and the boarding house."

"I wasn't aware of that, Charlotte. Do you know anything that might help Joe?"

"Only suspicions at the moment, Michael. When I link all the details, I'll let you know." She saw the disappointment in his eyes.

"There is something strange going on in the tunnels where Joe slept. If it is Joe, which I seriously doubt, anything I tell you might influence Joe's defence in a negative way."

"You're right, of course; silly of me to think otherwise. What about Nora? What happened, and why was Joe arrested?"

Michael related the story from when Joe phoned, and they met at the tunnel. "The inspector is convinced Joe committed the murder, and that I'm an accessory. Can you believe it? If I'm charged for anything, it should be to protect Joe from whoever killed Nora. The chief believes Joe lured Nora into the tunnel and worked her over." Michael felt a wave of powerlessness wash over him as he voiced his thoughts, "is he insane? Not sure, but I do know Joe would not hurt Nora. God, they've known each other since they were kids. That's about it, Charlotte, except the charges now include Magda and Brian as well as the others."

The clerk of the court announced to the public, "Court is in session. All stand." Charlotte's position in the press section allowed her full view of the court officials and defendant. Michael sat behind the defence counsel, eager to see Joe. Joe entered the dock, where a guard removed the cuffs. He sat when told and peered at his feet. *Could've done with a shine today. How absurd.* He couldn't remember when he last polished his shoes. *Ah! Yes! Shiny boots for parade before the march to the ships that transported eager young men off to war. What a fiasco, the silent dead or the wounded screaming in pain and then there were those who froze in battle.*

A tear dropped from his eye. He hastily brushed it away before tremors racked through his body. Withdrawal symptoms invaded his nervous system in an unexpected rush. He gripped the handrail to steady himself. Sweat oozed from his pores, saturating the shirt on his back, underarms and neck. His feet felt like he was back in the jungle of New Guinea fighting the Japs. *What a mess I've become.*

Joe sensed Michael's discomfort. Both men avoided acknowledgment of the other. There were no words to resolve the issue between them. Joe's future was at stake over the coming days. There was nowhere on earth he could hide. In fact, he didn't want to hide anymore. His addled brain still vowed revenge on Nora's killer and he vowed to keep his oath alive until the right time presented.

The judge ruled an adjournment until two in the afternoon. At least his friend Mick had the decency to appoint a reputable defence lawyer. Uncertain of the outcome, he had no choice but to heed the lawyer's advice. "Plead reasons of insanity, Joe. It's your only hope of sympathy from the jurors." Weak and miserable, Joe agreed. He had a better chance of getting out of a psych ward than prison. With that thought uppermost, he concentrated on the debate between prosecution and defence.

The hearing didn't last long. The prosecution held all the cards, and it depended on which way the dice rolled. A jury might find a lesser charge or, at best, not guilty if the judge accepted the insanity plea. Thoughts drifted in and out of his head; he remembered the night he phoned Michael about the body of a woman dumped near his bed. He had no explanation for the red shoes or the blood splatters up the opposite wall. *Body didn't get up and walk. Where did it go?* By this stage, he tried to convince himself that the body didn't exist. *But the shoes. Those fucking shoes. Jesus, why me?* Evidence piled up against Joe, his mind shifted to the scene in the tunnel. He was positive the red shoes belonged to the body. Next was Nora - damaged and lifeless. Joe knew how she suffered. He admitted he saw what had happened to Nora. His statement matched the coroner's report on her death. He had convinced himself that the Angels of Death were the culprits. He declared his innocence from the start. They were the ones he nicknamed the Trilbies, not Angels. Angels have wings according to the art world and religious societies. He sighed and clutched his ribs. Healing in that area of the body was slow. The bruises on his face had faded, but the scars marred deep within his soul.

Charlotte's statement proved useless. Her memory lapse about events before waking in the tunnels chipped away at his defence. He was in the vicinity when Brian died and with Nora the night she was brutally murdered.

The prosecutor's hypothesis placed Joe in and around the area where young women disappeared. Joe dry retched when the lawyers presented the ugly photographs of Nora's body to the court. He looked for Michael but only saw a grimace on his face. There was no eye contact. He trusted Michael, but found himself defenceless against the painful sting of betrayal.

The only point in Joe's favour was that not a droplet of blood marked his clothing. The prosecutor made no mention of this fact. The defence lawyer picked up on this deliberate omission of his opponent. Joe continued to analyse each moment of the past three months without conclusion. The Judge declared an adjournment for lunch.

Joe noticed Michael watching him leave the courtroom. How could he convince Michael of his innocence? He was an innocent bystander to sinister and evil acts. *Why didn't Mick own up about seeing the bloody faceless thugs?*

The courtroom was filled with reporters and public spectators. Joe nodded to Charlotte with her notebook ready and sitting beside someone he didn't know. It broke his heart when she turned away. *Bloody ingrate! Who knows where she might have ended up if it wasn't for me and Mick.* He asked the guard for some water to distract himself. He listened to the defence lawyer argue his case. "Joe suffered a nervous disposition from his years at war." He emphasised the trauma suffered by many of the returned men and women. His speech took a swipe at the government's ignorance of returned servicemen and women and their needs.

The lawyer admitted that circumstantial evidence pointed at Joe. He accentuated that none of the investigators examined his client's clothing or bedding. "The evidence presented to this court today is insufficient to convict a man for these crimes. What the prosecutor brought forward is all circumstantial." He argued the case admirably. He suggested that his client undergo a mental assessment in a psychiatric ward before a trial.

The judge called for both lawyers to approach the bench. He asked the prosecutor if he was in agreement. The prosecuting counsel agreed, although confident of the defendant's guilt.

The judge ruled "admission to a psychiatric ward for Joseph Moody to determine his state of mind. The trial will recommence at a later date." The few people in the court rose when the judge exited the room. Meeting Michael's eyes, Joe shrugged his shoulders in a way that revealed utter despair.

Back in a holding cell, Joe fell asleep, overcome by a mixture of emotions, fear, and exhaustion. A fit of tremors woke him. The duty officer in the cells recognized the symptoms of delirium tremens and rang the emergency bell. Before the nurse injected the syringe with a sedative, he said, "I got a solid case of jitters, Nurse. I missed Nora's funeral."

Chapter Fifty-Eight

Harold established a shoeshine stand near a men's barbershop not far from St James Station. He kept old rags, brushes and tins of polish in an apple crate. Men of all ages and backgrounds sat outside on an old wooden bench backed against the window to wait their turn. Harold polished the shoes of anyone willing to spend a few coins while they caught up on the daily news. Some well-dressed gents tipped with pound notes. A multitude of headlines to discuss. One particular incident occurred in his neighbourhood. The arrest of a man who committed murder in the tunnels. Opinions of a returned soldier's arrest for murder and abduction ensured lively discussions.

Some came for haircuts as well. A win-win for both the barber and Harold. The money he earned helped provide extra food for his homeless community. Courteous chit chat passed between the shoeshine man and his customers. Conversation, except with his regulars, narrowed to politeness. He kept rubbing at the leather until the shine returned.

He responded to discussions with his customers about the daily news. "No, sir, I didn't know about that." Or he asked questions. "How's the family? Did your son settle down after his return from the war? Yes, sir, too many lives lost and will the world be better off or have the powers looked at new methods of warfare? What do you think about rebuilding whole cities and how countries stake claims on others?"

Michael stood nearby. He leaned back against a store window with his hands in his pockets and head bowed. His double-breasted suit, limp from overuse, hung like an old rag on a peg. The past few days gave him little time to care about his appearance. His suit was crumpled and dirty as was his shirt. His tie end flapped in the wind smacking his cheek. He tucked the loose ends between his shirt buttons. He lost his tie pin somewhere in the tunnel. A gift from his dad. *Too late for remorse. It vanished as quickly as those girls.*

His hat brim sat low across his brow. He hid his face to avoid recognition from strangers. A recent photograph of himself glared from the front page of City News. No doubt Charlie's offsider took that snapshot. Movement along the bench. He had all day to wait. His excuse to talk with Harold.

The red and white striped barbershop pole stood silent and motionless, much like himself.

His childhood friends were gone or, in Joe's case, waiting for a medical assessment. *Any menace to society ought to have the book thrown at him. I let him down. I saw the bloody thugs in the tunnel, and we both rescued Charlie. What held me back? Fear, cowardice or lack of proof.* At the time, Michael withheld information about the Trilbies and blue lights in fear of ridicule or judgement or misrepresentation of the truth to protect his friend. A decision he regretted and found hard to justify. Nothing helped. Joe's arrest unnerved him. His will to explore the truth and locate proof of the Trilbies' existence increased.

Madness contaminated their lives in these past three months of hell. His superiors slapped him on the back with gratitude for solving Nora's murder, and then doubts about Michael's inclusion as a suspect crept into the investigation. Michael lived with his own doubts. The investigation ended.

Michael read the headlines earlier in the day before he left for the city to talk with Harold. The police got their man - Joseph Moody, a returned vet who suffers anxiety neurosis. What a load of bulldust.

Then, of course, the one who stole his heart. He missed Charlotte. He was miserable. He avoided work colleagues whenever he could. Loneliness possesses no shadow. *Maybe that's why Joe liked the tunnels - alone with only shadows and his nightmares. We all did our jobs to the best of our abilities. Have to put things right in all areas of my life. The first priority is helping Joe.*

Impatient for the last of the waiting customers to leave, Michael shifted from one leg to the other. He studied the men stepping in and out of the barbershop. *Anyone of these could be the killer?*

He was angry with himself for not taking the investigation further. He, too, had seen the Trilbies the night they rescued

Charlotte. He recalled she had no recollection of how she came to be in the tunnel. He and Joe waited until she woke from some drug-induced state. She believed they were the cause of those bizarre circumstances. *Who could blame her? Her statement would be prejudicial to Joe's cause. She suffered a bump to her head when she fell out of the grip of one of the thugs. A noteworthy bruise had also appeared on her upper arm.*

Harold's voice stirred Michael from his contemplation. "Yes, sir, it is a little chilly today. That'll be five bob, thanks." The gent paid Harold in loose change. Harold recognised his next customer. "Hello, Mr Devlin. How are things? Will you be seeing Joe today?"

"Not sure, Harold. I've got him in quite a pickle, don't you think? Is Joe capable of these crimes?" He had asked himself this question numerous times since Nora's murder. In a nervous impulse, Michael slid his palms back and forth along his trouser creases over his knees. His mind was restless, with time wasted while on suspension. Dark shadows accentuated his sleep-deprived bloodshot eyes.

"Can't rightly say one way or another, sir, war does strange things to a man. Joe's frequent bouts of wild behaviour petrified all the folk around the park."

Michael leaned forward to whisper, "Does he frighten you, Harold?" The detective hunched over and waited for a response.

"Nah, Mr Devlin. I know a lot of men like him, and it is all show no go. Now I'm not saying he did or didn't murder that young woman. Those tunnels are dark and mysterious, and Joe keeps to himself and hasn't made any friends there. He does talk with me sometimes about his past but not about his recent past except for his Angels of Death."

The answer was not what he expected, but his heart quickened with surprise. "Joe shared his visions with you?"

"Sure did. According to Joe, the men he talks about stalk the tunnels late at night and take bodies into a blue light. What a nightmare!" Harold ceased moving the cloth across Michael's shoes. He straightened his neck. "Odd how none of the others noticed Joe's angels of death unless they are more frightened of them than they are of Joe. People tend to keep to themselves down there. It's a private community."

"I understand, Harold. The constables had a hard time collecting information from the groups. I'm not sure what to believe myself, but he is my friend."

"You and he go back a long way, don't you?"

"Yes, we do. Bloody difficult to turn your back on a friend no matter what. I am torn about which direction to pursue."

"I'll tell you what. Why don't I keep my eyes and ears open and speak with a couple of the locals and see what I can find out? You meet me back here on Friday, and I will pass on any information I get." Harold leaned back to admire his work. "There, good as new, and the shine's on me, Michael!"

"Thanks, Harold, but here's a fiver to help. See you Friday."

"Thanks, Michael. Much appreciated. Oh! Just remembered, Joe said his angels wear Trilbies. Ain't that the oddest thing?"

"I reckon, Harold." Michael tucked his wallet into the inside pocket of his suit jacket and turned to head back home, leaving Harold to pack up for the night. A pretty good spot. Shoeshine while waiting for a haircut or shave - top to bottom treatment. Michael often paced along the streets, but this day he meandered along the pavement. Pedestrians rushed past him in all directions. He paused on the corner to stare at the bus stop where two of the girls had disappeared.

A strange odour wafted from nearby; the sensation unsettled him. A memory provoked him. *Charlie's mentioned a particular cologne before. What was it? Did it have something to do with the Trilbies? Time for a snoop around the tunnels. Suspended without pay until further notice. What a bloody joke.*

Any witnesses to inexplicable incidents inside the tunnels at St James were gone. Michael's guilt invaded his thoughts with each step. Michael failed in every aspect of friendship. He struggled to forgive himself for not defending Joe.

Chapter Fifty-Nine

Admission into a secure ward at the nearest hospital for mental diagnosis was quick. Joe struggled to free himself from the four burly men in white coats. A nurse jabbed him with a syringe containing a sedative. When the drug took effect, he was stripped and dressed in hospital pyjamas. A straight jacket secured his arms. He was lifted onto a small bed on his right side to enable staff to perform routine observations.

The psychiatric doctor walked into the room accompanied by Detective Devlin. Unprepared to see his friend bound and drugged, he asked, "Is this really necessary?"

"It's for his protection." The doctor removed his stethoscope with one swoop of his hands.

"Protection from what?" Michael demanded.

The doctor shrugged his shoulders. "Routine procedure. He can't harm himself or others while restricted. His health is well below par, but I believe Mr Moody possesses an underlying strength in his anger. After his outbursts, he denies mad behaviour. Under sedation, his true self will surface, despite your misgivings."

The doctor continued without convincing Michael of Joe's capability of violent acts. "We will conduct some tests here to determine the cause of the patient's fits and rages. Perhaps even use shock therapy if necessary."

"There'll be none of that, Doctor, without my consent." Michael was adamant that Joe needed his help more than ever. If it was up to him, Joe would be released into his care. Until the incidents in the tunnels were resolved, there was little he could do. Joe was in a semiconscious state but stared at the doctor. "Perhaps the police have some answers," Michael said aloud in case Joe could hear him. "Bye, Joe, I'll come by tomorrow, take care, and be good for the old doc, eh!"

Joe suffered agonising withdrawal pains from the alcohol his body had infused. His internal organs retaliated with such force he thought he would die. Constant sweat saturated his clothing as well as his bedding. The doctors helped as much as they could. Within a month, he was back in the ward with patients with various mental disorders. Now that he felt sober, his only chance of improving his fitness level was to rely on the army exercise regime. It was tough going, but he managed to set himself a goal between bed checks.

His escape from this place had yet to be planned, with only three weeks left to finalise the details before his court appearance. His body began to ache from extreme exercise as the withdrawal symptoms dissipated. He walked in the gardens each morning to strengthen the ligaments and muscles in his legs. His one desire, above all else, was to improve his physical condition. A task that was once easy now required mental stamina as well. An attainable goal based on his army training. His mission – revenge.

Heavy showers and gusty winds matched Michael's mood, so he decided to walk to the hospital. In hindsight, a taxi might have been a better choice, as the wintry weather did little to appease his anxiety. Michael buttoned up his trench coat to ward off the chill. Questions without answers rolled through his thoughts. Who would believe his and Joe's story of the blue lights concealing a passage to nowhere when his own mind strained to accept what occurred that night?

He wondered what might have happened to Charlotte if he hadn't been in the tunnel with Joe.

For once, the weather bureau was right. Discarded leaves tossed in all directions, and an overcast sky mirrored the gloom in his heart. His best friend was charged with murder. He entered the hospital, taking two steps at a time. Melancholy held his mood despite the physical exertion. Once inside the foyer, he inhaled deeply, then exhaled slowly to embrace the radiator's warmth. He loosened his coat and made his way to the front desk. His shoes squelched on the over-polished floor announcing his arrival.

"Yes?" The question came from the surly middle-aged woman seated at the desk. Her high-pitched voice in contrast to her build. The receptionist emphasised Michael report to the ward doctor or sister-in-charge before visiting.

Once the preliminary introductions passed scrutiny, Michael met with the doctor, who explained the results of Joe's blood tests. "Pathology reports show traces of an unknown substance, thus deemed self-made and requires further examination." After the doctor placed the papers inside his patient's file, he folded his arms across his chest. The next comment stirred the detective's principles of law enforcement. "I believe Mr Moody gathered substances for his own purposes and made a concoction which activates abnormal outbursts or performances of heinous acts at times outside his control."

Michael stared down the doctor in disbelief. The statement contradicted everything Michael knew about his friend. Drugs of any type played no part in his life. Alcohol annihilated the demonic nightmares haunting Joe, or so Michael believed. He supplied the amber fluid often enough to know his friend did not resort to other methods. Nothing in Joe's possessions resembled utensils required to experiment with drugs, let alone unknown types. Michael broke the silence between himself and the doctor. "I'd like to visit my friend."

"Yes, of course." The doctor moved to open the door, and Michael left the room without a backward glance.

Isolated for a week and in a ward, Joe sighted Michael enter the room. "G'day mate,"

"Right back at you, Joe. It's good to see you too. Got any good news? I hear you are getting the alcohol out of your system."

They made their way to the visitors' room. "Yeah, the tremors are bad." Joe leaned forward. "Why did you agree with the other cops that day? I told you what happened, and you said you believed me."

"That was the hardest thing I've ever done, Joe." Michael rubbed his hand beneath his collar. I had to get back up for your own good, and your safety was of utmost importance."

"So you say, Mick." Joe slouched in his chair.

"All I could think about was that you, my best friend, could have murdered Nora. I asked myself if you were unaware of your actions."

"Now look here, mate!" Joe's temper flared. A nurse hovered nearby; Joe saw the nod to a wardsman. He leaned back further and smiled - a fake smile.

Alerted by the shift in Joe's mood, he spoke with a calmness in conflict with his mind. "Nobody would have believed us, Joe." Michael checked his watch. He reckoned he had plenty of time left for the visit.

Both remained quiet. For a brief moment, the sun appeared between clouds to warm the earth and sparkle in puddles on the grounds outside. Peace ribboned between the men. Laughter peeled from across the gardens. "Long time since I heard someone laugh."

The visible pain in Joe's voice brought Michael back to the present. "Charlotte is a sort of witness, Joe. I know what we saw in the tunnel, and I know in my heart you did not murder anyone."

Joe was quick to pick up on the first bit. "What do you mean? Sort of?"

"She was unconscious at the time, remember, and she didn't know what had happened to her."

"I suppose so, Mick. That would explain her fear of us when she came round. Pity we didn't get help then."

"Hindsight's a wonderful gift."

Joe's nervous habit of rapidly shaking his leg returned. Joe shifted in his seat and looked straight at his friend. "Am I supposed to find that funny?"

"I will get you out of this, Joe, I promise. Be patient until your assessment is over for the hearing."

"Nah! I'll be gone by then."

"What do you mean, gone?" Shocked at the implication, he glared at Joe, who did not flinch. His plans were well underway. "Yep! Just that! I plan to get out of here one way or the other. The staff here bullies everyone in their care. I found a weak spot in the system. Watch this space!" Confidence emanated from Joe.

Michael attempted to make his friend understand the foolishness of his decision and pointed out the certainty of an unfavourable outcome. "Joe, be sensible for once in your life. No risks this time. Your life is on the line here."

Joe gritted his teeth, "This is warfare." He relaxed when he noticed the strain on his friend's jawline. "It's quite exciting to be back in the jungles outwitting the enemy."

Michael unclenched his jaw. "C'mon, mate, don't be thinking like that!"

"Why shouldn't I? Some creature murdered Nora. Right in front of me. And don't forget the corpse that disappeared without her shoes. The evidence stacks up against me. I hate this place and everything it stands for!" Joe jumped to his feet and paced back and forth, tightening his fists inside his pockets. The large open space of the visitors' room allowed small groups to gather in semi-privacy while nurses and wardsmen wandered the perimeter.

The murmur of conversations ceased at the sound of raised voices. All eyes turned toward the two men arguing about murders. Michael heard the squeak of rubber soles on linoleum floors edging from behind; he lowered his voice. "Let's take a stroll outside." Joe shuffled after him toward the open French doors into the garden. Chatter filled the room as they left.

Michael led Joe to a garden seat beneath an old fig tree. He wished they could be the carefree children they once were and climb the sturdy trunk. In silence, they sat listening to the hustle and bustle outside the walled garden. The sky turned a dull grey once the clouds dismissed the sun. Oversized striped hospital pyjamas and gown sagged over Joe's body. A wardsman brought a small blanket to wrap around his patient to ward off the afternoon chill as an excuse to ensure Joe had calmed down.

Michael spoke first. "Well, supposing you do get out, how far will you get?" He wanted to convince his friend of the futility of escape.

A sly grin broke across Joe's face "The other side of nowhere to search for Maddy."

Michael understood the meaning. "For Christ's sake, Joe, Maddy's been gone for over a year now; get over it!" He wanted to shake Joe to rid him of his senseless ideas.

"Aren't you just a little curious? If these Trilbies have taken Maddy, I intend to find her and bring her back. Just you wait and see, mate!" Bristled with determination, nothing would deter him from his plans.

"Jesus, Joe, you're not thinking straight." Michael rose from the seat and placed his hands in his pockets. He stubbed invisible stones where the grass had thinned. Perhaps Joe is the one to solve the puzzle of the mysterious Trilbies and their mission.

"My head has never been clearer since I came back. That old hag you talk about from the boarding house is likely involved in some way. All I have to do is get out of here and wait in the tunnel. If you don't want to help, I understand. The least you can do is deny we had this conversation. I'm not going to jail for something I didn't do. Best we do what we do well, eh, Mick."

Michael smiled and knew in his heart that Joe was on a mission. In the blink of an eye, Joe shouted obscenities at his visitor. Michael remained calm, understanding Joe's motives but unsure if the chosen path was right for anyone. An orderly appeared. Other staff rushed outside, but the burly wardsman restrained Joe in a wrestling hold. Joe could not move. Michael saw the grin on his friend's face as he relaxed to conserve his energy. "Leave this to us, sir." Joe jerked at the sensation of a syringe piercing his skin, and Michael left, wondering if all that was necessary. He reassured himself that Joe was a master of trickery and he would use the craft for a good purpose.

A patient whose bed was next to Joe's attempted to befriend him. "You trying to get back home?"

"Aren't we all?" Joe answered.

"You talk in your sleep, and I'm telling you I've seen those bastards you dream about. That's how I ended up here in the loony bin." The man shifted to his side to look at Joe.

"You don't say." Joe rolled away and thought the man insane to pick up on his nightmares.

"I'll help you get out of this place. You wait and see."

Joe raised his voice above a whisper. "Leave me alone. I don't need your help."

The next morning, during his walk in the garden, elation and fear tumbled through his mind - one after the other plunging him into despair. Sunshine streamed through the trees illuminating the thorned stalks in the rose garden and jaded hydrangeas in their last bloom. A headache pounded inside his temples. Frustrated by mixed emotions, Joe sought the dull interior of the common area indoors. An unforeseen opportunity arose during the evening's medication round.

Before lights out, Joe's newfound friend began pacing the room. "Time has come. The time is now. You will be free." His ranting and ravings disturbed the patients in the ward. The man upturned beds where fellow inmates slept. The room was in turmoil. Joe so wanted to knock this fellow's head off. He restrained himself from involvement. Through the strengthened glass window of the door, he could see the staff unlocking the door. His quick instincts noted the flaw. He made use of the knowledge. The staff blundered through and tackled the man causing the ruckus. Patients were lying on the floor, scared and with broken bones. Joe snatched the opportunity to move quickly through the door and close it behind him. In all the confusion, the staff member left his keys in the lock.

Joe noticed the grin on the man's face in the kerfuffle. A signal. Joe nodded and locked the door behind him. He punched the fire alarm to alert emergency services then waited outside in the garden. This was better than anything he could have planned; he needed to keep his wits about him. He ensured he was counted in the roll call and, when he was handed a blanket, made his way through the front gate and outside the grounds before anyone noticed. He had little time to escape. Michael's place was out of the question. That would be the first place the cops would look for him. He ran for his life to St James railway station; he had no choice. The tunnel held the secret for his chance to the other side.

CHAPTER SIXTY

Long strides between short sprints on wet footpaths gave no leeway for speed. Short of breath, with one more street to cross at St James tunnels. Joe stood on the pavement where shadows met between the street lamps. A hint of rain sweetened the night air.

Police stomped about Hyde Park to questioned everyone in the vicinity. Joe heard someone shout a warning. "A dangerous fugitive is on the run." He shuffled like an old man toward the bushy shrubs and jumped with fright when a skeletal hand gripped his elbow. "Easy! Boyo!" Harold whispered. "In a bit of strife, I hear."

Joe blended into the leafy shrub to stand beside Harold. "Yeah! More than a bit, some would say. I'm innocent, but they won't believe me."

"I know, Joe. How can I help, mate?"

Short of time to ask how he knew. Joe needed help to disappear. "I'm in a hurry. Got to get to the tunnels, mate.

Harold's sharp instructions prompted Joe to accept the offer to swap coats and hats. Joe agreed. "My slippers are scruffy enough, and if I stoop a little, we could easily pass off as the other."

"Okay, by me. I haven't had this much fun since before the war when a mate and I hoodwinked the sergeant. Here, take the knapsack as well and leave it inside the first tunnel. Off with you, lad, and we might see each other sooner than you think." Harold withheld his secrets.

"Thanks, Harold; I'll never forget this. I may not get back." The exchange was quick.

Harold kept his own thoughts. *The Angels of Death, I know them well. Never thought an angel could look like they do, especially angels who wear Trilbies. I think you are the man for the job.* "You ready, Joe? Let's lose these bloody wallopers. The blokes in the park could do with a bit of fun. We'll distract them long enough for you to get over the road and into the tunnels. Good Luck, Joe! And God Bless!"

Joe didn't hear Harold wish him a safe journey. The police runners headed their way. Harold was good for his word; he and his crowd created a ruckus whereby all the police converged on them. Harold danced in the fountain with the hospital blanket held high above his head. He whooped and shouted obscenities at all and sundry. The police believed they had found their man. Harold's mates from the park joined in, and soon it was a free-for-all.

A great visual memory to take wherever he was going. Joe managed to get as far as the tunnel entrance before a policeman spotted him. The officer's assignment to canvas the commuters on the platform placed him in full view of Joe. A shrill whistle pitched above the noise of the incoming train. Joe scrambled down the stairs as best he could against the rush of passengers heading for the exit. The constable could only watch the descent while he waited for his colleagues.

Joe knew exactly where he was going. He didn't know if he would survive or not; it was his only chance to avoid prison. He had no future if the police caught him. He heard the walloper's heavy boots pounding through the hollow chambers. Torch beams radiated arcs of light.

Joe removed the rucksack and left it as per Harold's instructions. He went straight to where he had stashed the piece of opal. The rock was rough and uncut. It was a chunk from a larger piece. The thought of what he was about to do almost overwhelmed him.

Shouts. No time to lose. He held his breath as he pressed the opal against the marks on the wall. Nothing happened. He looked at it. His hands trembled. He almost dropped it. It was the same piece he found on the floor the night Nora died. He had tested the piece one night when he couldn't sleep. Torch beams bounced off the walls. Fractured light on the rivulets of water seepage emitted images of scattered diamonds.

The front runners were about to catch up with Joe. The tunnels split in different directions. Like a wild pack of dogs on a hunt for prey, they re-assembled only to divide at a tunnel junction. Joe's muscles tensed with a heightened awareness of the proximity of those who chased him.

The menace of tentacles from torch beams reached out to snare him. His only thought was to open the gateway and step into the unknown. There was no guarantee of survival. The only sure thing was capture and a life behind bars.

For an odd reason he could not explain to himself, he recalled his father's death. *Why now? Am I taking my own life? Fuck! Maybe I am. But not in the cowardly fashion of my old man.* His thoughts rambled back to that day. He couldn't tell his mother what was happening in the shed that fateful day. He peeped through a gap in the wall and watched his father coil up a length of rope attached to a ceiling beam. He watched him put his head in the noose and then step off the chair as if alighting from a train. He saw the jerks and the bulging of his father's eyes as his face turned blue. Mesmerized, he stood silent, unable to move for what seemed like hours. He never saw his mother again. He was sent off to live with his aunt. His mother never forgave him. She could not understand why Joe did nothing.

In his child's mind, he thought it was a game. He didn't run or do anything to prevent his father's death. His feet planted on the spot. He stood in his own puddle of urine. He tormented himself with the knowledge that his father saw him peering through the wall. It was too late; he was past the point of no return. He struggled with his decision but finally convinced himself to ignite the lights without analysing the outcome.

He was about to step into the unknown. *Who knows, there might be freedom from my nightmares. Death or solace in another world, or better still, I might find Maddy.*

Blue flashes of light appeared the instant he placed the opal with the bright side against the markings. No second guess about his decision. He rushed into the vortex and disappeared, or so it seemed to the police who had pursued him. Vanished before their eyes. They had some explaining to do with their superiors.

Harold and a couple of others stayed in police cells overnight. "Misdemeanours in a public place." the officer said of the charges. Harold was questioned several times about the blanket and clothes he was wearing. He stuck to his story. He thought some angel left them because his clothes were getting so tattered. He also stated the angels of death collected Joe. The investigator thought otherwise.

Chapter Sixty-One

Michael woke with mixed feelings about the forthcoming hours. The thought of final farewells with Charlotte filled his heart with sadness. The dilemma he faced over breakfast was whether he pursued Charlie or left her to follow her own path. His toast burnt in the machine.

He tossed the slices in the waste. He drank his lukewarm tea while he mulled over his thoughts. His thoughts were only of her. She was leaving for good, and he wasn't ready to profess his feelings in a meaningful way. What am I to do? The sound of his own voice roused him.

Dirty dishes had piled in the sink over the past two days. He looked at them, hoping that they would disappear. Must get a cleaner. Not at all like Mister Neat and Tidy, as Joe used to say. Ah! And then there is Joe or was Joe. *Can't believe I'll never see him again. How will I cope without Charlotte? She knows as much as I do about the events of the past few months.* His mind retraced the steps that brought them together. Charlotte reported Magda missing.

His first interview with Charlotte was when Brian had asked if Madelaine's disappearance was linked to the latest missing girls. Magda was his sister's best friend and confidante. Perhaps he should revisit her file in unsolved records. Red shoes found in the tunnel were held as evidence. Charlotte's description of Magda's new shoes matched the pair found in the tunnel. Michael concluded that the body Joe saw before it disappeared belonged to Magda. Each recollection began to reflect a jigsaw.

The next crime put Charlotte in the tunnel, followed by Brian's death in the alley in front of Charlie. Was Charlie the target? He had no proof. The last crime was the most upsetting. Evil visited the tunnels the night Nora met her fate; what a horrible way to die with her friend Joe to witness the brutality.

Joe, my best friend from childhood, the only person I trusted and relied upon in our youth. I could blame the war. Maybe I should. It certainly affected Joe in a way I could never understand. His bloody Angels of Death wreaked havoc in our lives. I want to believe that he was not the killer. He couldn't be.

Michael paced the hallway back and forth until his thoughts cleared. *Of course, he is not the killer. I am a coward and looked after myself rather than defend Joe. I saw with my own eyes the men who carried Charlie out of those fucking lights. We rescued her, although she took some convincing. She had no recollection of how or why she was in the tunnels. Her last memory was a visit to the doctor. Joe's gone too, lured deeper into the shadows of the gaping tunnels. Lost forever? I hope not. Time to say goodbye to another. Perhaps she is wise enough to see a better future for herself and, of course, her safety. She would be at risk staying on in Sydney. I couldn't bear to lose her like the others.* The clock struck the hour. It was time to drive to the boarding house to collect Charlotte.

Charlotte waited on the porch for Michael to arrive. She and Mrs Park exchanged surly goodbyes. The woman's continual wringing of hands in her apron scrunched the fabric into knots.

"Home is where I need to be, Mrs Park. There are too many memories here. I look for Magda every day and if only she had…"

The landlady interrupted her. "All the ifs and buts won't bring her back, love." She clasped Charlotte's hand between her own. "None of us know what the future holds for us, dearie, none of us." Emotional, and her usual instinctive nature shut off, Charlotte missed the cold, calculated glare that belied the tone of the woman's voice.

The topic quickly changed, so her secrets would remain her own. "Well, I've to be at my brother's place in half an hour, so it's until we meet again. Did you leave a forwarding address?" "Yes, I left a note on the sideboard."

Urtha Park gave Charlotte one last look. "Take good care of yourself."

Charlotte withdrew from the landlady's offered hand and politely answered. "Goodbye, Mrs Park. I doubt if I will ever return to Sydney." Charlotte fumbled in her purse for a handkerchief to dab the welling tears. "Too much sadness here. Thank you just the same."

"Glad to have been a help. I told you I look after my girls. The angels bring them to me. I'll be off now."

Charlotte watched the woman walk along the path to the gate. Her suspicions remained unfounded. Without proof, the boarding house stood as it had been when Charlotte arrived. Only with new boarders. A shiver threaded along Charlotte's spine. *Was I wrong in my judgement of the missing girls from this place? How odd that Mrs Park should mention angels. Are they the same ones Joe often saw?* She dismissed this thought as nonsense. Charlotte was unaware of the physical changes to her body. She felt ill most of the day and blamed the sensation on her mental state. Too many deaths. Nobody could blame her for returning home after losing a friend, as well as acquaintances.

Mrs Park's attitude did puzzle her instincts. *The woman was my prime suspect for the missing boarders, so why was she so upset about my leaving? What changed? We weren't that close. I was a temporary resident and had only been here for a season. Perhaps the answers may surface when I am far away from Sydney and back home. At least time will be on my side, if nothing else.*

She adjusted her hat with the brilliant red enamel hat pin as soon as she heard Michael's car enter the street. Her suit was black with white trim. She twisted about to ensure her seams were straight on her legs, then patted down the crease in her skirt. She looked down at her new red shoes. *I'll never say goodbye to you, Magda.* She waved to Michael as he alighted from the car.

"You ready to go?" he asked.

Unable to contain her emotions, more tears trickled down her face. All she could do was acknowledge with a nod of her head.

He hugged her close. "It's ok. It's been a harrowing couple of months for us." His last opportunity to change her mind, he added. "You sure this is what you want?"

Her tears subsided, and she looked at his face. "I'm positive, Michael. This is right for me. I'll be able to rebuild my life."

He understood about the loss of friends. He thought that together they could conquer their demons. "At least you'll have no further trouble from the Trilbies."

They arrived at Central Station. Charlotte purchased some items from the cafeteria, including a small packet for travel sickness. She was a bit squeamish and rubbed her tummy. She had put on a little weight and dismissed the problem, blaming her need for comfort food.

Michael helped her with the tickets and got her luggage organised. She carried a small bag for the overnight trip. He waited with her until the signal to board. "I'm going to miss you, Charlie. Will you let me know your address when you get settled?"

She was nervous. "I'm not sure that's a good idea, Michael. I want to forget the past few months, and any contact with you won't do me any good."

He sensed she wished the station master would blow his shrill whistle. She looked at the steam engine, eager to expel its hot steam and its own whistle in response. He kissed her on the cheek.

"I'll wait until the train leaves if you don't mind."

She refused to succumb to her heart's desire to stay in Sydney and learn to trust again. Could she sacrifice herself again? A half-hearted smile curved her lips up on one side of her mouth. *Was going home the right decision? Yes, the right choice.* She forced herself to turn around and step into the carriage and leave everything and everyone behind.

Despite himself, he let her go. His last glimpse of her was a red shoe as she took the last step and disappeared from sight. The steam from the locomotive clouded his vision of her position by the window. He remained in the same spot until he could no longer see the train, then turned about and left the station. What does it mean to say goodbye? His preference was until we meet again. He knew he would see her again.

Chapter Sixty-Two

"1.00pm is the last free appointment, Miss Tyrell. A doctor can see you then. Will that time suit you?" The receptionist's voice was pleasant with a slight Irish lilt. The return train journey home had been fraught with a mixture of fear and emotions; that is when she wasn't sick. Travel sickness, she thought, except the illness lingered for days at the most inopportune times.

"Yes, thank you."

Charlotte shifted careers when she returned to her hometown. The daredevil attitude of a crime reporter altered after the tragedies in Sydney. In exchange for a quieter existence, she relinquished her dreams. Employment at the local library equipped her with a drive to remove memories from the past year.

A career in journalism lured her to Sydney three months ago, and after the deaths and murders of people close to her, she sought a fresh start. She sacrificed her dreams by returning home. Childhood friends had married defence force personnel and received transfers interstate or overseas. Others accepted bank transfers to outback towns. Young women, not wanting to be housewives like their mothers, relocated to the city in search of higher-paid jobs. Charlotte couldn't blame them. She tried to make her own mark on the world and deal with whatever life threw her way. With her background in journalism, she gained employment in the library's research department. The librarians utilised her skills at all levels, and her analytical mind discovered material held in archives. Charlotte kept her own counsel outside work. Hence the doctor's appointment.

In response to the doctor's first question, Charlotte answered. Yes, she was off her food, even though she noticed she had gained a little extra weight.

The doctor's expression did not change as he continued to ask more intimate questions. Charlotte was honest with all her answers. After a lengthy consultation, the doctor confirmed the problem was due to morning sickness. "Bit early to be sure, but all the signs are there." His smile broadened with what he thought was good news.

"A baby! But how?" Expecting a child unless - the abduction in the tunnel- Joe or Michael or both?"

"Now, Now, Miss Tyrell, you are old enough to understand..."

"Of course I do, but..." Her shoulders slumped. A multitude of tears poured down her cheeks; she grasped the handkerchief offered by the doctor. He allowed her the freedom of emotional release. Charlotte sniffled; her nose as puffy as her eyes; her hands twisted the cloth into knots. She looked at the doctor for a short time before she spoke. "There is something you need to know, but I don't know where to begin."

"Before you say anything, let me get my receptionist to delay the next appointment."

He wound the intercom handle and spoke tersely to the woman. "Hold all appointments, and cancel the last two in case. If they need urgent attention, send them to the hospital." He replaced the receiver. "Now, Miss Tyrell, start anywhere you like. Until I understand your situation, I'm unable to offer advice."

He leaned back in his leather chair and waited. Lines on his forehead furrowed deeper with each piece of her tale. He'd never heard a story as far-fetched as this patient. Although he understood how her career put her in the path of dangerous men. His first thought was to report a possible attack to the police. Charlotte told him that one of the men was a detective and the other the officer's friend - a derelict living in abandoned tunnels; therefore, any action was a waste of time. "What use would the police be in Queensland?"

He assured her of his support and advised that abortion was illegal; therefore, adoption might be suitable.

Charlotte listened to the doctor about applying for appropriate papers for legal adoption, or she could keep the infant. Single motherhood was not an easy option. Society frowned on young women having babies without a husband or family to support them. He added that she could use the excuse of a man not returning from the war. The doctor explained there was no rush, and perhaps she might like to keep the baby at the end of her confinement. Doctor Jacobs was willing to help her through the next seven months before she made her decision.

Back in her small rented cottage near the Ipswich railway workshops, she slumped into an oversized armchair. The plush cushions hugged her. Little to do except plan ahead. Did she want the baby or not? How would she manage? These and other questions plagued her night and day for the duration of her pregnancy. The months passed by without a fuss. She didn't like to tell lies, but she had told her employer her fiancé was missing in action.

Her news surprised her colleagues, and their excitement grew as fast as her size. Movement inside her womb heightened her sense of awareness of a new life forming. Sometimes she found herself caressing her abdominal region for no plain reason.

Chapter Sixty-Three

"You got your story straight, girl?"

Huddled in the corner booth inside St James' cafeteria, Lailah nodded, "I hear you, Harold." Both her hands cupped her extended belly. A new life shifted. "We've gone over this often enough. My priority is to protect my unborn."

"Right you are, Lailah. You're a brave girl." At the cafe's front door, the small bell tinkled.

"Here comes Detective Devlin. Please hold your tongue until I say otherwise."

"What can he do? What will he do?" Apprehension about the decision to seek help from a policeman turned to fear.

Harold stroked her back in an effort to release her anxiety. "Nothing he can do, child, but help you and your baby find somewhere far from Sydney. Hush, now, you wait here, and I'll bring him over." Harold walked toward Michael. Lailah remained seated in the booth, scared and alone. But the baby meant another life to save.

"Right on time, Mr Devlin." Harold's firm handshake belied his appearance of old age.

"Call me Mick. I'm off duty for a while."

"Yeah, I heard, suspended, eh? Pity, Mister Dev– er, sorry, Mick. Shame on your superiors; you're a pretty good detective."

"Cut the bull, Harry. The last case broke me."

"Oh. Come on, there's someone you need to meet." Harold turned about and led Michael to the last cubicle. The detective slung his coat over the high back partition and placed his hat on the table alongside Harold's felt cap.

A small girl with her eyes downcast was nestled in the corner. She stroked her lower abdomen with the gentleness of a mother to be.

"Mick, this is someone special. Let me introduce Lailah." Harold grinned. His approach worked.

This information stunned Michael. He slid across the high back bench, unable to speak and flattened his hat by accident. He averted his eyes to the crown of his hat while his brain adjusted to the news. "Lailah O'Brien? The same one, I assume?" He looked at Harold for denial. None came. "Christ, where has she been?"

The girl peered sideways at the detective, but Harold signalled her to silence. She obeyed. "I've ordered breakfast for us all; the girl needs nourishment after her ordeal."

"Ordeal? This girl's only having a baby. I've got girls missing, as well as Joe, and you want me to worry about a silly girl getting herself pregnant? Nothing doing, mate." Michael made to leave. Harold's extended arm blocked the way.

"Please, Mick. Wait until the lass over there serves our meals. I've a long tale to share with you. One you want to hear, especially when you find out about Joe."

Michael sat down, unsure if he could trust the man even though Joe had.

The swing doors to the kitchen opened. The back of the waitress came through the opening first. She struggled to balance the tray from tipping its contents to the floor. "Scrambled eggs on toast, three teas."

"Thanks," said Harold. To the girl, he said, "Tuck in, lass."

Lailah nodded and ate like a child to the point where she licked butter off her fingers.

Too young. Michael waited until the waitress returned to clear the table. "Now, Harold, where did you find the girl?"

"In Joe's tunnel. You know the one."

"How could I forget?" Michael leaned forward, hands clenched, "I've seen what happens down there, and it's my fault Joe's gone."

"Joe sends his regards, Mr Devlin." Lailah's soft voice caught the detective's attention.

"Did I hear you right? You've talked to Joe. How do you know Joe?" Questions fired as fast as bullets from a Gatling gun. Bewildered, he turned to Harold, "What's the meaning of all this? Who is she really?"

Upset by the detective's disbelief, Lailah excused herself from the table for the ladies' room.

Smooth as a cold beer on a hot day, Harold said, "Calm down, Mick. Let me explain.

Lailah disappeared before your reporter friend arrived in Sydney."

"Yeah, Yeah, I remember," Michael fidgeted. "Can't be the same girl, though."

"Listen, Mick, this is the same Lailah. Four months ago, she disappeared. One of the homeless blokes recently found her dazed and wandering in the tunnel where Joe used to sleep. He brought her to me 'cause he didn't know what else to do."

"You expect me to believe all this nonsense? Joe's dead, gone." Michael dipped his head and raised his palms to ward off Harold. "I know, I haven't got a body. I heard from the cops chasing him that he 'just disappeared'." Michael grabbed a serviette off the table and wiped his face to hide his tears. He blew his nose into the cloth and shoved it in his trouser pocket.

"Dead? What makes you certain he's dead, Mick?" Harold leaned forward. "I know for a fact he is alive."

Michael snarled. "Oh, sure. Prove it."

"The girl doesn't know how she got in the tunnels, but she carried a handwritten note addressed to you. Quieten down, Mick. Here comes Lailah."

Lailah moved toward the table and said, "It's no good, Harold; he doesn't want to help. I'll be on my way, thanks anyway."

"Sit, Lailah." Harold's firm voice broke her determination to walk away. "When Lailah was found, she kept muttering find Harold and Detective Devlin regards Joe Moody. This letter is addressed to you. It's from Joe."

Michael unfolded the sheet of paper and read the handwritten note.

Hey Mick,

I'm alive for now, and sober, would you believe. Difficult to adjust to changes. Can't tell you anything about where I am. Don't really know myself. Consigned my life here until things cool down your side of the tunnel.

I understand your reasons behind my arrest. I'm not sure I can forgive you for that decision. I am innocent, and I understand you tried to protect me but without evidence of those Trilbies, I got charged with all offenses which you and I both know didn't commit.

In the meantime, please take care of Lailah. Get her in protection as soon as you can. Her life is at risk, which means her baby is too.

The nature of the Trilbies and reasons for abductions is only a guess, and until I learn more, I'll stay here. You wouldn't believe me if I told you what it's like here, but it's what I imagine the Sydney area looked like before white settlement. I know that won't make any sense to you, but hopefully, I'll get to explain it one day.

Natives are restless. Stay safe. I'll send a Mayday if I need to reach you. Don't ask Harold. He won't tell else you put his life at risk.

Joe.

Chapter Sixty-Four

Memories haunted Charlotte whenever she was alone. She read about unsolved crimes of abduction that remained a mystery to Sydney investigators. Too few dared to believe the unexplained. A constant reminder of the past continued to torment.

The aroma of Divine7 cologne in the perfume section of the local department store taunted at irregular intervals. She faced new challenges since relocating. What appeared to be unsurmountable became a way of life, a turning point in her life. It was one she didn't want to face initially, but she grew more accepting as the months passed. She found she could accept this change and embrace it with every part of her being.

The lost hours between her visit to the Sydney doctor and when Brian died remained a mystery. Too many questions remained along with death or disappearances. By the doctor's estimated date of conception, Charlotte matched the time to when she and Magda got ill. Nothing much to pinpoint the conception but a hazarded guess and choice of three men - the detective, the war veteran and a doctor.

Her home life kept her busy. Almost a year had passed since she left Sydney. That time also created a blessing in disguise, even though regrets about leaving tampered with her thoughts. In good moments her mind drifted to times spent with Michael and Nora. She cringed thinking about Nora in the tunnels and Brian's death.

Michael and Joe tried to convince Charlotte about her rescue from the Trilbies. No matter how hard she tried, she could not understand why she was in the tunnel in the first place. With the discovery of Nora's body, something stirred in her mind's vision. All the confusion and hysteria at the time blocked out any resolution to unearth evidence. Her last two weeks in Sydney remained a blur.

A hint of recollection surfaced at inappropriate times, long enough to irritate her. Without any purposeful clues, a kaleidoscope of hues wove a myriad of images past her mind's eye. The only positive result was the small bundle of her infant son she held in her arms at night. Questions of who, how, when and why plagued her.

The local council had advertised a position for an archivist after the previous employee died from complications of a tropical disease contracted while serving with the army in New Guinea. Charlotte had jumped at the opportunity.

Working at the Town Hall, sorting and updating the archives kept her busy. Her neighbours Ian and Lottie Suffolk looked after Aiden when she decided to return to work. Single mothers remained a blight on society, but her little white lie and the cheap wedding band held her in high esteem within the small community. While in her workroom mid-afternoon in late July, a colleague entered. "Someone here to see you, Charlotte."

"I'll be out in a minute." She finished explaining the routine to the volunteers.

She paused near the front desk to brush lint off her twinset before her fingers raked her hair. The receptionist answered the telephone and pointed to the front door. "Him?" The girl whispered with her hand over the mouthpiece of the handset, "Yes! Him. Good looking too." She added before turning her attention to the caller. "Yes, sorry about that; what were you saying?"

Charlotte turned. She pushed the heavy door and shivered, not only from the change in temperature but apprehension. Inside the building, the air conditioning offered protection from external elements. The weather turned for the worse during the day. Outside, gutters overflowed, unable to contain the runoff from a sudden downpour. She heard his voice before she saw him. He stood beside a column supporting the portico. "Hello, Charlie."

Hesitation sucked the air from her lungs before she could answer. "Michael? What are you doing here? Never expected to see you again."

"I've retired from the NSW police force, and I've opened a private detective agency. I've tested my sleuth skills to track you down, and here I am! This is a small town, after all."

"Oh," was all she could say. Her mind filled with a jumble of words, none of which worked her tongue.

He spoke like a man in love. "Charlie, I've missed you and tried to stay away but realised I want you in my life, the rest of it actually." He reached for her hand and held it between both of his. "I hope you feel the same way."

Raindrops on his leather jacket sparkled like jewels beneath the portico lights. His damp hat offered little protection. She so wanted to leap into his arms, but the past flashed before her eyes. Her legs weakened. She thought she might faint. There was a lot to explain since she left Sydney. "Oh, Michael, I'm uncertain about my feelings for you. So much happened in Sydney, and try as I might, I have not forgotten what happened to our friends." She pulled away and let his hand drop. "Nor have I been able to piece together that night in the tunnels." Tears smudged her face. "Losing Magda, then Nora's death and then Joe's arrest and his disappearance, I didn't know which way to turn but home."

Michael moved closer to place his hands on her upper arms. "I understand, Charlie. I am remorseful myself about things we cannot change. I can explain more, but not here. I want to start over with you, and together we can perhaps forget the past. We can support each other through this."

"Michael, I need time" She wiped her tear smudged face. "I..."

"Take all the time you need, but in the meantime, a cup of tea wouldn't go astray. It's been a long day, and the night will be longer."

"For Christ's sake, Detective Devlin is that all you can think of when..."

"No longer Detective, Charlie," he smiled. "Let's share a pot of tea? Eh? No harm in that while I unlock that crime reporter inside you." He stood in front of her with his back to the lights, denying her visibility of any expressions on his face. "I checked that the cafe around the corner serves late. How about seven? And yes, your receptionist told me when you clock off. I'll wait for you there." He turned away and left.

At 7.00pm, Charlotte loitered for as long as she could. The night guard waited by the exit and locked the door behind her. She walked along the opposite footpath to the cafe before she drew the courage to cross the street. Michael, true to his word, sat on a stool at the counter and waited. His face lit up when he saw her. "I'm glad you didn't chicken out."

"Me too, I think." She tried to dismiss the pleasure of seeing him. Nervous by his nearness, she worried about her news. She sat beside him. He pecked her on the cheek. First, she needed to tell him about her child. A child conceived under questionable circumstances. A healthy son, she adored, Aiden, whose B negative blood type held no connection to her own. Did Michael or Joe, or the doctor have the same strain? She often wondered how this miracle came about. She shuddered at what she thought might have happened. Was she abducted and rescued as Michael wanted her to believe? What of Magda's or Nora's deaths? The boy was no secret in town, but how will Michael handle the news?

"I see you have a wedding band on your finger. Is there something I should know?" His thumb toyed with the gold band on her left hand. An abrupt 'No' put Michael on guard. "Well, are you married or not?" He asked.

"No longer."

"Widow then?"

"Can we talk about something else, please?" She turned to the waitress, who brought their pot of tea and cups to the table.

"Will there be anything else, sir?"

"Thanks, no."

A silence fell between the couple before they simultaneously uttered half-spoken words.

"You first, Michael." Charlotte was eager to hear his side of the story before sharing her news.

Michael's face muscles tightened on one side of his lips. "Don't know where to begin."

"From the start might be a good place." Her patience wore thin. Charlotte's fingers drummed her crossed forearms.

"Not sure if that is the right place to begin. The immediate past is where the story starts, and I'm worried you might not believe me." He looked for a signal. He knew she expected the truth and nothing less.

"Try me, Mr Devlin." She dared him.

"Brace yourself, little lady, for what I am about to tell will shock you." He uncrossed her arms and held her hands, and began his story.

Charlotte heard about the pregnant Lailah, who returned with a note from Joe from the unknown side of the blue lights. Her heart rate increased as her mind filled with dread. "Unbelievable."

"I know, but I met with Lailah and Harold. Joe is indeed alive and well somewhere else other than our world."

"But..."

"...Yes. Hard to believe but I would recognise his handwriting anywhere."

"Bloody Hell." Charlotte raised one hand to cover her mouth in amazement.

"There's more, Charlie. The night we rescued you, Joe and I made a pact to withhold information for your own good."

Charlotte's temper flared, "And what made you two decide to protect me?"

"Well, the fact is Charlie, Joe called me when the blue lights appeared that night. I was down there with Joe when those weird faceless men carried you back into the tunnel." He paused and waited for a reaction.

"You mean…"

"Yes, Charlie, I mean you had been on the other side."

"Oh God, no." She whispered.

"It's okay; nothing happened to you. We got you off those creeps."

"Did you say Lailah was pregnant?"

"Yes, why?"

"I…" tears rolled down her cheeks. She wiped them away with her fingertips before Michael retrieved his handkerchief. "We need to get out of here, Michael. I have something more to add to your story." Now was the time to tell him about her child and not inside a cafe. In her home, perhaps, but she would collect her son from her babysitter first.

First, she needed to tell him about her child. A child conceived under questionable circumstances. A son she adored. He was healthy and growing fast and soon would take his first steps. She shuddered at what she believed happened. *How will Michael handle the news?* They held hands as they walked, oblivious to their surroundings. Neither was aware of the danger lurking nearby. Neither saw nor heard the padded footsteps across the street.

Two dark clothed figures with trilbies perched low over their brows lurked in the shadows.

EPILOGUE

DEATH OR FREEDOM

Escaping his pursuers, Joe lunged into the swirl of lights he activated with the opal shard he'd found during Charlotte's rescue. The thought of dying in the process wavered beneath an overwhelming urge to freedom. The hypnotic rush of blue hues tampered with his senses where he heard colours, and tasted sounds. His limbs were pulled in all directions, but his soul demanded freedom over death. He struggled with the shift in his senses until - nothing but warm sunshine coated his body.

A calmness encased his mental state as he turned and faced an unfamiliar wall. He realised he was standing on the other side. *God dammit. I'm alive.* He hugged himself while he wriggled his fingers and toes to ensure they remained intact. He heard water rushing over rocks. *Nothing to fear here.* His body trembled. The adrenaline rush dissipated leaving in its wake an ache throughout his bones. Unstable on his feet, he edged across the path ahead and found a shady spot to recuperate.

He wanted to rest and regain his stamina but the rhythmical sound of the nearby stream lulled him to sleep. The gurgle of water blocked all other noise but not for long. He woke with a start. A hand closed tight over his mouth; a cold blade angled at his throat; his legs and arms pinned down by a bedraggled oaf.

His army training kicked in. *Survey the situation before making any rash decisions.* His motto, not his trainer's. To his left, he caught sight of a few men dressed in rags and tatters. A man with a blade signalled silence with the tips of his fingers pressed on his lips. On his right a woman's voice whispered in Joe's ear, she was so close he might bite off her nose. "There are others who threaten you, stranger."

He struggled to be free. Panic rose deep from within his core.

"Easy man," came the low voice of the owner of the blade at his throat. "We don't want to clean up the mess after I slice your throat."

The realisation of his own carelessness hit Joe hard. He quit the fight with a heavy heart and quickly resolved to stay alert. He cursed in silence while he studied his captors and the surroundings. Heat from the body atop him drew sweat from his glands. The thick undergrowth emitted an earthy scent, mixed with pungent odours that lingered on Joe's borrowed clothes. Joe's discomfort worsened with the stench of his nearest captor. Restricted movement induced painful sensations of pins and needles through his limbs. His skin itched as if ants crawled over every inch of his body.

Are these folk remnants from the war or another nightmare? He wanted to cough, sneeze or piss, whichever came first, just to get the oaf off him. *Stay focused. This is not a dream. This is real. I am on the other side.*

Hidden in the foliage, the camouflaged group crouched low. A woman leaned in. "If you value your life, stay still and quiet." Joe's ears pricked to the sound of voices near the wall, at least he thought the wall. He wondered if the newcomers were his pursuers or theirs. *If mine, then how did the wallopers get through? Did they follow me?*

Inside his back pocket, the opal's jagged surface almost embedded in his buttocks. Everyone relaxed when the knife wielder clicked his tongue. As the knife withdrew from Joe's throat, the other giant rolled away to rub stiffened muscles. The female in the group sat back on her haunches. Muscle stiffness and a prickling sensation prevented Joe from sitting.

"When you can stand, we will take you to a safe place." The eldest of the small band of misfits pulled a scarf from his neck and made to blindfold Joe. Joe stepped back and tripped over the extended leg of the thug who pinned him like a crocodile.

"Come." A hand extended to help him to his feet. "It's for your safety as well as ours."

"How do I know you won't kill me?"

"Trust stranger, trust. We have a lot of questions for you and here is not the place to linger. A patrol passes when the doorway opens. No one may enter without permits. You obviously came from the other side, and we need to know more." Joe shrugged his shoulders. The man's voice was low and ominous as he spoke. "A faceless guard will arrive soon to inspect the site."

"Faceless guard?" This statement intrigued Joe. He wondered if they wore hats. Trilbies to be exact. There would come a time to ask more. For now, he agreed to the blindfold as he didn't relish the idea of dying just yet.

CC Sullivan Cheryl Sullivan was raised and educated in Ipswich, Queensland. She began writing while nurturing three children as a single parent in Mooloolaba. In 2010 she moved to Brisbane for work and eventual retirement in Mitchelton.

Cheryl pursued her interest in creative writing at the Queensland Writers Centre where the idea for the series, Harvest of the Unborn, expanded during creative writing courses. She joined the Brisbane Writers' Group to practice the craft and later accepted an offer to co-ordinate the group.

Writing a psychological thriller set in the past challenged Cheryl but proved worthwhile. Her go to craft is painting with acrylics. The manuscript of her first book "Chasing Shadows" of the "Harvest of the Unborn" series was twice short listed for Queensland Writers Centre Adaptable to Screen - 2018-2019 and 2020-2021. In 2019 Cheryl was presented with the Brisbane Lord Mayor's Australia Day Achievement Award for encouraging writers of all genres through the writers Group.

You can find CC Sullivan at

E: chezasull@hotmail.com
amazon.com/author/cc sullivan